"The idea of seeing you was a big factor in my taking this job," Mac admitted readily.

To Ginger's dismay, his words caused her heart to leap with that same foolish joy she'd felt at nineteen when he'd first paid her attention.

"Mac, where is all of this headed?" Her voice caught in her throat. "Surely you don't have some whim that the two of us might get back together after six whole years apart."

"It's not unheard of for a divorced couple to reconcile after that length of time," he protested. "The fact that you hadn't remarried, either, gave me some grounds for hope."

Ginger took a step backward when he made a slight movement toward her. "False hope," she stated with emphasis.

I *am* over him, Ginger reminded herself weakly. Still, for him to have this power over her was maddening....

Dear Reader,

Special Edition welcomes you to a brand-new year of romance! As always, we are committed to providing you with captivating love stories that will take your breath away.

This January, Lisa Jackson wraps up her engrossing FOREVER FAMILY miniseries with *A Family Kind of Wedding*. THAT SPECIAL WOMAN! Katie Kinkaid has her hands full being an ace reporter—and a full-time mom. But when a sexy, mysterious Texas rancher crosses her path, her life changes forever!

In these next three stories, love conquers all. First, a twist of fate brings an adorably insecure heroine face-to-face with the reclusive millionaire of her dreams in bestselling author Susan Mallery's emotional love story, *The Millionaire Bachelor*. Next, Ginna Gray continues her popular series, THE BLAINES AND THE McCALLS OF CROCKETT, TEXAS, with *Meant for Each Other*. In this poignant story, Dr. Mike McCall heroically saves a life and wins the heart of an alluring colleague in the process. And onetime teenage sweethearts march down the wedding aisle in *I Take This Man—Again!* by Carole Halston.

Also this month, acclaimed historical author Leigh Greenwood debuts in Special Edition with *Just What the Doctor Ordered*— a heartwarming tale about a brooding doctor finding his heart in a remote mountain community. Finally, in *Prenuptial Agreement* by Doris Rangel, a rugged rancher marries for his son's sake, but he's about to fall in love for real....

I hope you enjoy January's selections. We wish you all the best for a happy new year!

Sincerely,
Karen Taylor Richman
Senior Editor

Please address questions and book requests to:
Silhouette Reader Service
U.S.: 3010 Walden Ave., P.O. Box 1325, Buffalo, NY 14269
Canadian: P.O. Box 609, Fort Erie, Ont. L2A 5X3

CAROLE
HALSTON
I TAKE THIS MAN—AGAIN!

SPECIAL EDITION®

Published by Silhouette Books
America's Publisher of Contemporary Romance

For Brian, my big, tall, handsome baby brother,
real hero material. And darned good husband
and father material, too.
(You owe me big-time for all these accolades in print!)

Also for my nephew, Jacob, who, like my
fictional little boy, Jonathan, started kindergarten
while I was writing this story.

 SILHOUETTE BOOKS

ISBN 0-373-24222-0

I TAKE THIS MAN—AGAIN!

Copyright © 1999 by Carole Halston

Printed in U.S.A.

Books by Carole Halston

CAROLE HALSTON

is a native of south Louisiana, where she lives with her seafaring husband, Monty, in a rural area on the north shore of Lake Pontchartrain, near New Orleans. Her favorite pastime is reading, but she also gardens and plays tennis. She and Monty are camping enthusiasts and tow their twenty-six-foot travel trailer to beautiful spots all over the United States.

Fans can write Carole at P.O. Box 1095, Madisonville, LA 70447. For a free autographed bookmark, they should send a self-addressed, stamped business-size envelope. Romance readers who browse the Internet can visit Carole's web site by first accessing the Harlequin Enterprises site (http://www.romance.net), where she is listed as a Harlequin/Silhouette author.

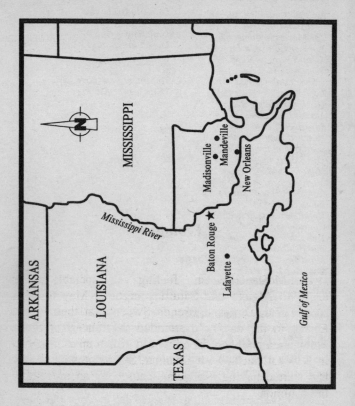

Prologue

Mac McDaniel wasn't feeling very sociable as he drove to Algiers one Saturday night in May to have supper with Don and Brenda Sweeney at their home. Earlier in the day he'd attended the funeral of Steve Flanigan, a boyhood friend who'd grown up as Mac had in New Orleans's Irish Channel. Six months ago Steve had started having headaches caused by an inoperable brain tumor.

What a sad event the funeral had been, Mac thought. Not to mention chilling. Life was so damned uncertain. Here he'd been drifting along in limbo for the past six years since his divorce. His next birthday he'd be thirty. *Thirty.* And here he was unmarried. No wife, no home, no kids. He'd always figured that by this stage of his life, he'd be a family man, not a damned bachelor.

Of course, he *hadn't* figured on a shotgun wedding at age nineteen when he was a sophomore in college.

The irony didn't escape him that he'd had an early shot at being a family man if he could have shaped up and made Ginger a better husband. But he'd been a sorry excuse for a husband.

Maybe if Ginger hadn't miscarried and they'd become parents, they would have stuck out their marriage longer and gotten through the rocky patch. Mac still grieved over that unborn offspring.

At the Sweeney home he jabbed the doorbell button, remembering Don's invitation a week ago. "Brenda says you're welcome to bring a lady friend," Don had said.

"I'll come by myself," Mac had replied.

He wasn't dating anyone. For a guy who'd been written off as a womanizer by his wife, Mac had dated damned few women the past six years. Okay, so maybe he'd been guilty of some innocent flirting while he was married, but he hadn't been unfaithful to Ginger. He hadn't even been strongly tempted to stray.

"Hey, come on in," Don said, opening the door.

He ushered Mac into the homey living room, where two-year-old Melanie was engrossed in a children's program on the big-screen TV. In response to Mac's greeting, she spared him a shy smile complete with dimples. Brenda appeared with cold beers for the two men and the promise that supper would be ready in about forty-five minutes. Shortly after she'd left to go tend to things in the kitchen, five-year-old Donnie entered with a hand-held computer game. His face lit up at the sight of Mac, and he came over and sat on the plaid sofa next to him.

Don was sprawled back in his recliner chair. Mac noted the contented expression on the face of his old football teammate and realized that Don had every reason to be content. Mac would look just as pleased in his shoes.

"What's this I hear about you considering a coaching job over on the north shore?" Don asked.

"You talked to Buzz Pichon," Mac guessed.

The other man nodded. "He came into the dealership last week. Said he was taking a teaching job down in the Lafayette school district."

Mac knew Don was referring to the New Orleans automobile dealership where he worked as a salesman. "Right," Mac said. "Patty is being transferred down there by the company she works for. A big promotion for her. Buzz called to let me know his job at Slidell High would be open if I wanted it. Or if I liked the richer end of the parish better, there would also be a coaching spot available at one of the Mandeville high schools."

Don chuckled. "Good old Buzz. You can't convince him that not everybody in the world wants to live across the lake. I'll bet you told him you weren't interested, and the words didn't faze him."

"Actually I didn't commit myself one way or another," Mac admitted. He shrugged when Don raised his eyebrows in surprise. "A change might do me good. I'm not feeling too satisfied with life in general these days."

"But the north shore? Isn't that where your ex lives?"

"As far as I know, she's there."

"Look, Uncle Mac, my team won," Donnie said proudly, holding his computer game in front of Mac.

"Great going, sport." Mac clapped the little boy on

the shoulder, not minding the interruption. There would be time later for adult conversation.

Brenda returned, carrying a glass of wine for herself. Since her high-school cheerleader days, she'd put on weight, but she hadn't lost the bounce in her step or her bubbly personality. It was obvious to Mac whenever he was around the Sweeneys that Brenda was still crazy about Don, who'd packed an extra twenty pounds onto his six-foot, big-boned frame. And Don still adored Brenda and let her boss him around like he'd done when they were high-school sweethearts.

"Sit down, hon," Don said, a husband's affection in his tone and in his warm glance at his wife.

She promptly perched on the arm of his chair, and he rested his hand on her hip. Mac fixed his gaze on Donnie's computer game, battling that bleak, lonely sensation that hit him more and more often when he was in the company of friends who were happily married couples. Mac was glad for Don, but damn, he envied him.

"Why do you guys have the TV muted?" Brenda asked curiously. "The news is on. Don't you want to hear it?"

"Melanie's been playing with the remote, punching all the buttons," Don answered, his tone indulgent.

"Want me to take it away from her, Mom?" offered his son.

"No!" Melanie stated. Still seated on the carpet, she hunched over and clutched the gadget to her small chest. "Mine!"

Brenda's gaze was fixed on the big TV. "Hey, isn't that Ginger?" she demanded, pointing at the screen.

Mac jerked his head in time to see a still shot of his ex-wife with a reporter. In a reflex action he sprang to his feet, meaning to get his hands on the remote. He froze in his crouched position as a commercial break began.

Brenda had already acted on the same urgent impulse and was bending over Melanie. "Give me the remote."

Melanie obeyed the no-nonsense order.

Slowly Mac sank back down, feeling like he'd been hit by a three-hundred-pound tackle.

"She was smiling. It's some kind of nice human-interest story," Brenda said, sitting cross-legged on the floor and pulling her daughter onto her lap. "Don't look so worried, Mac."

"Probably something to do with schools on the north shore." Don offered his own words of reassurance.

"Did Melanie cause us to miss the story?" asked his son, allying himself with the adult company who watched newscasts.

"No, that was just a preview we missed. There'll be a follow-up report," Brenda answered, giving Melanie a hug.

"Ginger looked good, didn't she?" Don commented.

Mac had to clear his throat to speak. "Yes, she looked good."

Brenda made a rueful face. "I'll bet she wears the same dress size."

"She hasn't had a couple of kids, hon," Don observed. "And maybe she eats her own cooking, huh, Mac? I'll never forget that spaghetti dinner Ginger made that none of us could get down. You ordered in pizza, remember?"

"Unfortunately I do remember." Mac cringed at the memory of his own lack of sensitivity. If he had it to do over again, he would eat a large plate of the nasty-tasting spaghetti. There were so many things he would do differently.

"Shh!" Brenda silenced them. "The commercial's over." She restored the volume as the newscast resumed with a close-up of the female anchor, who smiled into the camera.

"A high-school English teacher on the north shore, Ginger Honeycutt, has just been honored with a national award for her outstanding teaching. Larry Akins has the report."

"She took back her maiden name," Brenda murmured.

The reporter's interview with Mac's former wife lasted no longer than a minute and a half. Mac leaned forward, resting his forearms on his knees and staring intently at the TV, conscious of a yearning inside him. The sight of Ginger's pretty face framed by her vivid auburn hair, the sound of her voice, the familiar hint of reserve in her manner all fed that yearning and provoked a hundred emotions in his chest, chief among them pride. A husband's pride.

"That's great," he said, sitting back after the camera had switched to the station news anchors.

Don and Brenda both gave him surprised looks. His response obviously wasn't what they were expecting.

"You're a heck of a nice person, Mac," declared Brenda, her voice warm with sincerity. "Not many guys in your shoes would be genuinely glad for an ex-wife who'd—" She faltered as she searched for the right word.

"Who'd dumped them," Mac finished for her. "Not without some good reasons. I wasn't exactly a prize as a husband."

"Ginger wasn't exactly a prize as a wife, either.

Don't take all the blame on yourself.'' Don spoke up in stout defense of his friend.

"The whole marriage was unfortunate," Brenda said, sighing. "The two of you should probably have called it quits after the miscarriage, gotten a divorce and gone your separate ways sooner."

"The Honeycutts made that suggestion often enough." For the first time Mac's voice hardened with bitterness as he referred to his former in-laws. "Not that my parents were any more supportive," he added in fairness.

Brenda made a wry face. "I don't think I've ever known of a worse case of in-law problems."

"I've never known of a worse case of a jealous wife," Don stated. "Ginger didn't trust Mac out of her sight."

"Under the circumstances I can understand her being a little insecure," Brenda said. "Any woman would wonder, 'Would he have married me anyway?' It didn't help that you've always attracted women like flies, you handsome Irish devil," she said to Mac with a teasing smile.

When he couldn't muster a grin, her smile faded. "You're not over her, Mac?"

Mac shook his head. "Nope." He was making the admission to himself, too. God knows he'd tried to get over her. Their brief marriage had been hell in a lot of ways. But there had been snatches of heaven, too.

"I guess that's the reason you haven't found somebody else." Brenda's expression was full of sympathy. "Have you seen her or talked to her in recent years?"

He shook his head again and then shrugged. "She has an unlisted phone number. And, of course, her parents wouldn't dream of telling me how to contact her."

Before tonight he hadn't known the name of the school where she taught.

"How about supper, hon?" prompted Don in a transparent effort to rescue Mac from more well-intentioned probing.

"The pot roast should be done." Brenda put Melanie out of her lap and rose to her feet. From her troubled expression, her mind was obviously still on the conversation. "Ginger hasn't remarried, either. And I paid particular attention to her left hand. She wasn't wearing an engagement ring. Maybe she hasn't gotten over you. I've never seen a woman more crazy about a man than Ginger was about you." The last sentence was spoken over her shoulder as she left the room.

I intend to find out one way or another, Mac thought with sudden iron resolve.

If Ginger hadn't gotten over him, he would move heaven and earth to win her back. This time he would make her a good husband.

Chapter One

"The faculty meeting will begin in five minutes in the library. Teachers, please be prompt."

The school secretary's announcement came over the intercom in Ginger Honeycutt's classroom. Ginger worked faster at stapling a long strip of scalloped paper border to the bulletin board at the front of the room. When she'd finished, she took an extra few moments to step back and approve the overall effect. The bright red border framed the white butcher paper she'd stapled on as a background. After the meeting she would attach large letters cut out of construction paper, spelling out the eight parts of speech, each of which had a colorful cartoon picture depicting its function.

Designing bulletin boards wasn't a major priority to Ginger as a teacher, nor was it her biggest talent, but she believed in stimulating her students' minds in every possible way and using every teaching tool at her disposal. Eye-catching and informative bulletin-board displays could be effective tools of learning.

After the school year was under way, she turned over to her students the challenge of designing and putting up new displays to illustrate the subject matter being studied. She provided the materials and served as a consultant.

"This is *your* bulletin board and *your* classroom," Ginger always emphasized to her classes. Half the battle in teaching adolescents was getting them actively involved in their own education. That meant giving them some control over their classroom environment and allowing them to express their unique personalities.

The other half of the battle was not boring them to death. And not boring herself to death at the same time. Learning didn't have to be deadly dull. Ginger's list of learning activities included skits, homemade videos and original song lyrics performed for the class, poems and short stories and crossword puzzles. Mixed in were plenty of conventional in-class and homework assignments, but the key word was variety.

"That looks pretty good," she said aloud with satisfaction.

After retrieving her purse from a desk drawer, Ginger left her classroom and headed toward the library, admiring the highly polished floors of the corridors. By this time tomorrow afternoon the beige tile would be scuffed with the footsteps of students.

Coming abreast of the door to the teachers' lounge, she paused, wondering if she had time to pop into the women's rest room to run a comb through her hair and freshen her makeup. Better not, Ginger decided with a glance at her watch. It wouldn't do to walk in late to the first faculty meeting of the new school year.

The library seemed jam-packed with teachers. Ginger exchanged greetings as she made her way to an empty chair next to Sharon Hawkins, the librarian and a colleague whose company Ginger enjoyed. A tall, thin bleached blonde with an extroverted personality, Sharon was anything but the stereotypical prim librarian. A divorcée, she loved flirting with men. Today her smirk and the wicked gleam in her brown eyes were dead giveaways. Ginger knew without asking that there must be at least one eligible bachelor among the male additions to the faculty.

"What does he teach?" Ginger asked, smiling as she sank down into the chair. "Math?" One of the positions that had been open was in the math department.

"No, he's Larry Hebert's replacement." Larry Hebert had taught physical-education classes and coached football and basketball. "I thought I'd died and gone to hunk heaven when I laid eyes on him!" Sharon's smirk took on a dreamy cast. "Six feet tall, super build and a sexy grin guaranteed to make any woman tingle all the way down to her toes."

Not any woman, Ginger thought to herself. She doubted the new coach would make her tingle down to her toes. The description came too close to fitting her ex-husband, who was a high-school P.E. teacher and coach. Being married to him had given Ginger a built-in resistance to macho jock types.

Or perhaps more accurately, a built-in resistance to men. Ginger hadn't dated at all following her divorce and flight from New Orleans to the north shore until last November when she'd met Barry Whitfield, a CPA and Mac's opposite in every conceivable way.

The dozens of conversations creating a hubbub of voices in the library quieted as one of the assistant principals got the faculty meeting under way. He made a long series of announcements and then sat down, letting the principal, Bill Gary, take over. Short, bald and with a booming baritone, Bill gave his customary pep talk as a lead-in to presenting the several new faculty members.

"Last but not least," he said when he came finally to the cause of Sharon's excitement, "Coach McDaniel from New Orleans will be filling the spot in our P.E. department and bringing his considerable experience and expertise to our coaching staff. Some of you might remember his days of glory as a quarterback at SLU in Hammond."

Ginger had been giving her polite attention up to this point and smiling in a friendly manner when each new colleague stood and suffered the inspection of the assembled teachers. The words "Coach McDaniel" wiped the smile from her face and made her heart miss several beats. It can't be, she thought in befuddlement. There's some mistake.

"That's him," Sharon murmured as a black-haired man rose and turned around, his hand raised in a casual male salute. "Now, did I exaggerate? Is he a macho dreamboat or what? Drat it! You've already caught his eye, Ginger! Just my luck for him to like redheads!"

"I've no doubt whatever he likes blondes and brunettes, too," Ginger murmured, numb with the shock and confusion. It just couldn't be true that Mac was her colleague! This was all a bad dream!

Bill Gary brought the meeting to a close after a reminder that coffee and cookies would be served in the cafeteria immediately afterward. He got the point across without spelling it out that skipping the informal reception wasn't an option. Everyone was expected to attend and spend a few minutes socializing with fellow faculty members and welcoming newcomers.

"I don't need my arm twisted," Sharon declared cheerfully, standing up. "Just call me head of the welcoming committee."

Ginger joined the slow exodus from the library, struggling to get her emotions under control. A spurt of indignation finally came to her rescue. How dare Mac *do* this to her! She should be talking and laughing and sharing the general atmosphere of anticipation for the new school year about to begin at *her* school. Instead she desperately wanted to escape to her classroom and postpone a face-to-face meeting with him until she felt more prepared.

The *nerve* of him! Ginger had moved over to the north shore of Lake Pontchartrain, giving her ex-husband the entire greater metropolitan area of New Orleans as his territory. It simply wasn't fair for him to barge into her life like this. Getting over him had taken her five of the six years since her divorce. During that time she'd devoted herself entirely to her teaching. Finally she had a social life again and a caring relationship with a man she respected a great deal. Finally she was starting to feel happy and complete.

With *no* regard for her well-being, suddenly Mac showed up.

In the corridor several women separated from the crowd, heading for the teachers' lounge. Ginger had taken a step in the same direction when she brought herself up short. She would *not* go freshen her makeup. It didn't *matter* that her nose was probably shiny and most of her lipstick had worn off. Looking pretty for Mac hadn't been a worry for six whole years, and it wasn't a worry now.

Some of her indignation directed at herself, Ginger marched along to the cafeteria.

Taking her turn at one of two coffee urns, she filled a cup three-quarters full and added a packet of artificial sweetener. She was about to turn away, not even glancing at the plates of cookies, when Rosemary Wells, a good-natured African-American woman who taught business courses, spoke to her.

"Aren't you having one of these cookies, Ginger? They look delicious." Rosemary was busy placing several on a napkin.

"I'm resisting the temptation since I already blew my day's calories at lunch," Ginger replied. "I had an oyster poboy." Normally the cookies would be a temptation, but not today with her stomach in knots. She didn't even want the coffee. It was something to hold in her hands like a prop.

"You don't have a weight problem, girl," Rosemary scoffed.

"I can easily afford to shed five pounds."

"It wouldn't hurt me to go on a diet, but then I'd have to buy a whole new wardrobe. And on a teacher's salary, I couldn't afford that. So I'd better take one more cookie." Rosemary laughed merrily. "How was your summer? Did you enjoy your travels in Europe?"

"Very much." Ginger had spent the majority of the summer touring European countries as a chaperone for a group of high-school students on a travel-study program. It had been a marvelous opportunity for her, as well as for them.

"Tell me about Venice. One of these days I'm hoping to go there." Rosemary led the way to a spot some distance away and out of the traffic.

Under ordinary circumstances Ginger would have enjoyed sharing with Rosemary some high points of her stay in Venice. Instead it was an effort to stand there and chat, knowing that Mac was somewhere in the room. His very presence leached all the color and adventure from Ginger's summer experiences abroad. For him to still have this much power over her was *maddening!*

I *am* over him, Ginger told herself. Once the shock wore off, she would be fine. In the meanwhile she welcomed the resentment that boiled up when she spotted her devilishly handsome ex-husband, grinning and looking every bit as relaxed as Ginger was tense. Sharon, acting as faculty hostess, was glued to his side, and the two of them were circulating. It was only a matter of time before they reached Ginger.

Unless she slipped out…

No. Ginger sucked in a breath to conquer a flare of panic. She would *not* avoid him.

"Excuse me," she said to Rosemary and two other teachers who'd wandered over and joined them. "I should go over and say hello to Coach McDaniel. We were in a class together at Southeastern when we were undergraduates."

It was just one tiny piece of a story too painful to tell, the reason she hadn't confided in anyone on the north shore except Barry. He'd shared his own heartbreak with her.

Tonight they had a date, and Ginger would pour out this whole unexpected development to him. She wrapped that knowledge around her like a thin suit of armor as she wove her way through clusters of people to confront Mac.

"Hi, Ginger," Sharon greeted her brightly, eyebrows elevated in mild surprise. "Mac, this is Ginger Honeycutt, our celebrity English teacher. You may have seen her on television—''

''Coach McDaniel and I don't need an introduction, Sharon,'' Ginger cut in politely.

''No, we sure don't. How are you, Ginger?'' he said. ''It's great to see you.'' His deep voice she remembered so well resonated with a fervent sincerity, and he was gazing at her face as though he'd been hungry for the sight of her. When he made a slight movement with his hands, for a breathless second Ginger thought he was going to reach for her. Then he checked himself and extended one big hand.

''I couldn't be better.'' The answer she meant to be brisk came out sounding strangled. Reluctantly she raised her right hand. He promptly engulfed it with both hands, his clasp warm and strong. Ginger bore down on a painful squeezing sensation in her chest.

''Congratulations on that national award,'' he said, ''I caught the newscast about you this summer.''

His words answered one of the questions she'd wanted answered. He *had* taken the job with full knowledge she was on the faculty.

''Are you two old friends?'' Sharon asked. She was looking on with open curiosity.

Ginger tugged and managed to extract her hand, giving Mac a chance to answer. He kept his silence, looking at her questioningly. ''Old acquaintances, anyway,'' she said. ''We met when we were freshmen at Southeastern aeons ago.''

The sense of hurt that he hadn't spoken up and acknowledged her as his former wife was totally illogical. After all, she hadn't spoken up, either, acknowledging him as her ex-husband. To give him the benefit of the doubt, he might have been following her lead and respecting her privacy.

"It does seem like a long time ago, all right," Mac said soberly. "When I look back, I remember the good times, but I sure as heck wish I'd been a lot smarter."

"I'll bet." The main thing he undoubtedly would do differently was take better precautions and not get her pregnant.

"It sounds as though you two need to get together and catch up," Sharon commented.

"At some point I'm sure we'll have a talk, but not today," Ginger said with a grim note in her voice. "I have a few questions to ask Coach Mac, but they can wait." Questions like *Why are you here at my school?*

"How about later this afternoon?" he suggested. "I'll be tied up in a coaches' meeting for a couple of hours, but after that—"

Ginger interrupted, shaking her head decisively. "Sorry, I still have things to do to get ready for my classes tomorrow. Now, if you'll both excuse me, I need to say a word of welcome to my other new colleagues."

"Tomorrow let's have lunch together, Ginger," Sharon said to Ginger's back. *At which time, you can explain all this,* the librarian conveyed with her dry tone.

Mac said nothing, nor did he try to stop her, behavior that spoke louder than words to Ginger. Obviously he wasn't in any great hurry to be alone with her and explain his selfish actions. Undoubtedly he expected to be raked over the coals and was just as happy to let her anger die down.

True to her word, Ginger sought out each of the other newcomers and managed to socialize briefly before she made her exit from the cafeteria. A glance over her shoulder as she pushed through the plate-glass door verified that Sharon hadn't moved from Mac's side. The sight of the librarian's blond head paired with his darker head triggered a sharp, unpleasant reaction that was all too familiar. Ginger identified it without any trouble as the old jealousy that had plagued her during her stormy marriage.

The knee-jerk response seemed the last straw. "I won't *stand* for this! I'll go to Bill Gary. I'll go to the school board," she threatened under her breath as she made her way back to her classroom. Reaching it, she jerked the door open and closed it behind her with a bang of pure frustration.

It was too late to lodge a protest against the hiring of her ex-husband. If she'd known in advance, she might have gone to Bill Gary and explained the circumstances in confidence. But she *hadn't* been given any forewarning. Either Mac had suspected she might throw a monkey wrench into his plans and deliberately kept them from her or else he just hadn't given a darn about her feelings in the matter one way or the other.

Whatever the explanation, his actions were despicable. He'd placed her in an intolerable situation that she had no choice but to tolerate, at least for a semester. Because Ginger wasn't about to break her contract and leave her students in the lurch. Her teaching career meant too much to her.

A sense of resignation didn't translate into calm acceptance. Finishing up her bulletin-board display, Ginger applied vigorous pressure to the stapler, which emitted loud clicks. Casting dark glances at the door, she imagined herself hurling the stapler at Mac if he had the brass to come to her classroom.

But he didn't appear to serve as a target. Apparently

he'd taken her at her word when she claimed to be too busy to spare him fifteen minutes. Quite obviously he didn't care enough to be insistent. Out of sight, out of mind. Why seek out a hostile ex-wife when he had an admiring female in the person of Sharon, who would gladly spare him as much time as he desired with her?

I'm glad he has the good sense not to bother me, Ginger told herself. But she wasn't glad, and the realization only made her more angry and resentful.

Despite all the inner turmoil, Ginger persevered until she'd accomplished her list of tasks. At quarter to five she prepared to leave, packing up her leather tote bag, which doubled as a briefcase. The tote bag, complete with monogram, had been a birthday present from Barry. An expensive present, it had been chosen with his usual excellent taste. Today, like always, it brought him pleasantly to mind.

With more deliberation than usual, Ginger conjured up an image of Barry, visualizing his attractive, sensitive features, his sandy hair and hazel eyes. The mental picture soothed some of her feelings of hurt and rejection. Because yes, it *had* hurt that Mac was content to let the day end without having a private conversation with her. His behavior more or less confirmed that his taking a job here had nothing to do with her.

Which was a state of things Ginger should have wanted. And *did* want. It's just hurt pride, she told herself.

Most of the other teachers had already left by now. Ginger's car sat alone in its section of the parking lot, its closest neighbor a cherry red Camaro that hadn't been there when she arrived that morning. She would certainly have noticed it because it was a carbon copy of the red Camaro Mac had bought for himself against her objections a month before Ginger left him. The car had been just one more source of marital conflict between them.

By now he would have traded it in for a different racy bachelor's automobile. It wouldn't surprise her if he were driving a Corvette or a Porsche on his teacher's salary. Living within his means and building a nest egg hadn't been—and undoubtedly still weren't—priorities for Mac. They'd had numerous bitter arguments over managing their money, too.

The door on the driver's side of the Camaro swung open just as Ginger noticed that a man was sitting inside the parked automobile. She came to a halt, slightly uneasy. The north shore was a safe place to live, compared to New Orleans, but Ginger hadn't lost all her city instincts.

"Hi," Mac greeted her over the low-slung roof of the Camaro. "I was beginning to think I was staking out the wrong silver Honda."

"You startled me!" Ginger exclaimed.

"Sorry." He walked over to her and held out his hand, silently offering to take her tote bag.

Ginger clutched the handles tighter. "How did you know I own a silver Honda?" she demanded.

"I asked Sharon what kind of car you drove. I was hoping to catch you before you left school today. Could we go somewhere and have a cup of coffee and talk?" The invitation was humble.

"We can talk right here. It shouldn't take more than five minutes for you to make excuses for the dirty trick you've pulled. If you wanted to move to the north shore, couldn't you have gotten a job in another high school where at least we wouldn't be running into each other on a daily basis? You did know I taught here, didn't you?''

"Sure. I knew,'' he admitted readily. ''The idea of seeing you was a big factor in my taking this job instead of the one in Slidell.''

To Ginger's shame and dismay, his words caused her heart to leap with that same foolish joy she'd felt at nineteen when he first paid her attention. ''Well, I certainly wish you'd given me some say in the matter,'' she said. ''Because I would have insisted you take the Slidell position if I couldn't have convinced you not to take any job on the north shore. What brought about this decision to change jobs anyway? I thought you were happy with your coaching situation.''

"I haven't been exactly *happy* since we split up. In fact I've been pretty damned dissatisfied with my life, but I drifted along from year to year, not quite knowing what to do to get on track. Then this past May, Steve Flanigan died of a brain tumor. Remember him—he got roaring drunk at our wedding reception and almost fell into the cake?''

Ginger nodded. ''I read Steve's obituary notice in the paper and felt sad for his family.'' She'd also felt sadness for Mac, knowing how upset he must be.

"Steve's dying affected me like a wake-up call,'' Mac went on. ''Here I was close to turning thirty and divorced, with no wife and kids, no home. That same Saturday of Steve's funeral, I went over to Don and Brenda Sweeney's house for supper. Remember them?''

"Yes, of course, I remember them.''

"They have two cute kids. Don's doing well enough selling cars that Brenda was able to quit her job and become a full-time mom and wife, which suits them both to a T. At any rate I was sitting in their living room that night, envious as hell of Don, when all of a sudden your face flashed up on the TV screen. It hit me like a lightning bolt that, divorce or no divorce, I still felt married to you.''

Ginger wet her lips and swallowed to revive her vocal cords. ''Your Catholic upbringing.'' They'd been married in a Catholic church with a priest performing the ceremony. According to his religious faith, the marriage bond was holy and couldn't be dissolved by a civil divorce.

Mac raised his hands in a gesture of partial agreement. ''That's probably part of it. To fill in more of the story, Buzz Pichon had contacted me about a couple of openings at high schools on the north shore. You—''

''I remember Buzz,'' Ginger broke in before he could finish his question. ''Mac, where is this 'story' of yours headed? Why did you quit a coaching job with a top parochial school and move away from the city you swore would always be your home? Surely not on some whim that the two of us might get back together after six whole years apart.''

''It's not unheard-of for a divorced couple to reconcile after that length of time,'' he protested. ''The fact that you hadn't remarried either gave me some grounds for hope.''

Ginger took a step backward when he made a slight movement toward her. He checked himself and jammed his hands into his pockets. ''False hope,'' she stated with emphasis. ''It took me five of those years to get over you, but I *am* over you, Mac. You can rule out any thoughts about reconciliation. Our marriage was a big mistake to begin with. It was an even bigger mistake for me to try to hang on to you as long as I did. I should have set you free and let you sow your wild oats a lot sooner.''

''I disagree. We both should have stuck with our marriage. I was wrong for throwing in the towel and going along with a divorce.''

''Maybe so, but the fact remains that you signed those divorce papers. You were sick of the fighting, too. Sick of our in-law problems, our differences over money. Sick of my jealousy just like I was sick to death of *being* jealous and insecure.'' Ginger shuddered. ''Divorce was the best solution.''

''It wasn't all bad,'' he said. ''Was it?''

''No, it wasn't all bad,'' she conceded. ''But neither of us was happy.''

''I've matured and so have you. We could deal with the same issues a lot better now.''

Ginger easily conjured a picture of him and Sharon side by side at the faculty reception just a few hours earlier. She recalled the stab of jealousy. ''I would just as soon not deal with them ever again. Now I really have to go. I have a supper date.''

''With the CPA fellow you're dating?'' He shrugged when she blinked at him in surprise. ''I asked Sharon if you were involved with anyone. How serious is the relationship? You're not in love with him, are you?''

''I care about him. And respect him. And enjoy his company immensely.''

''Are you sleeping with him?''

''That's none of your business!'' Ginger edged past him to the driver's side of her car and inserted the key in the lock.

''I'd rather not know anyway,'' he said. His grim tone softened into pleading. ''Break your date, Ginger.

Please. Let me take you out to dinner somewhere so we can talk. For old times' sake, if nothing else.''

"We've already talked. And even if I didn't have plans, Mac, I wouldn't be interested in going to dinner with you. Not tonight. Not any other night.''

He allowed her to open the car door and slip under the wheel, making no effort to detain her physically, like the old Mac would have done. "You've got to give me a chance,'' he said.

"No, I *don't* have to do any such thing.''

"Can't we at least be friends?''

"No, we can't. I don't want you`for a friend.''

He sighed. "Don't think I'm giving up this easily.''

"I'm *not* playing hard to get, Mac. You were never the right kind of man for me.''

From his expression she might have slapped him hard. "And this CPA you're dating is?''

"Yes, I think he might be.''

"Drive carefully,'' he said in a disheartened voice. "I'll see you later.'' He closed the door and walked toward the Camaro, the set of his broad shoulders spelling out rejection.

Evidently he'd gotten her message loud and clear.

Ginger was glad he had. She just didn't *feel* at all glad.

Mac drove to his rented condo by a roundabout route, taking consolation in what Ginger hadn't said. She was too honest by nature to hurl lies like spears to wound him, like some women would do out of spite and revenge.

She *hadn't* said, *I'm dating a guy I love a lot more than I ever loved you, and I have every intention of marrying him.* When he'd reacted like a jealous estranged husband and demanded to know about her current relationship, Ginger *hadn't* informed him hotly, *It's none of your business, but,* yes, *I'm sleeping with him! And he's a lot better lover than you ever were!*

Her words had cut deeply enough, but they hadn't killed all his hope. Whether he succeeded or not in winning her back, he was convinced after seeing her today that he'd done the right thing moving to the north shore and making his best effort. God, he just prayed he hadn't waited too long and lost her forever.

Mac knew that he had to be patient and not crowd her. He had to make friends with her all over again and this time win her trust. Somehow he had to continue to exercise the same restraint that had held him back today when he managed not to take her into his arms, hug her tight and kiss away all the hurt and hostility. That had been Mac's old fix-it technique during their marriage, but it obviously hadn't proved effective. Curbing his natural instincts wasn't going to be easy. Mac was a demonstrative kind of guy who wore his emotions on his sleeve.

A romantic clinch scene might work in the movies, but not in real life. With or without an audience.

Chapter Two

Ginger's condo was located in a large real-estate development on property adjacent to Lake Pontchartrain. Her small, twenty-four-unit complex was the oldest and most modestly priced in the area. Ginger was able to apply her rent to make a down payment. The owner's asking price had been affordable on a schoolteacher's salary, and by that time Ginger had stopped expecting Mac to show up on her doorstep.

She'd also reached the point where she didn't panic when the telephone rang, didn't brace herself to answer it and hear his voice. With the easing of tension, something had died inside of her, some ember of futile hope. Safety had felt so terribly empty. And dull. Ginger had faced up to the humiliating truth—that she hadn't really wanted a divorce. Behind her actions had been some immature intention of proving to Mac—and herself—

how important she was to his happiness. Important enough for him to reform.

Instead she'd forced the truth out into the open. Mac could get along fine without her.

It hadn't been easy, Ginger thought as she headed into the development, but she'd learned to get along without him in her life. From this vantage point she could look back and see that her parents had been wise in counseling her to leave Mac and give up on a marriage that didn't have a prayer of lasting over the long term. A marriage that had come about solely because Ginger turned up pregnant.

To Mac's credit he'd taken full blame. Ginger would always be grateful to him for the way he'd reacted to her tearful announcement. Turning pale, he'd stated almost immediately, "We'll get married." And he'd stuck unwaveringly to that old-fashioned solution. A devout Catholic, he'd been horrified when Ginger's roommate raised the topic of abortion, something Ginger wouldn't have agreed to, either. He'd been just as quick to veto the course of action Ginger's parents strongly advised—for her to have the baby as an unwed mother and give it up for adoption. "No way. Not my kid," he'd said flatly.

Ginger had loved him that much more desperately because he'd shouldered the decision and made possible the choice that was actually her choice, too. It had only made her feel guiltier about his being trapped into marrying her when he carried out his role of bridegroom cheerfully. He'd insisted that eventually he would have proposed, after they'd both earned their college degrees. Ginger hadn't believed for a moment that she could have held on to him.

Ruggedly good-looking and likable, in addition to being a big jock on campus, he'd had his pick of girls to date. If Ginger hadn't gotten pregnant, she believed it would have only been a matter of time before some prettier, more outgoing cheerleader type had stolen him away from her.

Their marriage had lasted four years. Four stormy years during which Ginger had felt almost a complete failure as a wife. Finally she'd divorced Mac and set him free to make up for lost time and enjoy the single life-style he'd missed out on in college.

All Ginger had to do was visualize him and Sharon today to know she'd done the right thing. For him *and* herself.

The shock is already wearing off, she told herself as she parked her car and got out. A neighbor, Barbara Philips, had driven up with her five-year-old son, Jonathan. They both greeted Ginger in a friendly manner. She smiled and responded in kind.

"Hi, Barbara. Hi, Jonathan. How was your first day of kindergarten?" she asked the little boy, whose khaki shorts and striped polo shirt bore the evidence of a day of strenuous childish activity.

"My teacher's name is Miss Casey, and she liked the pictures I drew," he answered proudly.

Ginger inspected several examples of his artwork. He beamed at her compliments.

Barbara spoke up. "I wanted to tell you, Ginger, how much I admire the new sign. It really adds a touch of class."

"I was pleased with the way it came out, too."

Ginger followed Barbara's gaze to a flower bed in the center of a small lawn where a rustic wooden sign was mounted. A large anchor carried out the marine motif of the words etched in the sign and painted royal blue, Safe Harbor.

"Everyone appreciates what a good job you're doing as president of the condo owners association," Barbara said. "This place was looking run-down when you took over."

"I had my own best interest at heart," Ginger countered. "But thank you, Barbara. The only headache is collecting from the small minority who conveniently forget to pay their quarterly fee." The owner of D-1, Fay Novak, hadn't paid for the third quarter. A successful real estate agent, she'd recently moved to a fancier complex and put her unit up for rent.

Barbara seemed to read Ginger's mind.

"I ran into Fay Novak at the dry cleaners a couple of days ago, and she told me she'd found a tenant. A single man. He took a year's lease."

Jonathan had been fidgeting during the conversation that didn't include him. "I'm hungry, Mom," he complained. "You said you'd fix my supper as soon as we got home."

"I need to run, too," Ginger said, suddenly mindful of the time.

The pleasant encounter had served a good purpose, helping to get her mind off Mac for a few minutes. At least life will go on as usual away from school, Ginger thought as she hurried to her condo to freshen up before leaving for her supper date with Barry.

On the fifteen-minute drive to Madisonville, a neighboring town nestled on the Tchefuncta River, Ginger found she couldn't wait to arrive at Barry's renovated Victorian cottage to pour out her traumatic news. She called him on her car phone. Barry listened with sympathetic interest, occasionally uttering an exclamation or making a comment that encouraged her to relate the whole story in full detail. With some men she would have felt she had to summarize and hide her feelings regarding a past relationship with another man, but not with him.

Barry was truly a friend and a fun date, as well as a perfect escort for any occasion. Ginger's affection for him warmed her heart and brought to mind the statement she'd made to Mac that she thought Barry might be the right man for her.

"Has your ex-husband always exhibited a flair for the dramatic?" he inquired.

"What do you mean?"

"Well, his actions sound like those of a more imaginative type than your average high-school coach. You think he deliberately staged that faculty meeting, wanting to take you off guard?"

"Staged it? No, I think he just didn't go to the trouble to look me up earlier in the day and warn me he'd gotten a teaching job at my school. Sparing me the shock wasn't important enough to him. And he undoubtedly knew I'd be upset."

"If you wanted to give him the benefit of the doubt, he might have been busy himself preparing for students to arrive tomorrow. Possibly he would have liked to seek you out privately and didn't have the opportunity."

"Mac would have *made* the opportunity if seeking me out privately were a priority. It obviously wasn't."

"And I suppose there's no chance his courage could have failed him."

"Slim to none."

"Do you put any credence in his claim that he came to the north shore to reconcile with you?"

Ginger sighed. "I think he probably came with the

honest intention of going through the motions. He gave up pretty easily.''

Their phone conversation was interrupted by Ginger's arrival at Barry's house. ''I'm here,'' she said, parking behind his black BMW.

He met her at the door, a slender man of medium height. The apron he wore over his expensive tailored slacks and long-sleeved white shirt didn't detract from his well-groomed appearance.

''You've had a rough day,'' he declared, after kissing her lightly on the lips. ''Come into the kitchen and I'll pour you a glass of wine.''

Ginger accompanied him into his charming kitchen and perched on a tall stool. While Barry busied himself, chopping mushrooms with the skill of a trained chef, she sipped from a crystal wineglass and watched. Whatever the menu, she would be in for a treat. He was a gourmet cook and she was frequently his guest for excellent meals he'd prepared, usually from scratch.

Occasionally Ginger insisted on having him over to her place for lunch or dinner. Instead of cooking, she served take-out from one of the numerous good restaurants on the north shore. Her marriage had destroyed every bit of confidence in herself as a cook.

''I would offer to help, but all it would take to ruin our dinner would be for me to stir a pot,'' Ginger said glumly.

''That's a slight exaggeration,'' he chided. ''You're too intelligent not to be competent in the kitchen if cooking interested you.''

''I'm totally inept. I take after my mother, the queen of casseroles made with canned soup.''

Barry's smile was slightly pained. Ginger suspected he was recalling the specific meals he'd been subjected to at her parents' home. With his highly-developed palate, eating her mother's bland concoctions or, even worse, her dry-as-dust holiday turkey and tasteless dressing must have been torture, but, unlike Mac, Barry hadn't given a sign of any lack of enjoyment. His good manners were too ingrained. Afterwards he'd brushed off Ginger's apologies and never uttered a word of criticism, whereas Mac had always begun griping the moment he and Ginger were out the door, comparing her mother's cooking with his mother's, which he rated the best in the world. Insulted and put on the defensive, Ginger had inevitably gotten angry and they'd ended up quarreling.

The solution hadn't been a happy one for her, though it had come about at her suggestion following a big row. Mac had stopped accompanying Ginger to her parents' house in Metairie. In retaliation, she'd stopped going with him to his parents' home in the Irish Channel. The situation had been all the more horribly awkward since the Irish Channel was a New Orleans neighborhood and Metairie was a suburb of the city. There was no excuse for Ginger and Mac not to visit both sets of parents often.

Of course, more had been involved than the food issue. The Honeycutts hadn't approved of Mac as a son-in-law, and the McDaniels hadn't been satisfied with Ginger as a daughter-in-law.

"Unhappy memories?" Barry prompted, bringing Ginger back to the present.

"Sorry," she finally apologized, breaking an extended silence. "I'm not very good company tonight." He was chopping small fresh tomatoes from which the skins and seeds had been removed. "What are you making?"

"Marinara sauce with mushrooms and roasted red bell pepper. Over fettuccine. With a salad of chilled steamed asparagus on Bibb lettuce."

"Sounds delicious."

"Are you sure?" Barry asked, his tone lightly teasing. "When I mentioned marinara sauce and fettuccine, you seemed to wince."

Ginger mustered a smile. "Tonight almost any dish you mentioned would probably hit a raw nerve, although your version wouldn't be anything close to my disasters in the kitchen. It so happens that my most dismal failure was a tomato sauce with ground beef over spaghetti." She shuddered.

"You overcooked the spaghetti?" he suggested.

"It was mush. I served it in big clumps. But the sauce was worse. I poured in about half a bottle of garlic salt to make it highly seasoned. It was so nasty I kept adding sugar to kill the garlic flavor."

"So far you're not stimulating my taste buds," Barry admitted wryly.

"To make matters worse, we had another couple over for dinner that night. Mac's old football teammate, Don Sweeney, and his wife, Brenda. Don nearly gagged when he took his first mouthful, but he managed to swallow it. Mac spit his mouthful into his napkin and gulped down his whole glass of water. I was in tears by this point. I started picking up the plates. Brenda helped me. Mac went to the phone and ordered in pizza. It was definitely a low point for me as Suzy Homemaker," Ginger concluded. "I felt so completely inadequate."

"Afterward you weren't able to laugh about the whole episode with Mac and put it in perspective?"

"No."

"Surely he didn't try to make you feel worse than you already did."

"Probably not deliberately. He suggested that I should get his mother's recipe for spaghetti sauce and follow it to a T. And get directions from her on cooking spaghetti."

"You didn't do either, I assume from your tone."

"I didn't do either," Ginger stated grimly. "Nor did I ever cook spaghetti again, to this day."

Barry wiped his hands on a dish towel and brought the wine bottle to refill her glass. He paused long enough to give her a comforting kiss on the cheek.

"Thanks," she said gratefully. "You're a dear man to put up with me tonight."

"If the shoe were on the other foot and I'd run into Darleen today and was hit with the news that she'd upped and moved to the north shore, I think I could count on a sympathetic ear," he replied.

Darleen was his ex-fiancée who'd jilted him practically at the altar two years ago to marry another man. Between the private devastation and the public embarrassment, Barry had decided he couldn't continue living in his home city of Mobile, Alabama. He'd relocated to Louisiana and started anew in his profession as a CPA.

Ginger knew the whole painful story. "You certainly could count on me to listen and empathize," she assured him with heartfelt sincerity. "But I've already bent your ear enough. Let's talk about something pleasant. How's your new associate working out?"

"Great. Dan is really sharp, even if he is rather stand-offish."

"Maybe he's a little bit shy."

They exhausted that topic and talked of other things, but Ginger didn't enjoy the flow of conversation like she usually did. When she sat down to supper, she didn't relish the delicious food as much as she should have. She caught herself several times sneaking glances at her watch and became strongly annoyed with herself.

It was a poor reflection on her character to become so wrought up over Mac's sudden appearance in her life that a quiet evening with Barry could seem dull and Barry himself seem mild mannered. So what if Ginger's and Barry's relationship was a little lacking in excitement and passion? What they had going for them as a couple was *exactly* what Ginger valued in a man-woman relationship—mutual affection and respect. The *last* thing she ever wanted was to be swept off her feet again by a virile macho type like Mac. No, thank you. She could easily do without urgent sexual attraction.

If her relationship with Barry led eventually to marriage, she would count herself fortunate. He would make her a solid, dependable husband very much in the mold of her father. There wouldn't be any worries about women flocking around him. His and Ginger's marriage would be similar to her parents' marriage—the kind Ginger wanted the second time around—stable and comfortable, *not* a roller coaster of joy and despair.

Which was what her four years as Mac's wife had been.

At nine-thirty Ginger said goodnight and drove home. As she got out of her car, Ginger recalled that Fay had found a tenant for her unit. A single man. Had he moved into D-1 yet?

The parking lot at this end didn't give her a clue because the occupants of D had their reserved spots in the parking lot on the opposite end. Briefly Ginger considered walking along the well-lighted path and ringing the doorbell of D-1. She wanted to introduce herself to Fay's tenant, partly out of neighborliness and partly to carry out her duty as president of the condo owners association.

Better wait, Ginger decided. It was a quarter to ten, rather late in the evening to disturb someone unnecessarily.

In her upstairs bedroom Ginger undressed and slipped on her nightgown. She was standing at the sink in her adjoining bathroom, applying cleansing lotion to her face when the question struck her for the first time: had Mac moved to the north shore? Or did he intend to fight the traffic and commute from New Orleans?

By tomorrow Sharon could probably satisfy Ginger's curiosity. Mac might even be entertaining the librarian tonight in his bachelor pad, if he had one on the north shore.

"Who *cares* if he is? I sure don't," Ginger assured her reflection as she wiped vigorously at her face, removing every vestige of makeup.

Like a skeptical reply the doorbell chimed down below, making her start with surprise.

One of her neighbors must have come to report and ask advice about some maintenance problem. Ginger was used to being treated like a resident manager. Hastily she yanked the headband out of her hair and pulled on a modest wraparound robe styled like a kimono but made of a green-and-white-striped seersucker material. With shiny cheeks she hurried down the stairs barefoot, tying the belt of the robe around her waist.

"Who is it?" she called, her fingers on the key in the dead-bolt lock. At the sound of a familiar voice, she was prepared to unlock the door and admit her visitor.

"It's me. Mac."

"Mac?" Ginger's voice came out as a croak. She cleared her throat. "What do you want?"

"I need to give you a check."

A check? Ginger tried to make sense of his words and failed. Why would he be giving her a check?

"Please open the door, Ginger. I won't stay long."

"I'm not dressed."

"Put on some clothes. I'll wait."

For seconds Ginger stood there as though unable to move. Finally a surge of irritation at herself brought her out of her paralysis as she realized she was actually considering racing back upstairs, not just to throw on some slacks and a blouse but to comb her hair and apply lipstick. The very *idea* that she didn't want Mac to see her not looking her best! She should be *totally* unconcerned about whether he found her pretty and desirable.

"Couldn't this wait until tomorrow?" she demanded, unlocking and swinging the door open in one vigorous motion. He stood there, oozing rugged sex appeal in jeans and a knit shirt that hugged his broad shoulders. For the life of her, Ginger couldn't prevent herself from enjoying looking at him in a way she'd never enjoyed looking at Barry.

"I thought you said you weren't dressed," he said, sounding taken aback.

"I meant 'not presentable.' As you can see, I was getting ready for bed." Ginger gripped the doorknob tighter while his dark brown eyes continued to inspect her. "Are you coming in or not?"

He hesitated a second longer before he stepped over the threshold and entered her tiny foyer. Ginger spotted what appeared to be a checkbook protruding from his back pocket.

"I guess Sharon blabbed and gave you my address," she stated, pushing the door closed.

Mac half turned toward her and then apparently had second thoughts about carrying on a discussion in such close quarters. He moved toward the entrance to her combination dining room and living room, giving Ginger a rear view of him as virile and masculine as the front view. During four years of marriage she'd feasted her eyes on his bare upper torso when he'd stripped off his shirt, muscles rippling under taut skin.

And she'd gotten enormous pleasure from the sight of his bare torso below the waist, too. But it had been a possessive, jealous pleasure spoiled by the torment of wondering whether he took off his clothes with the same lack of self-consciousness under the lustful gaze of other women besides her. And spoiled also by the thought that even if he *wasn't* fooling around, he might be *wanting* to.

Mac finally got around to answering. "I didn't need to ask Sharon where you live since I already knew."

Obviously he just hadn't bothered to take advantage of that knowledge and drop in on Ginger before tonight.

"And how did you find out?" Ginger trudged along behind him, casting her gaze downward instead of ogling his build. The polish on her toenails was chipped. She'd been meaning to give herself a pedicure.

"From the real-estate agent I contacted here on the north shore. She was able to clue me in when I brought up your name and mentioned that you'd received a national teaching award. That was a really big honor. You don't know how proud I felt when I saw your story on the news."

"I was glad for the favorable publicity for our north-shore schools." Ginger's stiff reply was pure self-defense. His words meant far more to her than they should have.

Mac had paused in her dining area and was eyeing the glass-topped table with its silk flower arrangement gracing the center. "Is it all right if I sit here and make out the check?" he inquired.

"A check for what?"

"For the condo fee." He retrieved the checkbook from his pocket with his left hand while he pulled out a chair. "I was told to pay you."

"Told by whom? Not Fay Novak?" Ginger blurted out in disbelief. "You're not her tenant!" But he was indeed the single man in D-1. She read the apologetic admission on his face. "You can't do this to me, Mac. It's bad enough that you took a teaching job in my school."

"Don't jump to wrong conclusions," he soothed, holding up a big hand. "I swear I won't make a nuisance of myself."

"Of all the places you could have rented, *why* pick a condo in this complex?"

"The fact that it was available just seemed a stroke of good luck." With that meek explanation he sat down and opened up his checkbook. He extracted a plastic ballpoint pen clipped to the cover and clicked the end. "Do I make this out to you?"

Ginger suppressed her frustration. "No, you make the check out to Safe Harbor Condo Owners Association."

"What's the date anyway?"

She told him, and he scrawled on the check, but no ink came from the tip of the pen. Mac cursed under his breath and flipped back to the section of deposit slips. "Damned cheap pens never want to write," he complained, scribbling to try to start the flow of ink.

Ginger swallowed hard, the scene touching off a flood of memories. Their first whispered conversation in a college classroom had taken place because his pen wouldn't write. He'd borrowed a pen from her, forgotten to return it and sought her out in the library later. There were many other times when she'd supplied him with writing implements. Her graduation present had been an expensive silver pen with his monogram. He'd seemed so pleased with it and also seemed touched by the sentimentality. He hadn't used it but had tucked it away in the wooden cigar box that held treasured mementos like the gold cuff links his grandmother had given him when he finished high school.

Had he kept the pen? Surely not. He'd probably tossed it in the trash. The assumption shouldn't have hurt as much as it did.

"For heaven's sake, I'll get you a pen."

Ginger retreated to the kitchen.

"It's okay," he called. "This one's working."

She brought back a pen anyway and clutched it, watching him finish writing the check. The sight of his bold penmanship, so familiar, tugged sharply at her emotions.

"When did you move in?" she asked.

"Yesterday. I rented a truck, and Don Sweeney and Chuck Alario gave me a hand. You remember Chuck?"

"Yes, I remember him."

"I rang your doorbell a couple of times, but I wasn't able to catch you home."

"I was gone all day yesterday. Mac, why are you *doing* this to me?" she burst out. "Don't you have any sense of fair play? It wasn't easy leaving New Orleans and everything that was familiar. I had a lot of adjustments to make. I deserve to be happy with my life."

"The last thing I want is to make you unhappy," he said, his expression downcast.

"Then find another place to live! It's bad enough having you on the same faculty!"

"I signed a year's lease." Carefully he tore out the check, laid it on the table and stood up. After making a movement to return his checkbook to his hip pocket, he apparently changed his mind and gripped it in his hand instead as he started for the foyer. His errand accomplished, evidently he was in a big hurry to go. "And I meant what I said earlier," he spoke over his shoulder. "I won't bother you, however much I might want to."

"Your presence will bother me!" she blurted out in protest, following after him, her frustration level rising again to an almost unbearable level. "Why didn't you drop this latest bombshell on me when you waylaid me in the parking lot at school? It would have been a lot more considerate than paying me a visit at bedtime. I could use a few hours' sleep tonight."

"You didn't give me much of a chance to tell you anything," he replied. "You were in too big a hurry to keep your date with another man." His tone held its own accusation.

"I'll hazard a guess that you didn't spend the evening alone tonight yourself." The words popped out on their own. "Not that I care if you did or not."

"I met Sharon at a local restaurant, and we had dinner. But it wasn't a date. I'm not interested in dating her or anyone else. The only woman I want to be with is you."

"Oh, sure."

"It's true."

"No, it's *not* true. People don't change their basic

personality, Mac. You could no more stop charming every female in sight than you could stop breathing.''

He'd reached the door. Grasping the doorknob in one hand and still gripping his checkbook in the other hand, he turned to face her. "I agree that people don't change their basic personality, and I haven't changed mine. What I have to change somehow is your opinion of me as some kind of Don Juan type who can't keep his pants zipped.''

"My opinion of you doesn't *matter* anymore.''

"Yes, it does matter. It matters like hell.''

"The best thing you could do to raise yourself in my estimation is to show some regard for my feelings. I intend to steer clear of you at school, and I'm asking you to follow my example.''

He expelled a breath and nodded, agreeing without any argument to her terms. "This is even tougher than I anticipated," he said, his voice rough. He was looking at her hair, her face, her figure. Ginger's breasts grew heavier, and the muscles in her abdomen tightened in response to the hunger in his gaze. "Here we are within reach of each other after all these years apart, and I don't dare put my arms around you, don't dare touch you or kiss you—''

"No, you *don't* dare," she broke in, wrapping her arms tight around her waist to suppress the sharp longing he'd aroused. "There's someone else in my life to hold me and kiss me. Good night, Mac. The next payment of the condo fee will be due the first of October in case you're still Fay's tenant and are responsible for it.''

"I'll pay it on time.''

He left, pulling the door closed behind him.

Ginger stood in the same spot, overwhelmed with a

sense of letdown. Of course, his dinner with Sharon had been a date. He'd enjoyed the librarian's company and would undoubtedly go out on more dates with her, dates with lots of other women whether he termed them dates or not. That was his prerogative. He was single. But how could he look Ginger in the eye and say so earnestly, "The only woman I want to be with is you"?

"And I have some waterfront property in the desert to sell you," Ginger said aloud, twisting the key in the dead bolt.

Her cynicism didn't change the fact that her foolish heart had melted at Mac's declaration. It was a knee-jerk reaction, the result of frayed nerves.

Fortunately he wasn't sincerely bent on reconciling with her, despite statements to the contrary. Otherwise he would have behaved entirely differently. He wouldn't have been so restrained, not touching her once on three different occasions, except for a handshake.

Mac's way of healing rifts and smoothing over arguments had always been to take her into his arms, kiss her, use his strength to manhandle her gently until she'd succumbed to the sheer joy of physical contact with him.

No, he was only going through the motions, whatever his underlying reasons. Probably he couldn't really analyze them himself.

And I'm afraid to believe him. Ginger had been hurt too badly to ever trust her heart to Mac a second time.

Chapter Three

The buzz of Ginger's alarm clock interrupted what was more an exhausted stupor than restful slumber. She hadn't managed to fall asleep until well past midnight and hadn't slept well. Groggy and clumsy with fatigue, she knocked the clock to the floor trying to turn off the alarm. Then she bumped her head hard on her bedside table, fumbling to retrieve the clock, which still buzzed insistently.

With silence finally restored but the noise reverberating in her head, she dragged herself out of bed and headed for the bathroom, moving with the coordination of a drunk taking a sobriety test. "Ouch," she muttered as she grazed her hip on the door frame.

After turning on the shower and stripping off her nightgown, she stood with her eyes closed, yawning and rubbing both her head and her hip. Her fuzzy thoughts were resentful. *Mac knows darned well I'm one of those* people who can't function without eight hours' sleep. He lived with me for four years. I'll bet he went back to Fay Novak's condo last night and fell fast asleep. Right now he's probably still in bed, dead to the world. He'll sleep another thirty minutes, jump up as cheerful as you please and hop into the shower....

Images all too vivid and all too alluring filled Ginger's vacant mind. Mac asleep, the sheet down around his waist and his whole upper torso bare. Mac stepping naked into the shower, the water coursing down his face and his broad shoulders and muscular chest, down the rest of his big, rugged body.

"So help me, if I had his phone number, I would call him and wake him up," Ginger grumbled, yawning as she pulled the shower curtain aside and stepped into the tub. She shrieked when the cold spray hit her. The fact that she'd apparently accidentally twisted the temperature knob to the right seemed like her ex-husband's fault, too.

It didn't improve her dark mood one bit to know that her nipples had already been hard and goose bumps had already risen on her skin *before* the icy dousing. Ginger was highly exasperated with herself that after a horrible night and feeling as dragged out as she felt, she could get turned on by visualizing Mac's naked body.

The exasperation grew when she found herself taking special pains with her hair and makeup. "For heaven's sake, this is the first day of school, not your high-school prom!" she informed her reflection in the mirror.

The caustic lecture must not have sunk in. Fifteen minutes later she came to her senses standing in her walk-in closet, reaching for first this garment and then that one, caught up in indecision about what to wear.

With an impatient exclamation Ginger pulled a moss

green skirt off a hanger and donned it and a cream-colored blouse with an embroidered neckline. Out of principle she couldn't wear blue because Mac had always liked her in blue, especially vivid shades.

Finally dressed, Ginger quickly made her bed less neatly than usual and hurried downstairs. The sight of the check lying on her dining table played further havoc with her normal early-morning efficiency. She put the check away out of sight in a drawer, shoving the drawer closed none too gently, and next placed the chair where Mac had sat back in place, but to no avail. His presence still lingered so strongly that she could have easily summoned his apparition. For a crazy moment Ginger contemplated taking the time to wipe away his fingerprints on her furniture with a polish cloth and run the vacuum to remove any traces of his footsteps.

Too rushed by this point to top a bowl of cereal with fresh fruit, she made do with plain cereal and milk for breakfast. In pouring the milk, she slopped some on the counter, a mishap causing another flare of irritation. Vowing that tomorrow morning her life would be completely back to normal, she ate standing in her small kitchen.

Her departure definitely didn't restore any sense of normalcy. When she stepped outside, Mac's footprints might have been painted in red, forming a trail from D-1 to Ginger's entryway and then a trail back to his own entryway. Ginger's privacy had vanished overnight. The very name of the condo complex, Safe Harbor, had become a ludicrous joke. She felt like a fugitive who'd been tracked down.

The high school had become a whole different environment, too. A much less pleasant environment fraught with tension and dread. The change that bothered Ginger most, though, was the change in *her*. Her hard-earned serenity and contentment with her life had deserted her. She had butterflies in her stomach as she pulled into the faculty parking lot.

"You're just shaky from lack of sleep. And haven't recovered from the shock. That's all." Ginger was searching for a cherry red Camaro as she spoke these words of hollow reassurance to herself.

Since Mac hadn't barged into her classroom yet, she didn't encounter his ghost when she entered and was able to push thoughts of him aside. Or for a short while until the bell rang and the room filled up with students. Her ears seemed to pick out snatches of conversation about the new coach and his rugged good looks.

In his own insidious way, Mac had invaded her classroom without even appearing in person!

The adrenaline that flowed with her righteous indignation served a good purpose, helping to flush away her fatigue and allowing her to generate the enthusiasm and positive energy that made her a successful teacher. Each of her first three classes of the day went well, but by the time fourth period came, Ginger was glad she had a free hour for her plan period and then lunch.

I need a cup of coffee to perk me up, she thought as she tiredly erased the chalkboard.

There was coffee in the teachers' lounge. But what if Ginger walked in and found Mac there? For all she knew, he might have fourth period off, too. One glance at her and he'd see she hadn't slept. He'd spot the dark circles under her eyes, notice her pallor under her makeup. When Ginger encountered him, she needed to be at her best, her strongest.

And look her best, her prettiest.

"I can't believe you're acting like such a bimbo!"

Ginger told herself disgustedly, creating a puff of chalk dust as she slapped the eraser down.

With the handles of her tote bag gripped in one hand and the strap of her purse slung over her shoulder, she headed down the corridor to the teachers' lounge, formulating a new resolution. She would *not* alter her usual habits at *her* school because her ex-husband was on the faculty. She would *not* try to avoid him as she'd indicated last night she would do. Let their paths cross whenever they happened to cross. Ginger would take in stride seeing him. He soon would get the message that she was completely over him.

Mac wasn't in the lounge. Nor did he wander in, although it turned out fourth period *was* his plan period. Sharon revealed this information when she stuck her head in the door and made no bones about the fact that she was looking for him.

That's good that he stayed away, Ginger told herself. I'm glad he's avoiding me. And she *was* glad, not disgruntled. Her sense of letdown came from being geared up to contend with his unwanted presence.

The very fact that he was finding it so easy to keep his word and avoiding contact with her proved that he really *hadn't* moved to the north shore because of her.

''The secret of weight control is an active sex life,'' Sharon said, biting into her chicken sandwich. ''Which brings up a subject I'm dying to discuss. What's the scoop on you and Coach Mac? I can't get to first base with the guy because he's too busy grilling me about you.''

Ginger opened her carton of milk and inserted a plastic straw. ''I have it from a good source that he took you out to dinner last night. Sounds like you're halfway to first base.''

''He didn't 'take' me to dinner. We met at Rooster's, ate and went our separate ways. You were the main topic of conversation.'' Sharon took a big bite of her sandwich and chewed. ''Who's the good source? I didn't see a soul I knew there on a school night.''

There were more questions Ginger had wanted to ask about the dinner date, like who had actually initiated it. But whether Mac had asked Sharon or she'd asked him, he was obviously open to a relationship with the librarian.

''Mac told me himself when he rang my doorbell at quarter to ten last night. He dropped by to pay his condo fee,'' Ginger added.

''Condo fee?'' Sharon was feeding herself fries, her befuddlement not affecting her appetite. ''I don't get it.''

''He didn't mention he's my neighbor?''

''No, he didn't say where he was living. He bought a condo in your complex?''

''Leased, not bought.''

''Come on, Ginger! Spill the beans,'' Sharon implored. ''I'm dying of curiosity. What's the history between you two? Is he an old boyfriend?''

''More than an old boyfriend. Try ex-husband.''

The other woman choked on her food. ''Ex-*husband!* But neither of you gave the slightest *hint!* You've got to fill me in!''

Ginger complied, telling just the bare facts. ''We met at Southeastern in Hammond, married when we were sophomores and divorced four years later after we'd both gotten our education degrees and taught in different high schools in New Orleans for a year. I moved over here, and he stayed in the city. Until yesterday we hadn't seen each other or spoken for six years.''

''No efforts at reconciliation on either side?''

''None.''

Sharon had consumed her fries. She eyed Ginger's plate. ''Are you serious about not eating those?''

''Help yourself.'' Ginger handed her plate over and watched without regret while her fries were raked onto the other woman's plate. Maybe there would be some benefit from all the turmoil she was experiencing. She might just lose those five extra pounds without exerting a lot of willpower.

''You did get some advance notice that your ex was taking a job on this faculty, didn't you?'' The other woman resumed the conversation as she continued to devour her lunch.

''My first inkling was when Bill introduced him yesterday.''

''Mac apparently expected to find you among his new colleagues when he stood up yesterday. He didn't show any surprise. He must have found out.''

''Yes, he knew.'' And evidently didn't care what havoc he created in her life.

''So what's the situation? Does he want to be friends? Is he still carrying a torch for you?''

''There's no chance we'll be friends, and no, he isn't carrying a torch for me.'' He never *had* carried a torch for her.

Sharon hesitated. ''Are you still hung up on him?''

''Absolutely and positively not. Be my guest if you want to date him.''

''You sure?''

''I'm sure.''

The librarian looked satisfied with the emphatic answer. "Okay. I'll take that as a green-light signal then. Any objections to me letting Mac know when your name comes up again that you've confided in me?"

Ginger shook her head, giving her permission. "I would just as soon you didn't tell anyone else." Let Mac spread the word he'd once been married to her, if he wished.

"That goes without saying." Sharon finished her sandwich and drained her carton of milk. Sitting back in her chair with a contented sigh, she patted her flat stomach. "I was starved, and I had a big breakfast this morning. I made myself bacon and pancakes. I usually don't go to the trouble unless I'm cooking for two." Her wicked grin filled in the details. Her breakfast guests at those hearty morning meals were male and had spent the night.

Ginger could have shared the information that Mac's favorite breakfast had once been bacon and pancakes. Sharon would undoubtedly find out on her own whether it was still his favorite. And soon. In a week's time the tall, thin, man-hungry blond woman would probably know all of Mac's preferences, including intimate likes and dislikes.

The knowledge shouldn't have been painful. But it was.

It shouldn't have made the old jealousy curl through her, as sharp as razor wire on a prison fence. But it did.

Mac's words played like a recording: "I've matured and so have you. We could deal with the same issues a lot better now." Undoubtedly he had matured in many ways, and Ginger certainly had, enough to know that she didn't want to revert to her old self. Her adoration of Mac hadn't been a healthy emotional attachment. It hadn't made her happy, hadn't made her feel good about herself.

Ginger *wasn't* falling into the same old pattern.

"Here you are. Coach Sanders said I'd find you in the gym."

Mac looked over his shoulder at Sharon Hawkins, who approached with a book in her hand, low heels clicking on the hardwood floor. "Hi, Sharon. I was just about to leave," he said, pocketing his keys and double-checking to make sure the door of the equipment room was securely locked.

"How did your first day of coed P.E. classes go?"

"Fine. Although it's going to take some getting used to, after teaching all boys," he admitted. "I'd forgotten how much teenage girls giggle."

"Giggling is a measure of feminine excitement at that age."

Mac's grin was rueful. "In that case the level of excitement ran pretty high."

"You do realize that your girl students are the envy of all their girlfriends who drew other P.E. teachers?"

He eyed her skeptically, figuring she wasn't serious. Mac wasn't comfortable with the whole line of conversation. "Is the book you're holding the one on the history of baseball we were talking about last night?" he asked, getting them started toward the gym door. He didn't want to be rude, but he was ready to leave.

"Yes, it is. You said you'd like to read it, so I took the liberty of signing it out to you."

"That was nice of you. Thanks." He accepted the book from her and tucked it under his arm. "I'll return it in a few days and get it back in circulation."

"Keep it until you've finished reading it."

"Hey, I'm not a slow reader, despite being a jock back in high school and college," Mac said dryly. Besides, I'll probably have a lot of time for reading at night, he reflected to himself with an inner sigh.

Sharon laughed. "No insult intended. I just meant it's a thick book." They'd reached the door of the gym. "Does a cup of strong, fresh-brewed coffee sound good to you?" she asked as they stepped out onto the paved, covered walkway. "It does to me. I was thinking of stopping at Rooster's for an espresso. Care to join me?"

"I'd better pass. I still have some boxes to unpack."

"Isn't moving a pain? Incidentally I had lunch with Ginger Honeycutt today, and she told me you're her neighbor."

Mac automatically slowed down. With the mention of Ginger, the librarian suddenly had his full attention. "Not her next-door neighbor, but I'm renting a condo in the same complex where she lives."

"In case you're wondering, Ginger also filled me in on some confidential background information that explained her odd behavior yesterday at the teachers' meeting. Odd to me, not you. I'm sure you understood and probably weren't surprised that she treated you like you had a communicable disease."

No, he hadn't been surprised, but he'd been sick with disappointment. It wasn't something he could talk about with anyone but Ginger. "Could you spell out what this 'background information' was?" Mac asked, wanting to make sure Sharon wasn't pumping him for details Ginger hadn't divulged and didn't want known.

They'd come to a complete stop by now. The librarian glanced around. No one was in sight, but she lowered her voice anyway. "The gist of it was that you're her ex-husband. By the way, I'm not talking out of school, pun intended. Ginger gave me her permission to let you know she'd confided in me. She also gave her blessing.''

Mac frowned. ''Blessing?''

''I believe her exact words were 'be my guest if you want to date him.' Wouldn't you rather continue this discussion over a cup of coffee?'' Sharon suggested.

''I'd rather not continue it period, but a cup of coffee is seeming like a good idea.'' Mac needed to go somewhere long enough to recover from the hurt of Ginger's quoted words. He didn't trust himself to drive directly to his condo. Instead of sticking to his plan to give her space and gradually win her respect and trust, he might find himself ringing her doorbell and spilling his guts. And ruining his chances with her.

Mac had to win her back.

He couldn't explain why she was the woman for him, but she was. She had a special quality about her that had attracted him from the beginning. And, of course, he'd found her to be pretty and sexy. He still did.

The spark was still there between them. Now that they'd both grown more mature, they could be good together.

It was just a matter of hanging in there and convincing her.

Barry wasn't at home when Ginger phoned at five-fifteen. After listening to his recorded voice, she left a message and then tried his office number on the chance that he might be working late. Again Ginger got a recording.

''Where are you?'' she said in dismay, hanging up. It was ridiculous, but she felt entirely alone and vulnerable. Talking to Barry would help put things back in perspective.

While she waited to hear from him, she flipped on the TV and tried to watch the news, but she couldn't concentrate for wondering whether Mac was at his condo by now. Maybe he'd returned and left again. Or maybe he'd invited Sharon over tonight.

"Don't *think* about him!" Ginger exclaimed, and got up to go and take a couple of aspirin for her headache.

Finally at six o'clock the phone rang, making her jump. That's probably Barry, she thought. But what if it wasn't Barry? What if it was Mac? The possibility made Ginger's throat dry.

Barry's voice came over the line. "Hi, you okay?"

"Now I am," she replied. "Did you just get home?"

"I just this minute walked in the door. Dan offered to buy me a beer when we were leaving the office. It was his first friendly overture in the month since he became my associate, so I said sure. We went to Rooster's Café and ended up having two beers."

"That's Sharon Hawkins's hangout."

"As a matter of fact she was there having coffee with a guy. She saw me and waved."

"What did he look like?" Ginger already knew what the description would be.

"Big. Tall. Black hair. Brown eyes."

"Too bad Sharon didn't bring him over and introduce him. Then you would have had the pleasure of meeting my ex-husband."

"Ah, that explains why I caught him glaring at me when I looked over in his direction. I didn't know if I reminded him of his worst enemy or Sharon had mentioned I was a CPA and he had a grudge against his tax accountant. Instead she must have pointed me out as the fellow you were dating.''

''More than likely.''

''So that was McDaniel. He does work fast in starting up a new social life, doesn't he?'' Barry's observation held tinges of both male admiration and male envy.

'''Work' implies effort, and there's no effort required. He just smiles and exudes his macho aura, and women flock to him.''

''He wasn't smiling much today. He seemed rather brooding.''

''Sharon will find a way to cheer him up. This wasn't their first date. He had dinner with her last night.'' Ginger went on to explain how she'd gotten the information and filled him in on Mac moving to the complex, leaving out nothing except shameful, humiliating details. Like the way her body had hummed to life in response to Mac's nearness last night. It didn't seem fair that Mac had gotten even more ruggedly handsome since the divorce. He'd been handsome enough.

''What gall,'' Barry marveled. ''Or daring. I'm not sure of the right word.''

''Gall,'' Ginger decided for him.

''Before we hang up, did you get better acquainted with Dan this afternoon?'' She'd been too busy relating the latest installment in her personal soap opera to give him a chance to say whether he'd made inroads into his new associate's standoffishness.

''He thawed out quite a bit. We discovered several common interests, including wine. He's quite knowledgeable on the subject and has an extensive library with some books I don't own. He very generously offered to lend them to me.''

''Gosh, you two do have a lot in common. I'll bet

you and Dan will become good friends. Over time,'' she added when Barry wasn't quick to respond. Obviously some doubt lingered.

It was a case of mutual reserve, Ginger suspected. From Barry's comments she'd surmised that his associate was cautious in warming up to people, and Barry tended to be the same way. He was rather proper and polite according to today's standards, but she found those qualities charming. Probably all the more so, admittedly, because Mac's brand of courtesy was so entirely casual by contrast.

After she'd gotten off the phone, Ginger turned on her CD player and microwaved a frozen low-cal dinner for her supper. Then she settled down to accomplishing some schoolwork. Or more accurately, settled down to attempting to accomplish some schoolwork. She found it difficult to concentrate.

Any second the doorbell could ring, and Mac could be standing outside her door. Likewise the telephone could peal to life, she could answer and hear his voice in her ear. Ginger found herself rehearsing what she would say, imagining just how she would behave.

Ten o'clock came without a visit from Mac. Without a phone call from him. Wearily Ginger went upstairs and got ready for bed.

But she didn't fall asleep. She lay there, eyes tightly closed against images of Mac and Sharon having dinner. Had they gone to her place afterward? Was he still there? Would Sharon be cooking him breakfast in the morning? Questions whose answers had *no* relevance for Ginger crowded her mind.

The ringing of the phone brought her eyes wide open. She sat up in bed and tried to make her hello sound drowsy, just in case the caller was Mac. Not for anything would she give him the satisfaction of guessing the truth—that he'd given her insomnia.

A click followed by the dial tone told Ginger the person at the other end had hung up. A wrong number. Or was it? A phone call was one way of finding out whether anyone was home.

"What are you *doing?*" Ginger murmured as she punched the digits for local information.

"What city, please?" inquired an operator.

"Mandeville."

A recorded voice intoned Mac's phone number and then repeated it.

Ginger pressed the digits in sequence.

Ring. Ring.

He wasn't home. He was at Sharon's. The dismayed certainty welled up.

"Hello." His deep voice came over the line, the male cadences slurred with sleepiness.

He was home in bed. The phone had awakened him. But he would go right back to sleep.

Ginger gently clicked the disconnect button, turned off her bedside lamp and fell into exhausted slumber.

Chapter Four

"Today's a new day," Ginger cheerfully informed her reflection in the mirror as she applied makeup the next morning. A good night's sleep had done wonders for her morale. Yesterday with its failures and emotional merry-go-round was behind her, thank heaven. She felt able to cope with whatever the day held.

That included encountering her ex-husband at school.

Her life *could* and *would* go on as usual. It was simply a matter of getting used to his presence on the north shore.

As a statement of being firmly in control, Ginger donned a royal blue suit dress. Blue was one of her best colors. She'd liked blue long before she'd ever met Joseph Patrick McDaniel. She wasn't going to stop wearing blue outfits because he'd barged upon the scene and might make the wrong assumption that she'd dressed to please him. Let him think whatever he liked.

This morning there was time to make her bed up neatly before she went downstairs. There was time to sit down at the dining table in her usual spot and watch a few minutes of a news program on a New Orleans station while she ate a nutritious breakfast of cereal topped with a sliced banana.

Ginger's routine was back to normal. Soon *she* would be back to her normal self.

On her arrival at school, Mac's car wasn't in the parking lot. Its absence already seemed the norm. He would habitually arrive a few minutes later than she did, and his coaching duties would probably keep him there after she'd left. In time I won't even look for a red Camaro, Ginger thought.

Some of the newness had also already worn off when her classes trooped in. Individual faces looked familiar. She was able to connect a lot of names with the faces. The collective excitement had settled down to a more manageable level. The handsome new coach apparently was yesterday's news. Ginger's ears didn't catch the first mention of Coach Mac.

When fourth period rolled around, she left her classroom, breezed into the teachers' lounge to buy a canned diet drink and was walking out the door when she came face-to-face with Mac. He wasn't alone. And naturally he hadn't accompanied another male P.E. teacher from the gym.

"Hi, Angie." Ginger directed her first greeting to the trim brunette who coached the tennis team. Then she spoke to her ex-husband. "Hi, Mac, how are you?"

"Are you leaving?" he asked, reaching out as though he meant to grasp her arm. Then he quickly dropped his hand, evidently having second thoughts about detaining her.

"Mac was just telling me the funniest incident that happened in his first-period class," Angie said, laughing.

"Too bad I don't have time to hear it." Ginger waved the folder she held. "I'm off to make copies of some handouts."

"Mind if I come along? I haven't managed to locate the copy machines yet," Mac said.

"They're not hard to find. They're in a room right off the main office."

"I'll show you where they are," Angie spoke up. "Have a cup of coffee first, Coach. I want to hear the rest of your story."

Frustration showed on Mac's face, but when Ginger hurried on her way, he didn't follow after her. She assumed he went into the teachers' lounge with Angie. Getting to know his new female colleague better plainly took priority over trying to get in his ex-wife's good graces.

Sure, he moved to the north shore to be near me, Ginger reflected cynically.

It would get easier and easier to run into him. Eventually her heart wouldn't leap into her throat and her whole body wouldn't go into shock. Maybe in time she would even develop a total immunity to his rugged good looks, his deep voice, his easygoing masculine charm. In time she could see him, talk to him and feel nothing but a calm detachment.

In the meanwhile the fact that her pulse fluttered at the sight of him and she melted inside when she looked into his eyes didn't shake Ginger's conviction that she'd made the right decision by divorcing him. Intense physical attraction wasn't a sound basis for a marriage. There had to be trust and devotion. Mac was a great guy in a lot of ways, but it just wasn't in his personality to be the kind of husband Ginger required.

As she passed through the office of the school secretary, Ginger waved to Nora Burky, who was talking on the telephone and had students ringing her desk. A stout, big-bosomed woman in her fifties with teased silver gray hair the size and shape of a football helmet, the secretary was as kindhearted as she was stern and efficient, but she was like a bloodhound when it came to scenting gossip. In Ginger's present state of mind, she was just as glad to avoid chatting with Nora.

Second on Ginger's list of people she preferred not to have to talk to right at the moment was Sharon Hawkins, who looked around with a big welcoming smile when Ginger entered the small room with the copy machines. Fortunately Rosemary Wells was also present, but the personable business teacher didn't stay long to act as a buffer. She soon departed with several stacks of materials.

Sharon immediately went over and closed the door.

"I wouldn't do that," Ginger said, making her tone lightly ironic. "Poor Nora will be all in a dither."

Sharon laughed. "She'll pop over to the library later and put me through the third degree. I'll make up some juicy gossip." She returned to the machine she'd been using and began straightening a stack of papers. "Did Barry mention he'd seen me yesterday afternoon at Rooster's?"

"Yes, he said you were having coffee with a man. From the description I gathered it was Mac."

"It was. Who was the guy with Barry, at the bar?"

"His new associate. It's kind of a trial partnership thing."

"I see. He's an accountant, too."

"A CPA." What was behind this interest in Dan? Ginger was wondering. She'd been expecting the librarian to have Mac, her new love interest, on her mind. "I haven't met him. Is he good-looking?"

"Very attractive. In the same way Barry's attractive," Sharon added almost hesitantly. "Expensive clothes, immaculately well groomed, a cultured air about him. My gut instinct as a woman says he's probably gay."

"You can't tell that from just looking at a man!" Ginger scoffed.

"Not always." Another hesitation. "Obviously I was wrong in my snap judgment of Barry. Or I assume I was wrong, since you're dating him."

Ginger's mouth fell open. "You certainly *are* wrong! Just because a man isn't macho *doesn't* mean he's gay." Her sharp tone expressed her objection to making snap judgments about another person's sexuality.

"Not so loud," Sharon cautioned, holding up her hand. "I'm not being judgmental. Honest. I love gay men. As friends. It's just…well, you're a teeny bit naive sometimes, Ginger. I'd hate for you to be hurt. You *have* slept with Barry?"

"Yes. Several times." Her answer didn't erase the concern in the other woman's expression.

"Only several times? You've been dating him for what—eight or nine months?"

"Sex isn't the key element in my relationship with Barry, the way it was with Mac." Honesty compelled Ginger to add, "Not that I didn't enjoy Mac's company a lot when we were getting along."

"Was he the jealous type?"

The question took Ginger by surprise. She thought a

moment before answering. "He never had reason to be jealous."

"Yesterday he gave me the impression he'd like to go over and punch Barry. I wondered if it was a knee-jerk reaction."

"You pointed Barry out to him?"

"Mac saw me wave to Barry, so I just casually mentioned that Barry was the guy you were dating. I didn't think there was any reason for secrecy."

"There isn't."

"Ginger, are you sure everything's over between you and Mac? He's showing an awful lot of interest in you."

"I *am* female, even though I'm his ex-wife. At the present moment he's in the teachers' lounge showing a lot of interest in Angie Packard."

"I'd better go break that up. See you later," the librarian said, hastily scooping up her materials and departing, a woman on a mission.

Ginger pushed the door closed again. She was grateful when no one joined her while she was completing her task, using all three of the copy machines to speed things up. The route back to her classroom took her past the teachers' lounge, but a glance through the large glass pane in the top half of the door was enough to quicken her steps. Seated on a sofa, Mac held a section of newspaper open in front of him. Obviously he wasn't getting much reading done, with Sharon perched beside him and Angie sitting nearby on an adjacent sofa. Several other people were also in the room, but Ginger barely registered their identity.

Eventually scenes like this in the teachers' lounge won't bother me, she told herself, her fingernails biting into her palms.

There would be many similar scenes with her ex-husband ringed by women admirers. Ginger could count on that as much as she could count on the sun rising in the east. The thing to do, she knew, was not walk on past, but pop in for a while and subject herself to the unpleasantness as a curative measure.

Maybe tomorrow. But not today.

Back in her classroom Ginger busied herself doing schoolwork. She was standing at a file cabinet, arranging brightly colored folders into sections for each class, when the quiet tapping of a visitor made her heart leap. She looked around, half-expecting to see Mac standing on the threshold.

The person who opened the door and stepped inside was a man, sure enough, but he wasn't Mac. Earl Pritchett, who taught social studies across the hall, had come in search of staples, which she readily supplied. Ten minutes later another colleague, in this instance a woman, dropped by to ask a favor. Ginger agreed to swap lunch duty with her.

The bell rang, ending Ginger's plan period, an hour during which Mac could have sought her out. But he hadn't. True, she'd asked him to steer clear of her at school, but that wouldn't have stopped him if seeing her were really important.

Sharon was dead wrong in thinking that his ex-wife held any more interest for him than the other single women on the faculty and staff. Out of sight, out of mind.

That afternoon when she was leaving school, Ginger spotted Mac out on the football practice field, conducting drills. Even at a distance she could read in his body language his enthusiasm for coaching, which apparently hadn't died. He fervently believed in the value of team sports and the importance of fostering school spirit in youngsters and teenagers. He believed that regular physical activity was essential for good health and that physical-education classes were as important as any others in the high-school curriculum.

Or he *had* held all those beliefs. Probably he still held them. Ginger doubted he'd changed in any essential way. More than likely he'd continued his free-spending ways and lived from paycheck to paycheck, with a big credit-card balance. He was probably still generous to a fault, quick to dig into his wallet and lend twenty dollars, quick to pick up tabs. His favorite viewing on TV was undoubtedly still live sports events. He probably still upheld his mother's cooking as the best in the world. He probably couldn't be bribed or enticed to attend a ballet or an opera and would have to be dragged to art openings and serious plays and movies.

In addition to those traits, he had other more redeeming qualities. He would come to the aid of a friend or a family member in a second. He loved children. He was patriotic.

If only you'd been a complete rat, it would have been easier to get you out of my system, Ginger thought, sighing. "Would be easier," she corrected herself aloud.

Plainly she hadn't entirely gotten over him in six years. Now she could complete the process.

Returning to her complex later that evening after having dinner with Barry, Ginger drove around to the parking lot at the opposite end, where residents of buildings C and D had their reserved slots. D-1's slot was empty. Mac was probably out with Sharon or Angie or possibly even another woman he'd met who was their competition.

But *not* Ginger's competition. She'd withdrawn from that particular contest for good.

Last night's tension was gone as Ginger got ready for bed. Her ears didn't strain for the sound of the doorbell. She wasn't braced for the ringing of the phone. Barry had observed accurately that she was remarkably calm, but it was a calmness arising out of a sense of anticlimax.

Her feeling of emptiness was similar to what she'd felt after the divorce when she'd realized she no longer had to dread Mac's putting in an appearance in her life.

It was almost ten-thirty when Mac pulled into his parking spot. He'd gone to an action flick and afterward killed another forty-five minutes having coffee and a piece of pie at Rooster's Cafe.

Well, you got through another long evening, he thought to himself, getting out and quietly closing the door of the Camaro.

The four buildings of the small complex, two on either side of a central lawn, all faced inward. A flagstone walkway running the length of the lawn intersected individual walkways leading to each entrance.

Mac bypassed his walkway when he reached it and continued toward the far end until he'd come abreast of Ginger's building and had a clear view of her parking lot. Her car was back in its spot. It had been gone at six-thirty when he'd gotten here, following football practice.

He'd known in his gut that she was with the CPA fellow, Whitfield. For a few crazy minutes the pressure had gotten to Mac. He'd gone berserk, considering one desperate plan after another to track her down, kidnap her and take her somewhere private where the two of them could *talk* to each other and get things straight between them. Start making up for *lost* time, dammit!

Mac had reasoned himself back to sanity and faced up to the realities. While he wasn't a violent person by nature, in the heat of the moment he might deck Whitfield if the guy came on as Ginger's protector. That would be setting a great example for his students if Mac ended up with assault-and-battery charges being brought against him. Most importantly he'd only be sabotaging his chances with Ginger by using brute force. She would come down on Whitfield's side, not Mac's. The publicity would cause her embarrassment.

So damned much was at stake. He *had* to be patient and follow his game plan of earning her respect and trust.

I didn't know it would be quite this much hell, Mac reflected, gazing at Ginger's condo. A faint glow behind the blinds on the second story told him she was still up. She was probably getting ready for bed, dressed in a nightgown and doing her nightly routine of cleaning her face and brushing her hair. When she finished, her skin would be fragrant and soft, her hair silky to the touch.

Mac let himself remember…

He was lying in bed, drowsy and content. Ginger flipped off the bathroom light and came into the bedroom, her bare feet making no sound on the carpet. She slipped under the sheet on her side, reached and clicked off the lamp. Then she scooted close to him and said softly, in that tone that turned him to warm mush inside, "Good night. I love you."

"Same here," he replied, his emotion making his

voice gruff. Turning onto his side, he wrapped his arm around her waist and she snuggled even closer.

"You have football practice tomorrow afternoon?" she asked, her words muffled by a yawn.

"Every day this week. Don't expect me home before five-thirty or six." Mac's words were muffled, too, because he was nuzzling her forehead, her cheek, planting kisses and savoring the softness of her skin and her feminine scent.

"I'm sorry I'm so pooped out on week nights," she said.

"I'm beat on most week nights myself. Teaching takes it out of a person."

"We could set the clock earlier and make love in the mornings."

"Haven't we had this conversation before?" he asked, threading his fingers through her hair. "I'm not feeling sexually deprived because we're making love less often than we did when we were students in college. Honest."

She breathed out a sigh.

"Go to sleep, worrywart," he chided, hugging her tight.

Soon her breathing was even and her body relaxed in his arms. Mac drifted off to sleep himself, optimistic that his young wife's anxieties would fade when she saw they had no substance.

Mac sighed, returning to the present. In retrospect he should have taken Ginger's anxieties more seriously and dealt with them better than he had. "Give me another chance," he said aloud.

The glow in the second story of her condo suddenly

went dark. He retraced his steps, heading to his own dark condo and his empty bed.

When fourth period rolled around the following day, Ginger put Operation Cure into practice. Carrying her tote bag stuffed with several batches of papers to grade, she went directly to the teachers' lounge, where she took up her station at a long table that served the dual purpose of a work area or an eating area.

Angie Packard strolled in about ten minutes later, but today Mac wasn't with her. After drinking a cup of coffee and browsing through the north shore edition of the New Orleans *Times-Picayune*, Angie departed. Other teachers, including Rosemary Wells, came and went.

Mac didn't show up at all.

Ginger had finished grading her papers by the time the lunch bell rang. By that time she was also fuming. Here she'd gotten herself all geared for an encounter with him and no encounter had materialized.

Is he doing this to me on purpose? she asked herself, stuffing the bundles of student quizzes into her tote bag so roughly that she popped two rubber bands.

Today was the day she'd agreed to do another teacher's noon duty. Ginger patrolled her area of the school grounds, working off steam. Minutes before the bell rang, ending the lunch period, she spotted Mac's red car tooling into the faculty parking lot and glimpsed him hurrying toward the gym. Evidently he'd gone off campus somewhere to eat.

Alone?

Hardly.

It occurred to Ginger that Sharon hadn't so much as poked her head into the teachers' lounge during fourth period. Had the librarian known Mac meant to make himself scarce in the teachers' lounge today? Had they met somewhere for lunch today?

So what if they had? It was no business of Ginger's, no concern of hers.

That afternoon when she was leaving school, Mac was out on the football practice field like the previous afternoon. He happened to turn his head and evidently recognized her car because he lifted an arm and waved. A horn tooted a cheery salute behind Ginger, and she glanced in the rearview mirror. Angie's sport-utility vehicle was following her.

Mac had probably been waving at Angie, not her. Or maybe at both of them. The more the merrier, Ginger reflected cynically.

The following day she stayed in her room during her plan period. She couldn't see subjecting herself to another hour on tenterhooks like she'd spent yesterday in the teachers' lounge, watching the door.

Friday afternoon finally rolled around, signaling the end of the first week of the new fall semester. Everything had gone well with Ginger's classes, but her nerves were frayed. She needed to recoup over the weekend.

And yet how was she to relax with Mac as her neighbor?

Mac wasted no time pulling on running shorts and a T-shirt when he got up on Saturday morning. A long run would help to work off some of the frustration that had been building up in him. Dammit, he *had* to have another one-on-one talk with Ginger during the weekend, preferably today.

He was starved for the sight of her. Just the thought

of fifteen minutes of gazing at her and carrying on a conversation with nobody else around filled him with more eagerness than he could contain.

Surely he'd earned fifteen minutes of her company. All week he'd restrained himself and hadn't tracked her down at school. Night after night he'd managed not to show up on her doorstep.

Mac deserved a reward.

Setting out from Ginger's parking lot, he came eventually to Monroe Street, where he took a right and headed into the heart of Old Mandeville. The traffic was light, allowing Mac to lope along and take in his surroundings, noting the abundance of large, stately shade trees and the neatly painted, old-fashioned frame houses set in lush yards planted with azalea shrubs and glossy-leafed camellias and beds of daylilies.

The high-rent district of Old Mandeville, Mac reflected, automatically favoring the gracious older homes with their big, inviting verandahs. He might have been more impressed if he hadn't peddled his bicycle past the mansions on St. Charles Avenue in New Orleans when he was a boy and later driven past them in his first old wreck of an automobile as a teenager. He'd delivered newspapers to posh homes in the historic Garden District, which was only a few blocks away from his parents' house in the Irish Channel, in itself a historic neighborhood settled by Irish and German immigrants in the past century. Magazine Street formed a dividing line between the two neighborhoods, one white-collar and one blue-collar.

Mike and Mary McDaniel still lived in the same house in which they'd raised their four boys. They were none too happy with Mac that he'd moved to the north shore, which might have been Outer Mongolia as far as they were concerned.

If Mac got back together with Ginger, they were going to be even less happy. Nor would his brothers be overjoyed, for that matter. The whole clan would just have to change its attitude, because this time around he wasn't letting his family—or hers—come between them.

The sound of male voices distracted Mac from his sober thoughts. A group of men, all obviously serious runners, entered Lakeshore Drive from a side street just as he was coming abreast of the intersection. He picked up his pace to match theirs and ran along with them. He stayed with them on the rest of their ten-mile loop. It felt good to push himself.

When he headed back along Monroe Street, returning to his condo, his T-shirt was wet with perspiration, as was the bandanna he wore like a sweatband around his head. As he walked the last few blocks of the side street leading to the Safe Harbor complex, Mac's heartbeat picked up instead of slowing down when he decided to take a quick shower and then ring Ginger's doorbell and ask her out to breakfast. If she didn't accept right away, he would wheedle and beg, resort to bribery, whatever it took.

"Dammit!" he cursed in disappointment when he came within sight of the parking lot at her end of the complex. Her car was gone.

Had she met Whitfield for breakfast somewhere? Mac wondered, his hands balled up into fists.

"I can't take much more of this," he muttered between clenched teeth.

His frustration was back full strength. So much for the benefits of his seven- or eight-mile run.

A small boy was playing on the lawn between Ginger's building and the one opposite hers. He looked to be about five years old.

"Hi, mister," he greeted Mac. "Look how good I can catch a pass." He tossed a toy football several feet into the air and clutched it to his breast when it came down.

"Not bad," Mac said. He'd paused to watch, arms akimbo, welcoming the diversion.

"Want to see how fast I can run?"

"Sure. Take off."

The little tyke dashed about fifteen yards, made a circle and dashed back.

"You're pretty fast, all right."

"I can throw real good, too, when I have somebody to catch my pass."

Mac couldn't hold back a grin at the blatant hint. "Well, let's see you do your stuff."

The boyish face lit up with pleasure. Rearing back, he hurled the undersized ball. It sailed wide and high, but Mac leaped sideways and snagged it with one hand.

"You might try holding the ball like this," he suggested, and demonstrated. "Here. I'll show you. Catch." He sent the football gently spiraling through the air. The tyke grabbed at it, but it struck his chest and fell to the grass. "You almost had it," Mac said.

"Next time I won't miss."

He didn't miss, sure enough, and he beamed in response to Mac's words of praise.

While they were tossing the small-scale football back and forth, a little girl who appeared to be about six or seven years old appeared and came up to them. "Hi, Jonathan," she said to the boy.

"Go away, Melissa," he replied, otherwise ignoring her.

"Can I catch the ball, too?"

"No, girls don't play football. Just boys."

"Please." The entreaty was directed at Mac, who was about to include her anyway. His mood had improved considerably during the past ten minutes. Kids were fun. One of these days he was hoping to have some of his own to spend time with.

"Hi, Melissa," he said. "Sure, you can join in. Right, Jonathan?"

Jonathan's glance toward her was sulky, but he relented.

Melissa caught the ball on the first try when Mac gently tossed it to her. He smothered a grin when Jonathan's face fell. The little boy had obviously hoped she'd fail miserably and make him look good.

It also amused Mac that the addition of a female resulted in more sociable chitchat. She'd obviously overheard adult conversation about him and verified that he lived in D-1 and wasn't married, that he was a high-school teacher and coach.

"What's your name?" she asked. "I don't know what to call you."

After some discussion of their polite options, the two children decided that Mr. McDaniel was too much of a mouthful. They opted for addressing him as Coach Mac.

"Hey, there's Miss Ginger," Melissa announced just as Jonathan was executing a pass to Mac. "That's her car."

The ball fell right through Mac's hands onto the ground. His head had snapped toward the parking lot. Sure enough, Ginger's silver gray compact car had pulled into its slot. Joy leaped up in his chest as she got out, wearing navy slacks and a green-and-white-striped knit blouse. Even if she'd met Whitfield for breakfast, she wasn't with him now. She was here, and Mac was going to get his chance to talk to her.

"Hi," he called to her.

"Hi, Miss Ginger," childish voices hailed her in unison.

"Hello," she answered, making her greeting general.

"Come and play with us, Miss Ginger," Melissa urged. "Then we'll have two boys and two girls, and it'll be even."

"Yeah, Miss Ginger, come and play with us." Jonathan seconded the invitation.

"I wouldn't be very good at throwing and catching a football," she protested.

"What the heck, I just missed a pass myself," Mac declared, bending down to pick up the toy ball. He gestured broadly with his arm, beckoning her to join them, prepared to break up the game if she didn't. No way was he going to lose this chance.

"Please, Miss Ginger."

Melissa's plea seemed to tip the balance. Ginger walked over and dropped her shoulder bag on the grass. The rays of morning sunshine glinted on her auburn hair.

"Throw the ball, Coach Mac," Jonathan prompted.

"Sure thing," Mac said. He was feasting his eyes on his estranged wife, feeling better about life in general than he'd felt in years. They *would* get back together.

"Coach Mac passes to us, and we pass back to him because he can catch the ball no matter how bad our passes are." Melissa explained the impromptu rules of the game. "Throw to Miss Ginger first."

Mac complied.

After about five minutes had passed, Jonathan's mother, a thirtyish brunette whom Ginger introduced as Barbara Philips, appeared to collect the little boy and take him off to run Saturday errands. Melissa departed, too, suddenly recalling that she and her mother were going shopping.

Hardly able to believe his good luck, Mac found himself alone with Ginger.

"Well, I'd better go inside and clean up my condo," she said.

"That can wait an hour or so, can't it? Let's go out and have some breakfast. I can just taste a big stack of pancakes and a couple of strips of crisp bacon." Mac immediately wished he'd left off the mention of pancakes and bacon, which for some reason seemed to strike an unpleasant chord with her.

"I made myself some toast earlier," she said.

"Then you can't be too full to eat a ham-and-cheese omelet. I remember you always ended up ordering one of those."

"And savoring every calorie-laden bite."

"You don't have to worry about counting calories," he scoffed. "I doubt you've put on an extra pound."

She looked flustered, suffering his approving inspection of her figure. It was impossible for him not to gaze at her like a husband because in his heart and soul, he *was* her husband still.

"I can easily afford to drop five pounds just like I could when we were married," she said, summoning her poise. "But even if I were as slim as Sharon, I would say no to going out with breakfast with you, for obvious reasons."

He could guess what the biggest reason was. Her CPA boyfriend, Whitfield. At the moment Mac just couldn't stomach bringing up the guy's name. He didn't want to get into a tense discussion. He just wanted—needed—some time with her.

"How about a glass of orange juice? That's on your diet. Come on. I have a gallon jug in my refrigerator." Mac took a step, willing her to accept. "We'll sit out on my patio. It's nice and shady in the mornings."

"Just a small glass, and I won't stay long."

"The longer, the better. Once you leave, I'll have to do some cleaning myself."

His stride was buoyant as he accompanied her to his door. There she halted instead of preceding him over the threshold. "Mac—"

"What?"

"I'm here for orange juice and nothing more." She met his gaze, but only briefly, pretty pink color flooding her cheeks. "In case there's any question in your mind."

"Hey, I'm all sweaty." A factor he was depending on to help him resist the powerful temptation to take her in his arms, kiss her, hug her tight. "If I came close, you'd probably faint."

"I'm serious."

"I'm dying of thirst. I probably covered eight miles this morning."

"*Eight* miles? Where did you go?"

Mac ushered her inside as he answered, describing the route he'd taken and telling her about the group of men he'd met along the lakefront. It occurred to him that he would have been a different man, a far happier man on his morning run, if he'd known what a treat lay in store for him. Because it *was* the biggest possible treat to spend time alone with Ginger, especially when he didn't have to corner her.

She'd voluntarily come to his condo. All his restraint and patience were paying off. The last thing Mac wanted to do was blow the progress he'd made. That meant keeping his hands off her, no matter how much he wanted to touch her and take her into his arms. It meant not making a wrong move.

Chapter Five

"Sorry, but all I own are these one-size-fits-all drinking glasses," Mac said with cheerful apology, setting two large tumblers on the counter with twin clunks.

From her station in the doorway of the small kitchen that was a duplicate of hers, Ginger got a glimpse inside the cabinet before he flipped the door closed. Only one lonely glass remained on the shelf. Below that shelf sat three thick white plates that looked like restaurant ware.

"Just fill mine half full." This is Operation Cure, she reminded herself to counteract the intense pleasure of watching him. A pleasure that shouldn't have felt this familiar after six whole years apart. His movements were so thoroughly masculine. "You've certainly kept yourself in good physical condition," she remarked. Voicing the compliment gave her further excuse to ogle his body.

The burgundy running shorts he wore struck him high

on thighs that were corded with muscle. Ginger tried
not to remember touching those thighs and comparing
them to steel, but her fingertips tingled with their own
memory. So did her palms as she noted the way his
gray T-shirt molded his broad shoulders and taut back.
Keeping her gaze above the neck was no help, either,
because his black hair was mussed with unruly locks
falling forward on his forehead, and the back of his head
still bore the imprint of the bandanna, now dangling
from his pocket, he'd used as a headband. It seemed
more like yesterday than six years ago that she'd had
the right, as his wife, to step up close and use her fingers
to comb his hair.

Those intimate pleasures hadn't been enough to com-
pensate for what was lacking in their marriage, she reminded herself.

"Here you are." Mac handed her a tumbler. It was
closer to two-thirds full than the half glass she'd re-
quested. But his serving measurements had always been
generous.

Ginger preceded him into his living area, which
looked larger than hers because of the scarcity of furniture. He had no dining table. Obviously he ate his
meals at the breakfast bar sitting on one of the two bar
stools. Or maybe he balanced his plate on his lap as he
sat on the man-size brown tweed sofa or the recliner
upholstered in beige leather. A square coffee table
strewed with magazines and newspapers, a tall reading
lamp beside the recliner and a TV and VCR on a stand
completed the furnishings.

The only item Ginger recognized was the sole wall
decoration, a charcoal portrait of her hanging over the
fireplace. The sight of it was unexpected, transporting
her back to a hot summer day in the French Quarter.

She'd walked along Jackson Square with Mac, her arm around his waist and his arm around hers. Against all her protests he'd propelled her over to a canvas director's chair to pose for a street artist.

"I'd completely forgotten about that silly portrait of me," she said, shaking off the spell of bittersweet memories. "I'm surprised you kept it when you didn't keep anything else, from the looks of things. I left you our furniture and dishes, such as they were, so that you didn't have to set up housekeeping from scratch."

"I sent you word through your parents that you could have whatever you wanted. Didn't they pass the message along?" His voice had a hard note at the mention of his former in-laws.

"Oh, yes, they told me you said to take what I wanted before you called Goodwill and had them come and clean the place out."

"I was mad and hurt because you'd packed up and left me."

"Things had gotten so bad between us we were hardly carrying on a civil conversation anymore. You kept coming home later and later. It didn't help matters that one of your old high-school girlfriends started chasing you."

"Dammit, Ginger, I wasn't sleeping with Trudy Miner. Nor did I have any intentions of doing so."

"It's immaterial now, Mac."

"No, it *isn't* immaterial. It's important that you believe me. I admit I wasn't entirely without fault. In retrospect I guess I should have done more to discourage Trudy."

"Didn't you start dating her after we split up? My parents saw you at a restaurant with a sexy blonde a week or two after I had moved out. From the description

I guessed she was Trudy. They left without being seated," Ginger added.

"And hurried to the nearest phone to call you," he stated harshly, not making a denial. "I'm sure it made their evening to be able to report that their no-good son-in-law was out with a woman."

"You didn't answer my question."

Mac sighed. "I dated Trudy for a couple of months. Until she gave up on me as a lost cause."

"A lost cause?"

"She wanted to get serious."

"She should have taken a page out of my book and gotten herself pregnant. I'm sure you would have done the decent thing and married her, too." The cynical words popped out. Ginger bit her lip, but she couldn't keep herself from asking, "You did sleep with her once I was out of the picture?"

His guilty expression was answer enough. "The sex didn't mean anything." He sighed again, shoving his free hand through his hair. "I didn't intend to get into heavy discussions today."

Ginger moved over to the fireplace and bought some time to get her emotions under control while she studied her portrait critically. "That artist was quite a con man, wasn't he? He made me as pretty as the movie actresses he painted from photos and displayed as examples of his art."

Mac had walked over, too, and stood to one side several feet away. "I don't agree. I think he painted you the way you looked."

"I wish. It's a very flattering likeness."

"Not to me. You were every bit that pretty in my eyes."

"So you said at the time, which thrilled me no end."

Ginger sipped her orange juice while a similar thrill subsided. Once a fool, always a fool, she thought. "One thing I have to give you credit for. You're certainly a man who sticks to his original line."

"It wasn't a line," he replied.

Ginger sucked in her breath, and her heart fluttered as he made a movement toward her, lifting his hand. He meant to come closer, meant to touch her, *finally*. Longing welled up, almost drowning her flare of panic. "Mac—"

His hand closed into a fist, and he turned away abruptly and walked over to the sliding glass door leading onto the patio. He slid it open with a vigorous motion. "Let's sit out here in the fresh air."

The disappointment was almost overwhelming. "I think I'll take a rain check," she said when she trusted herself to speak. "I have a lot of chores to do."

"Stay a few minutes," he pleaded. "Long enough to drink your orange juice. Please."

Ginger followed him outside. There was no reason in the world to stay, but she didn't want to leave.

"My landlady sold me this patio set," Mac explained as he pulled out a black metal chair with a waterproof cushion in a floral design. The bright colors of the cushion were slightly faded. "It has a few spots of rust, but a wire brush and a can of black spray paint will make it like new. That's one of my weekend projects." He gestured for her to have a seat.

"I hope Fay gave you a reasonable price," Ginger said as she sat down in the chair and set her tumbler on the round metal table. "A couple of people here in the complex were interested in buying it, including Barbara, but Fay was asking way too much."

Mac had settled into the chair on her right-hand side

after dragging it farther away from her. But Ginger still had a full view of his big body, his thighs sprawled open in a masculine posture that made it impossible not to notice the bulge of his crotch. She felt the stirring of feminine desire.

"You'd be proud of me," he stated after he'd taken a big swallow from his glass. "I got her to knock off a hundred bucks."

"Did you really?"

He raised his hand to mimic taking an oath in court, then lowered it. "I've learned to manage money. On a teacher's salary I'll never be rich, but I've accumulated some savings and even have a few investments in mutual funds."

"That's wonderful."

"I've worked on all my shortcomings." He grimaced. "Or most of them. I still watch a lot of live sports on TV, when I have time to watch TV."

"Watching sports on TV is nothing to apologize for," Ginger answered. "After all, you're a coach."

"Coaches need to be well-rounded people, too. Looking back, I can't believe I let my brothers' ribbing get to me when I went to a cultural event with you. I would go without grumbling now," he added.

Ginger sipped her orange juice while she considered how to answer. "I don't get to very many operas and ballets myself, maybe one of each during the winter season."

He scowled at some thought. "Whitfield goes with you?"

"Yes, he especially enjoys theater. And he's a film buff, too. We see a lot of movies."

The scowl deepened. "How successful is he, anyway?"

"As in income?"

"Yeah, as in income."

"I've never asked him, but he can apparently afford a fairly upscale life-style. He wears nice clothes, owns a lovely house that he renovated, drives a late-model BMW."

Mac shook his head disgustedly. "A BMW. What color? Black?"

"Yes. How on earth did you guess?"

"One was parked at Rooster's the afternoon I saw Whitfield there. Something told me it belonged to him."

"Your instinct was right." Ginger's voice was flat. He'd been with Sharon at the time he was scrutinizing the parking lot. The reminder was like a reality check.

"How serious are you about the guy?" he demanded. "I need to know what I'm up against."

"You're not 'up against' anything, Mac. If I broke up with Barry tonight, I still wouldn't get involved with you again."

"Tell me anyway."

Ginger thought and answered with a resigned note. "Barry and I haven't talked about marriage, but we're very companionable. It won't surprise me if our relationship develops into a permanent commitment. He's the kind of man I would want in a husband, if I remarried."

Her final statement, which she hadn't meant to be cruel, made him flinch. He rubbed a hand across his face, slumping a little deeper into his chair. His deep voice held discouragement as he asked, "Is this week unusual? Ordinarily do you spend nights with him, at his place or yours?"

He was admitting indirectly that he'd kept up a surveillance during the week and knew she'd slept alone at her condo. Ginger shouldn't have been thrilled that he'd gone to the trouble, but she was.

"No, Barry and I both are the types to be aware of appearances. One of his next-door neighbors, whom he's quite fond of, is an elderly woman. He wouldn't offend her for the world. And I'm old-fashioned enough to be concerned about my reputation. I think teachers should try to be good role models."

The too long explanation seemed to cheer him slightly. He downed the rest of his orange juice and set the glass on the table. "Let's do something together today, for old times' sake. What do you say?"

"Do something?" she repeated.

"Anything. Take a ride in the country and have a picnic. I've heard of Folsom all these years and have never been there." Folsom was a rural community thirty miles to the north with rolling hills and Thoroughbred horse farms.

"I can't. Not today," Ginger heard herself adding and not sounding nearly definite enough. It was so hard to say no to him, especially when, God help her, she wanted to say yes. She got up and shoved her chair back into place, the legs scraping on the concrete. "I really have to clean my condo."

He'd stood up, too. "Clean it tomorrow."

"Tomorrow I'm going over to Metairie to visit my parents." They hadn't been informed yet that their detested ex-son-in-law had relocated to the north shore. Ginger hadn't been able to bring herself to tell them over the phone and dreaded telling them in person. They would be appalled and distressed. Thinking about their reactions helped to restore her common sense. "I'm *not* going on any picnics with you, Mac, not today, not ever. Thanks for the orange juice."

His expression spelled out resignation. "My pleasure."

Without any further efforts to persuade her, he accompanied her inside. The old Mac wouldn't have given up like this and accepted her firm refusal.

"You *have* changed in some ways," Ginger said.

"For the better, I hope," he replied soberly.

"There's your phone." She brought attention to the obvious as the combination telephone and answering machine on one end of the breakfast bar pealed to life. "I can find my way out."

"If it's important, whoever's calling can leave a message."

They'd reached the foyer when the caller's voice blared out, "Hi, handsome, this is your friendly school librarian. If you're at loose ends today and want to do something wild and reckless, by all means give me a call. I'm open to suggestions. By the way, you left your sunglasses in my office yesterday."

"Sharon," Mac said as though Ginger hadn't made the identification for herself. "I looked everywhere for those damned sunglasses."

"You're going to need them if you take a drive to the country and have a picnic. The sun's already bright outside."

"I'm not going on a picnic by myself," he protested.

"A lot of men might have trouble setting up a date on the spur of the minute, but not you, Mac. Have fun." Knowing it was best to end the conversation right there, Ginger departed.

"If you change your mind and decide to goof off, I'll be around," he called after her.

I would need to change my mind in the next thirty minutes, Ginger thought. He would be around, all right, but only long enough to shower and change clothes and go off on a Saturday excursion with Sharon. Or Angie. Or some other female unknown to Ginger yet.

Maybe she was his first choice. Or maybe he'd just asked her first because she was convenient when the idea hit him. Either way he would enjoy himself just as much once other arrangements were made. The knowledge shouldn't have hurt as much as it did. You're not special, she emphasized to herself.

Being clear-sighted and pragmatic still didn't keep Ginger from feeling cheated because she'd done the wise thing and turned Mac down. Operation Cure certainly didn't seem to be working. The more she was around him, the more she wanted to be around him. She seemed to get more vulnerable instead of less vulnerable.

The phone was ringing when Ginger walked into her condo. Her heart leaped as she wondered whether it was Mac.

The caller was Barry. To her shame the sound of his well-modulated voice coming over the line instead of Mac's deeper voice came as a disappointment. Silly fool! she berated herself.

To make up for the slight to Barry, Ginger put extra warmth into her greeting and readily agreed when he suggested coming over during the afternoon and bringing a video of a vintage Italian film Dan had lent him.

"You wouldn't believe his collection of foreign movies," Barry remarked with a tone close to awe. "He has all the great ones that are out in video."

"Gosh, you two certainly do have a lot in common. Come over any time after two o'clock. That should give me plenty of time to finish my cleaning."

"The movie has subtitles," he warned. "I know you find those distracting."

"I'm sure I'll enjoy it anyway," she insisted with much more enthusiasm than she actually felt.

If Barry had been bringing over a movie she actually wanted to see, she would be looking forward to his arrival more, Ginger told herself. Her lack of anticipation *wasn't* boredom with his company.

Barry pulled up just as she was watering an oversize terra-cotta planter in her entryway. He got out of his BMW, looking well groomed in khaki slacks and a striped cotton shirt with its button-down collar open at the neck and long sleeves neatly folded back several turns. Both slacks and shirt were crisply ironed from the cleaners. He wore leather deck shoes styled like loafers and had omitted socks. The outfit was Barry's version of weekend casual.

A picture of Mac that morning in his running shorts and damp T-shirt flashed before Ginger's eyes. He would have changed into jeans and a knit shirt, garments that had probably come straight from the dryer and hadn't been ironed. Ginger banished the comparison, summoning a bright welcoming smile.

"Hi," she called. "Your timing's perfect."

A movement caught her attention, and she glanced over to see Jonathan emerging from his condo in the building opposite. He carried the toy football. As he spotted Ginger, his little face lighted up, and he trotted over in her direction.

"Hi, Miss Ginger!" he hailed her. "Want to play another game of catch with me?"

"Another time. I have company." Barry had walked

up by now, a grocery sack in one arm and a video in the other hand. "You've met Mr. Whitfield before."

"Hi, Mr. Whitfield."

"Hello, Jonathan." Barry glanced at her small neighbor with an abstracted smile.

"You and Mr. Whitfield could both play," the little boy suggested hopefully. "We could throw the ball to him, and he could throw it back to us."

"That's generous of you to be willing to include me, Jonathan," Barry said. His note of amused irony was for Ginger's benefit. "But I wouldn't make a very good playmate when it comes to tossing a football. Check back with me when you take up an individual sport like golf or tennis. Okay?"

"Mr. Whitfield doesn't like football," Ginger explained gently to erase the little boy's confusion with Barry's refusal, which had been couched in language that was too adult for a five-year-old.

"I have a softball," Jonathan offered, still holding out hope. "I can run and get it."

"That's very sweet, but Mr. Whitfield brought a movie for grown-ups for him and me to watch."

"Oh. Okay." Jonathan turned and walked away, his posture expressing his disappointment.

"That's the problem with all the emphasis on kids playing team sports," Barry commented. "They don't learn to entertain themselves."

"It's normal for children to enjoy playing with someone," Ginger protested. "I'd rather see them participating in any kind of group activity than just sitting in front of the TV for hours on end. Or a computer, for that matter."

"I'm not sure I agree. There're some very educational TV shows for children. And a computer opens up

the whole spectrum of knowledge with the right pro-
grams. What's there to learn from a brutal contact sport
like football, other than a taste for violence and the
drive to win by any means?''

''Football has rules. And it instills principles that are
important to society, like cooperation, for example. It
teaches discipline.'' Or all those things were true with
a dedicated coach, like Mac, who genuinely cared about
kids of all ages. Mac would never have dealt with Jonathan as Barry just had done.

''Ideally, perhaps,'' Barry conceded. He shrugged,
indicating that he didn't have enough interest in the
whole subject to pursue the debate. ''Shall we go inside? The beer I bought to go with our popcorn is getting warm.''

Ginger knew without being told that it was imported
beer. Barry wouldn't even pause beside the popular domestic brand that she'd glimpsed in Mac's refrigerator
when he was getting out the gallon jug of orange juice
that morning.

If Ginger had accepted Mac's offhanded invitation to
ride to Folsom and have a picnic, he wouldn't have
thought twice about packing up a cooler with generic-
brand soft drinks, tossing in a couple of beers for good
measure. Nor would he have hesitated to pop open a
can and hand it to her without a glass, something Barry
would never do. Ginger didn't have a single doubt, either, that she could have enjoyed every swallow, sip-
ping straight from the can, if she'd been foolish enough
to put aside all the lessons of the past.

But she hadn't been that foolish. She'd acted wisely
and was far better off, spending the afternoon with
Barry. On that thought, Ginger accompanied Barry inside, not feeling either fortunate or wise.

The movie turned out to be more than two hours long, and it seemed to drag on interminably. The black-and-white cinematography struck Ginger as bleak. The storyline was obscure, and the characters difficult to identify with. There was virtually no action. Her mind wandered, and she kept reliving scenes that had actually occurred that day, with Jonathan as a little real-life actor.

In the first she saw herself returning during the morning from her trip to the post office and joining the game of pass-the-football with Mac and the two children. Some minutes earlier Mac must have gotten back from his run to the lakefront. Sweaty and thirsty, he'd stopped and taken the time to entertain his small neighbors. Driving up and seeing him, Ginger had been reminded of how he'd always made time for children, even when she'd first met him in their sophomore year. It was one of his endearing traits. His nieces and nephews all adored him and had flocked to his side at those McDaniel family get-togethers she'd attended before she stopped going to them and he stopped going with her to her parents' house.

Whatever his flaws, Mac would make a wonderful, loving father. She wasn't so sure she could say the same for Barry. The recent episode with Jonathan brought home the fact that Barry didn't find children very interesting. He barely noticed them when they were around. Of course, he might be entirely different around his own son or daughter. Ginger tried to conjure a picture of Barry holding an infant. Barry swinging a squealing toddler up into the air. Barry down on the floor playing a board game with a preschool offspring who resembled him.

None of those mental snapshots would come into

clear focus. Troubled, Ginger stirred to attention with a sigh as the movie ended and the credits scrolled. As always, Barry watched them intently, speaking only when the long list of foreign names had reached the end.

"With a small screen you lose some of the impact," he said regretfully, rewinding the tape. "Fantastic cinematography, though, wasn't it? And superb directing."

"I'm not much of a judge," she replied, not committing herself.

"You seemed absorbed."

"Actually I wasn't that absorbed in the story," she admitted. "My mind drifted."

"I'm sorry you didn't enjoy it."

"Don't be. I wasn't miserable or restless. I was just doing some thinking."

"About what?"

Ginger hesitated only a second before answering truthfully. "Having children."

He raised his eyebrows in mild surprise. "Don't tell me you've suddenly started hearing a biological clock ticking."

"No, not yet. But I do want to be a mother before my biological clock ticks down. It occurred to me that as well as I know you, I couldn't venture a guess as to whether you want to be a father eventually."

"Remind me not to subject you to any more foreign flicks with subtitles." His quip was lightly ironic, but Ginger could tell from his expression that he was mulling over the idea of himself as a parent. She waited for him to speak. "I can't quite imagine myself in the role of Dad. But I assume most single guys feel that way." He went on with a matter-of-fact candor, "When I see families out in public and a kid tugging on a father's hand and acting a brat, it's not a sight that makes me envious.''

"That's understandable.'' But what about those other times when a child was well-behaved and a father was reaping the rewards of fatherhood?

"Speaking of brats, some local teenagers spray-painted vulgar words on every picket fence on my block last night. The police caught them in the act.''

Barry had quickly lost interest in the subject of parenthood. Ginger didn't pursue the discussion, but it had shed a different light on their relationship. A harsh light that revealed defects.

"How serious are you about the guy?'' Mac had demanded hours earlier, referring to Barry. She'd answered something to the effect that she wouldn't be surprised if she and Barry ended up getting married at some future time. Ginger recalled that she stated, ''He's the kind of man I would want in a husband, if I remarried.''

But was he? Her ideal husband was a man with at least latent paternal instincts. Perhaps Barry had them. There was still lots of time to explore the issue and make sure she wouldn't be making another big mistake if she married him. Before taking such a step, they would have many in-depth discussions.

Still, Ginger could no longer drift along, comfortable with the idea that her relationship with Barry was headed generally in the direction of a permanent commitment. It might be headed nowhere.

This disturbing new insight made her feel that much more vulnerable in coping with Mac's presence in her life.

Chapter Six

I wish I had a mild case of flu, Ginger thought when she awoke the next morning. Normally she enjoyed visiting her parents, but today she would have been grateful for any legitimate excuse to cancel. They were going to be so horribly upset when they learned their ex-son-in-law was back in her life. She dreaded telling them. Yet sooner or later they would have to know.

Get it over with, she advised herself resignedly and took extra care with her appearance as she got ready. It was important to convey the message that she was coping very well and they need not be concerned about her.

Today's visit included attending the eleven-o'clock worship service with John and Ellie Honeycutt, so Ginger dressed accordingly, choosing a silk print dress that her mother especially liked on her. It was more feminine than her schoolteacher outfits, most of which tended more toward a career-woman look. She donned sheer panty hose and had just slipped on dressy pumps with heels when the phone rang.

"That's probably *not* Mac," she said aloud, impatient with herself for her own panicky reaction. "He hasn't called you once so far."

Nor was he calling her this morning. Fay Novak's voice came over the line, gushingly friendly and yet reproachful. After apologizing for disturbing Ginger on a Sunday morning, Fay got to the point, requesting that Ginger remove her name from the posted list of condo owners delinquent in paying their fees.

"My tenant assures me he gave you a check days ago," the real-estate agent said.

"He did," Ginger was forced to admit. "With school starting I got busy and simply forgot. I'll do it right away."

"I would appreciate that. Isn't my tenant a handsome thing, though? I figured all you single women at Safe Harbor would thank me for renting to an eligible bachelor." The slight emphasis on "all" hinted that at least one of Ginger's female neighbors had expressed appreciation. Ginger opened her mouth and closed it, disgusted with herself for not making some reply to discourage Fay from passing along a tidbit of gossip. "Last night I was driving by the Burger Shack and saw Mac escorting Barbara Philips and little Jonathan inside. I felt like a real do-gooder," Fay declared.

"Do-gooder?" The syllables had stuck in Ginger's throat.

"Well, you know how man-shy Barbara is after her divorce. And you can't blame her. She was married to a rat who took off for parts unknown to avoid paying any child support. It's been rough on her, but she needs to move on and find a dad for that cute tyke of hers.

There's my other line, Ginger,'' Fay said hurriedly. ''It was nice talking to you. Have a good day.'' She cut the connection without waiting to hear any parting words in reply.

''Now just how am I supposed to handle *this?*'' Ginger wondered aloud with a kind of weary despair about Mac's newest romance. Her female co-workers were worldly enough to take care of themselves. However, Barbara seemed more at risk, for those very reasons Fay had mentioned.

Plus there was little Jonathan to consider. He'd already been through enough without having his mother fall for a charming man who might not be a good prospect for a husband. The experience might leave Barbara that much more bitter and disenchanted with men.

What a mess. It wasn't right of Mac to put Ginger in such an untenable position.

With an extra five minutes to spare before she headed for the causeway, Ginger decided to carry out her promise to Fay Novak without delay. After getting in her car, she drove to the parking lot at Mac's end of the complex, where the bulletin board hung. Before Mac had moved into D-1, Ginger had taken the slight inconvenience in stride. Now she regretted being forced to notice whether Mac's reserved parking slot was empty or occupied.

This morning the sunlight gleamed on his red Camaro, waxed to a high shine. Ginger turned her back to it and focused on her task, noting the sound of footsteps on the paved walkway leading to the parking lot. Finished, she turned around, expecting to see a man, but not expecting to see Mac, who wouldn't be wearing leather-soled shoes that made audible footsteps.

Ginger blinked in surprise and then gazed with reluctant admiration. The man striding toward her *was* Mac. He was wearing dress slacks and a dress shirt with a tie and carried a sport jacket slung casually over his shoulder. In his more refined attire he was every bit as virile and rugged as he'd been yesterday in his running shorts and sweaty T-shirt. Ginger's stomach muscles tightened, and suddenly the silk of her dress felt buttery soft against her skin.

His low whistle of appreciation for her appearance brought her out of her trance. "You look very pretty," he said, giving her a male once-over that repeated the compliment. "I like that dress on you."

"You look quite sharp yourself." He was standing close enough for her to get a whiff of his shaving lotion and recognize the scent as the same one she'd always liked him to use. It had the same effect on her, awakening feminine pleasure.

"Sharp enough for you to invite me along?" he asked hopefully.

"I'm on my way to Metairie to attend church with my parents. I doubt seriously you would want to go along."

"Try me."

Ginger searched his dark brown eyes and saw that he was serious. "You were going somewhere yourself," she said, indirectly stating her question: where was he going all dressed up?

"I'm headed across the lake to a christening."

"Whose child?"

"Larry's. He and Sally had their fourth kid, a little girl."

Larry McDaniel was the brother closest in age to Mac, who was three years younger than Larry and the youngest of the four McDaniel boys.

"You *were* bluffing, inviting yourself along with me. You'd be on the blacklist with your family for the rest of your life if you didn't show up for a christening. I guess afterward you'll all be going to your parents' house for one of your mother's big dinners."

He nodded. "The whole gang will be there. My three brothers and their wives and the twelve grandchildren. Probably a few aunts and uncles and cousins, for good measure."

Ginger raised her eyebrows questioningly at his glum tone. "I thought you thrived on big family get-togethers."

"That was before I moved to the north shore. The main topic of conversation will be raking me over the coals."

"Oh, I see. You're a traitor because you left New Orleans."

"There's more to it," he explained reluctantly. "They know you're living on the north shore. The news story about your teaching award reminded everyone you'd moved over here."

"Say no more." Ginger had the full picture. "All your relatives—and especially your mother—are worried that the Protestant witch you married might trap you into marriage again. Right?"

He restated her ironic assessment of the situation more diplomatically. "They're smart enough to figure out what the main attraction on the north shore was for me."

"Mac, don't give me that line of bull!" she burst out.

"It's not a line of bull."

"Yes, it is. You've been out on dates with at least two other women this very week."

"No, I haven't." His denial came readily. "It's been well over a year since I've dated anyone."

Ginger rolled her eyes in exasperation. "You told me yourself you were out with Sharon on Monday night. The following afternoon Barry saw you with her. Fay called this morning and mentioned she spotted you last evening with Barbara and Jonathan."

"None of those were *dates*," he protested. "I ran into Barbara and Jonathan outside the Burger Shack."

"You didn't arrange to meet them there?" Ginger skeptically probed his definition of "ran into."

"I was as surprised to see them as they were to see me. We all sat at a table together," he went on to admit. "It was either sit with them or eat alone."

"Of course, you paid for their food."

"No. I offered to, but Barbara refused to let me."

"What about Sharon? Did she split the bill with you?" Ginger knew darned well her librarian co-worker hadn't even reached for her purse.

"What if she didn't? That still doesn't mean I was out with her socially. Dammit, Ginger! You know I like people in general, and half of the people in the world are women!" he exclaimed, frustration in his voice and expression.

"And half are men. Did you notice that Barry was having a beer that afternoon with his male associate? You'll never change, Mac." Ginger turned to leave.

"Is he going with you today?" As he uttered the harsh question, his hand closed on her shoulder, stopping her. "Did you get all dressed up for Whitfield?"

A wild, unreasoning joy had exploded inside her. He'd finally reached for her, finally touched her, his fingers strong and pulsing with his male vitality. Ginger opened her mouth to speak an honest denial and then said instead, "It's really none of your business."

"You're wrong. It *is* my business, dammit! Divorce or no divorce, you're still my wife." He muttered a violent curse at himself. Then his grip gradually eased. Before he took his hand away, he caressed her shoulder. Shivers of pure delight spread through Ginger's body all the way to her fingertips and toes. "Sorry, I shouldn't have grabbed you like that," he apologized gruffly.

"It's okay." Her voice came out sounding as weak and defenseless as she felt. "I should have answered your question. I'm going to my parents' house by myself." She bit her lip but couldn't keep from asking, "What about you?"

"I'm going by myself, too."

There was no reason whatever for her to suddenly feel more light-hearted about the day ahead, but she did.

His Camaro was right behind her as she took the most direct route to the Lake Pontchartrain Causeway, which was just minutes away. At one of the toll booths, she paused to pay a male cashier the correct amount, a dollar bill and two quarters.

Mac pulled up at the same toll booth after she'd gone ahead. Ginger glanced in the rearview mirror and saw him handing over a bill and having to wait for his change. No doubt he would exchange a few friendly words with the Causeway Commission employee.

He *did* like people. All races. All ages. Male and female.

And people, young and old and in between, were drawn to Mac because he was so likable and such a genuinely nice guy. It was his popularity with women that Ginger hadn't been able to handle. And apparently would still have trouble handling, a major reason all by itself for not even considering reconciliation. Add the same old in-law problems and different philosophies about finances to the mix, and you were looking at disaster all over again.

No way could Ginger subject herself to marrying Mac a second time and divorcing him a second time. And that's what would happen. She just *knew* it in her heart.

"Divorce or no divorce, you're still my wife," he'd said. The problem was that she never should have been his wife in the first place. Ginger hadn't been his type. She was too quiet and reserved, too studious and serious minded for him.

After her miscarriage she'd known the best thing for him was to set him free. It had been weak and selfish of her not to. She'd paid the price herself and subjected Mac to a lot of misery and, no doubt, guilt for lusting after other women even if he hadn't actually been unfaithful. He was still struggling with guilt, caught up between being attracted to other women and obeying his conscience by trying to reconcile with Ginger because he felt tied to her by his marriage vows.

"What a mess," Ginger said with a sigh, glancing in her rearview mirror again. The Camaro had zoomed up behind her. She waited for it to roar pass, but Mac slowed down, matching his speed to her staid fifty-five miles per hour, the posted speed limit that was widely disregarded by causeway travelers.

To Ginger's surprise he stayed several car lengths back across the entire twenty-four-mile-long bridge. It was oddly companionable. When they'd reached the south shore, he headed off for New Orleans proper.

Good luck, Ginger found herself thinking with empathy.

More than a dozen people were waiting for him to show up, while only her two parents would be glancing at the clock, marking the time until their daughter—and only child—arrived. The situations were entirely different and yet similar in that she and Mac both were dreading their family visits.

"I had my menu all planned, but your father insisted on taking us out to eat," Ellie Honeycutt explained when they were back in the car following church service. She patted her husband's knee affectionately. "Isn't that sweet of him?"

"Very sweet," Ginger agreed.

"This way your mother doesn't have to cook and you girls don't have to clean up the kitchen," John declared.

"It always seems like a holiday when you come and visit on a Sunday like this," Ellie said happily. "How's Barry? I thought you had said you might invite him to come with you today."

"Barry's fine. But I decided I would invite him another time. Actually I wanted the opportunity to talk to you and Dad about something that's come up recently."

"Oh? Something that involves Barry? Such an attractive, pleasant young man. So well mannered and neat as a pin. Your dad and I both like him. Don't we, John?" She paused long enough for Ginger's father to respond in the affirmative. "And he's a Methodist, too. That makes it nice."

"He's got a good head on him," John put in. "You don't become a CPA if you're a dummy."

"All that money he makes!" Ellie exclaimed, and

then clapped her hand over her mouth, giving her husband an apologetic look.

"Dad, I hope you didn't *ask* Barry what his income is!"

"The subject came up kind of naturally when we were discussing filing income tax. I asked him what bracket he was in."

Ginger cringed with embarrassment.

"What was it you wanted to tell us?" Ellie asked with a coy note. "Something to celebrate?"

"No, nothing particularly exciting and nothing relating directly to Barry. It can wait until later." All the complimentary remarks about the man she was dating and her parents' obvious approval of him as a future son-in-law made bringing up Mac that much more difficult. That coupled with the fact they had been talking earlier about a Protestant wedding they'd recently attended meant the kindest thing to do—as well as the most cowardly—was to further postpone filling them in until after the Sunday meal at a restaurant. Ginger's news would definitely kill the festive spirit.

She found herself wondering how things were going for Mac today just as she had earlier in church. Oddly, thinking about him as he fended for himself amid his large family made her own quite different ordeal more bearable. Part of Ginger's dread, she realized, was not wanting to hear her parents attack him yet again.

And attack him they did. The scene in John and Ellie's cozy den a couple of hours later was even worse than Ginger had imagined. At first shock rendered both her parents speechless.

Typically her mother found her voice first. "There must be something you can *do* legally!"

"Damned right there's something you can do!" John roared. "Get an injunction against him!"

"Dad, calm down," Ginger pleaded, alarmed that his face had turned bloodred. "Everything's okay."

"Everything's *not* okay!" he yelled, banging his fist on the arm of his recliner. "The dirty so-and-so took advantage of you and got you pregnant. The least he could have done was make you a halfway decent husband. But instead he ran around on you. He has the morals of a tomcat."

"I never had any proof that he ran around on me. I was probably overly suspicious of him. And he's not bothering me now. Honest. Please, Dad, nothing's worth your having a heart attack."

"Ginger's right, John. You don't want to give that Irish devil the satisfaction of putting you in the hospital." Her mother's words fortunately had some calming effect. He shook his head, still visibly upset, but his fury had subsided to a safer level.

"There's nothing for either of you to worry about," Ginger said. "I'm coping very well with the situation."

"Of course you are," declared Ellie stoutly. "You're completely over him and dating a nice man who would make you a *good* husband." As opposed to the bad husband Mac had been. "You would never get mixed up with the likes of *him* again." She shuddered. "Remember how he criticized your cooking," Ellie said. "Remember all those times you called me up or came over here in tears?"

"I was a pretty rotten cook." And shouldn't have been so quick to call her mother and go running to her house for sympathy. A tendency that had justifiably been a sore point with Mac.

"Money burned a hole in his pockets." John added

to the list of husbandly failings. "Nothing would do for him but he had to go in debt and buy that flashy red car instead of saving up for a down payment on a house."

"He'd never had a decent car. His parents couldn't afford to buy him a new car when he was sixteen." As her parents had done.

"I'll bet he didn't even get it paid for before he traded it in on a new one. What's he driving now on a teacher's salary? A Corvette?"

Ginger winced because she would have made the same scornful conjecture a week ago and been just as wrong as her father was. "Would you believe he's still driving the red Camaro? It looks beautifully well maintained."

John frowned and uttered a grunt.

The frown would deepen, Ginger reflected with a sigh, if he knew that Mac had followed behind her all the way across the causeway that morning and she hadn't objected in the least.

Both her parents would be even more aghast if she'd confided that their ex-son-in-law wanted to erase his "ex" status and take them on as in-laws again.

Chapter Seven

"Nothing was wrong with my old job, Ma," Mac replied. "It was a good job, but so is my new job."

"You're running after *her.* That's what this is all about."

The collective indrawn breaths could be heard around the table.

"Now, Mary," Mike Sr. began.

"Let him answer, Pop." Mike Jr.'s grim words quieted his father's peacemaker attempt.

"You hit the nail on the head, Ma," Mac said. "I moved to the north shore because of Ginger and no other reason."

His mother's outcry of genuine dismay rose over the groans and murmurs and assorted curses. The entire range of reactions around the table conveyed disapproval and opposition to the idea of a reconciliation.

Mary threw up her hands. "But *why* would you want

her back? She was a terrible wife! She couldn't cook. She didn't fit in with your family. She put on airs. Attending operas and ballets, like she grew up in one of those mansions on St. Charles Avenue instead of out in Metairie.'' With a snort of disdain Mary slapped the air. ''Talk some sense into your brother!'' she implored her other three strapping sons, who didn't need much prompting. They jumped on him, going by seniority.

''Ginger walked out on you, man,'' said Mike Jr. ''Left you without so much as saying goodbye. Don't you have any pride?''

''You must be out of your mind!'' declared Keith.

''And those parents of hers.'' Larry took up the argument. ''You want them as in-laws again? Come on, little brother.''

Mac let them talk themselves out. Finally his mother exclaimed in frustration, ''*Say* something! Don't just sit there!''

''I wanted to let everybody else have their say first. Because I don't intend to listen to any of this again. Okay?'' He looked from scowling face to scowling face. ''I'll be thirty years old my next birthday. I'm old enough to know what will make me happy. I *haven't* been happy the past six years. I want my wife back. And if I'm lucky enough to get her back, I don't want to hear the first word of criticism about her from any member of my family. Is that understood?'' He looked meaningfully at his mother, who tossed her head and gazed away with an injured air, quivering lips pressed together.

Mike Sr., who'd been quiet until now, cleared his throat loudly. ''You made your point real well, son.''

Mac looked gratefully at his father, sensing that he

at least had his support. "I guess I'll shove off," he said, pushing back his chair.

"Like hell," said Keith, balling up his paper napkin. "You don't get away from here with your pockets full of change, little brother. We're gonna have a Boo-ray game." Boo-ray was a south Louisiana version of poker.

"I haven't forgotten you cleaned me out the last time we played," Larry said to Mac.

"Cleaned us all out," Mike Jr. added. "We want our revenge."

And they didn't want him to leave and break up the family gathering with everyone's emotions raw. Whatever mistakes he made and however badly he messed up his life, he was still their brother.

Mary got up and began gathering dishes, clattering them together. Her daughters-in-law rose, too, and began helping her.

"Ma, are you too mad at me to send me home with some leftovers?" Mac asked gently.

His request obviously soothed her ruffled feelings. "I'll fix up some containers," she said. "Don't forget them when you go."

"Don't worry. I'm not about to forget them. Your roast beef and gravy only get better warmed up."

"Your ma's roast beef is the best in the world," declared Mike Sr., and all his sons, including Mac, added their vocal agreement.

"My wife's is second-best," Keith was quick to add, snagging Meg around the waist and giving her a conciliatory hug.

Larry and Mike Jr. followed suit, making the same claim, and each gave his spouse a hug or kiss.

Mac watched, feeling envious as hell.

He doubted Ginger would ever cook roast beef or any other food half as well as his mother did, but he frankly didn't give a damn.

The visit with her parents had left Ginger feeling depressed. The return trip across the causeway seemed twice as long as the earlier trip with Mac cruising along behind her. Ginger doubted that he had left his parents' house in the Irish Channel this soon, but she kept a watch in her rearview mirror for his bright red Camaro. It would have been a cheery sight, lifting her spirits, Ginger admitted to herself.

None of her emotions concerning Mac had ever been mild—and still weren't. But strong emotions didn't mean happiness and contentment, not in the face of the kind of problems that had kept her and Mac from making a go of their marriage. Those same problems still existed. Ginger didn't dare forget that fact for a moment or she might let herself start to hope Mac *had* moved to the north shore because of her.

His parking spot was occupied, she noted, detouring past the parking lot at his end of the complex. However, the automobile wasn't his. Balloons outside of a condo in Building C explained why all the visitor parking places were also taken. The couple in C-6, the Ezells, must be having a party, and their guests had parked in every available spot.

Maybe the party would be over by the time Mac arrived home, Ginger reflected. It was his situation to deal with, not hers. As president of the Condo Owners Association, she wasn't responsible for policing parking infringements. Knowing Mac, she doubted he would be as upset as some people might be.

By contrast there was ample guest parking in the lot

at her end, and her arrival seemed to spark an exodus of her neighbors in Building A that would create more empty reserved slots, too. She was talking to two of her neighbors when she noticed a car that had just pulled into a guest spot.

Ginger did a double take, her heart leaping with a foolish joy as she recognized the car. Mac's Camaro!

She replied absently to her two neighbors' parting words and stood there as Mac strode toward her, carrying a stack of food containers. He'd taken off his tie, undone the top two buttons of his dress shirt and rolled the sleeves back to his elbows.

"Hi," he said. "You're just getting back, too." His deep voice had a lilt of the same gladness she was battling.

"Yes. I passed the parking lot at your end and saw that it was full."

He'd reached her. "Apparently there's a party going on." He sounded and looked unconcerned. "Did you have a nice visit with your parents?"

Ginger made a little face. "Up to a point."

"The point where my name came up?"

She nodded. "I hadn't told them before about your moving to the north shore."

"It wasn't good news, needless to say."

"No." Ginger sighed. "My father got so upset I was afraid he might have a stroke or a heart attack. Of all things, he wanted me to get an injunction against you. As though you'd been a wife-beater."

"He never liked me from the beginning. Aside from the fact that I got you pregnant, I had two other black marks against me—I was Catholic and I wanted to be a high-school coach and physical-education teacher. In your father's eyes that was wasting a degree since I'd never make a lot of money.'' Mac's voice had hardened and so had his expression. "I'll bet he's all for your marrying Whitfield.''

"He and Mother both like Barry. Barry's Methodist, which is a big plus for them.''

"He's also a CPA and earns double or triple my income. Another big plus,'' he stated grimly.

"It's not a minus,'' Ginger conceded. "Barry has better social skills than a lot of men and puts himself out to make my parents like him. You'd never guess he doesn't enjoy my mother's cooking, for example, and he's a gourmet cook himself.''

"In other words, he's a better phony than I ever was.'' Mac was scowling fiercely. "Dammit, I put myself out to make your parents like me during the first year or two we were married.''

"And I put myself out to make your parents—and your brothers and their wives—like me. How was your visit with them?''

It was his turn to grimace. "Pretty tense. We had a family free-for-all that helped a little to clear the air.''

"Did my name come up?''

"You were mentioned more than once.''

"And not with fondness by a single person. Especially not by your mother.''

His failure to make a denial confirmed that she'd accurately summed up the situation. "I made it crystal clear that they didn't have any influence over how I lived my life,'' he stated soberly. "If I could win you back, by hook or crook, I would. They could like it or not like it, as they chose.''

"Nothing's changed, has it? We *won't* be getting back together, but if we did, we would have the same in-law problems.''

"So what if we did?"

"Mac, you wouldn't be happy with a rift between you and your family. You know you wouldn't."

"Over time—"

"Over time the same thing would happen again! And I'm not up to another divorce. We're just not suited to each other. We never were." Ginger didn't dare stop talking and let him get a word in. "You have a lot of great qualities, but you're too popular with other women. I would be as jealous as I was before. I don't *want* that."

"I wouldn't give you any reason to be jealous," he argued. "Everything would be different this time around, if you'll just give me another chance." He made a move as though he meant to set his stack of food containers down on the ground and free his hands. But before he could, a woman's hysterical voice cried out his name.

"Mac! Thank God you're here!"

Barbara staggered out of her unit toward them, carrying Jonathan in her arms. The little boy was sobbing. A towel was wrapped around one of his hands.

"Barbara! What happened?" Mac thrust the containers at Ginger, and she took them from him, equally alarmed as he was. He rushed toward mother and son, whose faces were both chalk white.

"Jonathan sliced his hand with a knife! I need to take him to the emergency room! Could you drive us in my car?"

Mac had reached them and held out his arms for Jonathan.

"You might get blood on your clothes," Barbara warned.

Heedless of the caution, he gathered the little boy

gently to his chest and headed across the grass. "We'll take the Camaro."

Barbara trotted behind him, leaving her condo door standing wide open and talking with the same shrill note of hysteria. "He knows he's not supposed to use knives. He decided to core an apple for himself. And not with a paring knife, but a filet knife."

"I didn't mean to cut myself, Mom!" Jonathan's pitiful wail wrung Ginger's heart.

"Your mom's not fussing at you," Mac said. "She's just upset because you're hurt. We'll get you stitched up, and you'll be good as new."

Ginger felt immensely soothed by his words and was sure that Jonathan and Barbara were affected the same way. Barbara sounded more like her normal calm self as she stated fervently, "I really appreciate this, Mac."

He ignored her expression of gratitude and instructed, "You get in on the passenger's side and hold our young quarterback on your lap. Good thing it's your left hand, huh, sport? You'll be able to throw a football while it's healing."

Barbara obeyed, moving quickly. Mac wasted no time getting in behind the wheel and driving off in the low-slung automobile that had once been a point of contention between him and Ginger.

In retrospect she'd probably been wrong to make such an issue. The Camaro had turned out to be a good purchase for him, providing reliable transportation and pride of ownership. My main objection was that I didn't want Mac driving a flashy car that would catch the eye of every female on the prowl, Ginger reflected as she went to close Barbara's door. It locked automatically.

"What am I supposed to do with these?" she asked herself, hefting the containers of Mary McDaniel's leftover Sunday dinner. The question was rhetorical. Since she didn't have a key to Mac's condo, she would have to stow the food in her own refrigerator, which was little enough to do as her part in coming to little Jonathan's and Barbara's aid.

The phone rang just as Ginger was pushing her refrigerator door closed on the unlikely sight of her ex-mother-in-law's plastic ware sitting on a shelf.

"Hi, how was your day?" asked Barry.

"Eventful. I arrived home about a half hour ago in time for an emergency. Jonathan cut his hand on a knife."

"Jonathan?"

"The little boy who wanted you to play football with him yesterday afternoon."

"Oh, sure. What was he doing with a knife?"

"Evidently he tried to core an apple for himself. Luckily Mac happened to be around. He drove Barbara and Jonathan to the emergency room."

"Why didn't someone just call 911 and have the paramedics come?"

That would have been Barry's solution, a solution that didn't require him to get personally involved. If he had been the one present minutes ago instead of Mac, he wouldn't have taken the same swift actions that Mac had. Actions motivated by caring about other people.

"The nearest hospital is only ten minutes away. And Jonathan's life wasn't in danger. Taking him for medical treatment seemed the logical thing to do."

"Maybe the experience will teach him not to fool with knives. How was the visit with your parents? As bad as you expected?" Barry's voice held sympathy that he hadn't wasted on a small boy who'd suffered a trauma.

As Ginger answered, filling him in, there was no doubt in her mind which man she would want nearby in an emergency if given her choice of Mac or Barry.

"What did you do today?" she asked.

"I attended church. Then this afternoon I got together with Dan. He showed me through the house he's renovating in Old Covington. He's making one room into a library with real wooden paneling." Barry's enthusiasm shone through as he described the architectural features of the house and outlined Dan's plans for turning it into a lovely and comfortable home.

"It sounds wonderful," Ginger said. "Am I going to get to see the before stage so that I can appreciate the finished product?" She was growing more and more curious to meet Dan himself.

"Dan had a professional video made, and he's taking pictures at every stage of the work. He's actually quite an excellent photographer himself. I sure wish I'd thought of having a video made," Barry lamented.

So much for my hint for a tour, thought Ginger. "Is Dan dating someone special?"

"He hasn't mentioned anyone. Are you coming over?" he asked. "I made some raspberry sorbet that's to die for. With fresh raspberries."

"Save some for me. I want to stay here and wait for news on Jonathan." It was too complicated to explain about the food in her refrigerator that Mac would be coming to claim.

Even without the food as an excuse, Ginger knew she would have wanted to stay there. There was no point in lying to herself and pretending that the inclination she felt to spend a few hours in Barry's company was any match for the urge to see Mac even for a few minutes.

Operation Cure was a bust. Being around Mac wasn't

helping one bit to get him out of her system. Quite the contrary.

What *would* do the trick? Getting involved with him again and proving to them both that their personalities didn't mesh? It would mean breaking off with Barry, a less exciting—and, yes, less sexy—man who might make her a good, steadfast husband.

Greatly disturbed by the whole train of thought, Ginger went upstairs and changed her clothes. Instead of slacks she put on a pair of black jeans, knowing full well that Mac had always liked her in jeans.

An hour passed, and Mac didn't return with Barbara and Jonathan. Ginger fidgeted and watched the clock and worried. What was taking so long? Was the injury more serious than she'd thought? Had Jonathan been rushed into surgery? She wished Mac or Barbara would phone and give her an update. They must realize she was concerned.

Another hour passed. The doorbell pealed just as Ginger was looking up the number of the nearest hospital to call the emergency room and try to find out what was going on.

Closing the phone directory, she rushed to the door and opened it to see Mac standing on her threshold. He'd obviously already been to his condo to change clothes himself because he was now wearing jeans and a knit shirt.

"I've been pacing the floor worrying about Jonathan!" she exclaimed. "How is he? Did you bring him home? Is he still at the hospital? How bad was the injury?"

"He's home. We got back about thirty minutes ago and got him settled. He sliced his hand pretty deep, but there's no serious nerve damage. He was feeling good enough that he wanted a take-out kids' meal, so we swung by a restaurant on the way.''

"I'm so glad he's okay. What took so long?"

"There was a major accident on Interstate 12, so we had to wait our turn. A nurse checked out Jonathan's hand and bandaged it to stop the bleeding.''

"I was starting to imagine all sorts of complications.''

"I'm sorry. I would have called you, but I don't know your phone number and Barbara didn't have it with her.''

"Oh.'' Evidently he hadn't gotten her unlisted number from Sharon.

"Can I come in?''

"Certainly.'' Ginger stepped back for him to enter. "Your food is in my refrigerator.''

"Thanks. Remind me to take it with me.''

Instead of brushing past her and leading the way into her living area as he'd done on his one previous visit, tonight he paused inside her foyer while she closed the door. Ginger gestured for him to precede her, but he didn't budge. "Have you changed your mind about coming in?'' she asked, her heart drumming in her chest as she met his gaze.

His grin was forced. "I was just waiting for you to go first so that I could get a rear view of those black jeans you're wearing.''

"Mac, you'd better just take your leftovers and go.'' Ginger edged around him and slipped into the kitchen. Before she could jerk open the refrigerator door, his arms came around her.

"Just one hug,'' he said, his voice low and full of pleading. "This is such torture.''

His arms tightened and Ginger sagged against him, surrendering to his strength. A soft moan of delight came from her throat.

"You feel so good in my arms," he whispered, his words muffled by her hair. "God, I've missed holding you."

Ginger opened her mouth to utter a protest and couldn't form any words other than his name. "Mac."

"I'm sorry, but I'm human." His apology was spoken against her neck. He was planting kisses, his breath warm against her skin. Ginger's head tilted sideways, giving him access, shivers of pure delight rendering her helpless. "Turn around and kiss me. Please. Just one kiss," he urged, his mouth against her cheek.

No.

But her body didn't heed the weak message from her brain. She twisted toward him and when she was half-turned in his arms, his lips had taken possession of hers with a repressed hunger and incredible tenderness.

You're making a terrible mistake. Don't do this. The voice of her judgment couldn't keep Ginger from kissing him back. It didn't keep her arms from going up around his neck, her palms from stroking his face, her fingers from plunging into his hair with a kind of frenzied joy. It didn't prevent her tongue from mating with his or her mouth from returning the pressure of his mouth. There was no point in lapsing halfheartedly, since this was the one and only time she would act so foolishly. She would carefully avoid temptation in the future, which meant not being alone with him again.

He groaned, lifting her against him. Ginger could feel the hard evidence of his desire. You'd better call a halt or there'll be no stopping, the voice of sanity nagged. She didn't want to listen to that voice. She didn't want to stop. She wanted to keep kissing him. She wanted to make love with him. Just one more time. One more glorious time.

"Mac." She pulled her lips apart from his with the idea of making her position clear before they went any further.

"I know. I've had my kiss I asked you for." He rested his cheek against hers, drawing in a long, ragged breath, his chest rising and falling against her breasts. "Just let me hold you a minute while I recover, okay?"

"You're not the only one who has to recover."

"Are you turned on, too?"

"Of course I'm turned on." The old Mac would have discovered for himself when he unzipped her jeans and slipped his hand inside, claiming her femininity. Ginger bore down on a wave of sexual frustration.

He slowly set her down and looked searchingly into her face. "You did intend for me to stop, didn't you?"

Ginger stepped free of his loose embrace. "Actually I intended for you to pause long enough for me to make sure you didn't read any significance into what was happening."

"Go on."

"Making love one time wouldn't change anything between us. It wouldn't be a first step toward reconciling."

"In that case I'm glad I put on the brakes," he said quietly. "When we make love, I want it to mean we're on the road to getting back together."

"In that case it's better that you showed some self-control." Ginger's words came out sounding aggrieved. To her annoyance Mac gazed back at her, looking almost cheerful at some thought that struck him. He backed away and leaned on the counter, folding his arms across his chest.

"You're not sleeping with Whitfield, are you? Not on a regular basis."

"How is that relevant to the discussion?"

"Highly relevant from my point of view. If you were sleeping with him, you wouldn't think of jumping into bed with me for a one-night stand. You would be faithful to him."

"For all you know, my morals have slipped," she said defensively.

"I doubt that." He straightened and rubbed his stomach. "Have you eaten supper? I haven't, and I'm getting hungry."

Apparently enough had been said on the subject of her intimate relationship with another man. He was perfectly content to drop it and move on, having made a much quicker recovery from aroused desire than Ginger.

"No, I haven't eaten supper." Her reply was irritable. "I was too concerned about Jonathan to think about food."

"You want to go out for a hamburger? Or I could go pick up something," he said, reading the refusal of his first suggestion.

"I've had my quota of calories today already. My father took my mother and me out to a restaurant after church. I'll just make myself a tuna-salad sandwich after you've gone. And you have your leftovers you can warm up." In his own microwave oven in his own condo.

"How about making me a tuna-salad sandwich while you're making yours?"

"You don't like tuna-salad sandwiches," she reminded him.

He shrugged. "They're not my favorite, but I eat one occasionally."

"Why force down something you won't enjoy when you could fix yourself a sandwich with your mother's roast beef?" It was a safe assumption that one of the containers held Mary's mouth-watering roast beef.

"Because I don't want to eat by myself. I'll help you make the tuna salad if it's not made," he bargained, and began opening up top cabinets. "What size bowl do we need?"

Ginger's resistance eroded completely. "You can fix yourself a roast beef on a bun," she said, pulling open the freezer compartment and getting out a package of whole-wheat buns. "Or however many you want."

He took the package from her. "Only if you're sure you don't mind."

"It's no problem that the roast beef came from your mother's kitchen, if that's what you mean."

"That kind of surprises me," he commented. And obviously pleased him, too.

They both went to work in the small kitchen with their separate preparations. Ginger got a six-ounce can of tuna from her pantry, while he retrieved one of the plastic containers from her refrigerator.

"Do you have a covered microwave dish I could use?" he asked.

She set her can of tuna down near the electric can opener and supplied him with the dish and a large spoon. Instead of returning to her portion of the counter, she paused a minute to watch him transferring slices of roast beef dripping with rich brown gravy. The aroma made her mouth water.

"Can I talk you into having one of these? There's plenty for both of us," Mac said.

Ginger's taste buds got the best of her. "Maybe I will. I didn't have a roll and butter today with my dinner. And I ordered trout. Of course, it was trout amandine," she added guiltily. "Not exactly low-cal."

"Your weight is perfect for those jeans."

"They're snug."

"In all the right places."

She was returning the tuna to the pantry and glanced over her shoulder to catch his appreciative male inspection of her rear end. Under his gaze the jeans *did* fit perfectly. Her figure became lush rather than padded with an extra five pounds. Mac had always had the ability to make her feel sexy and desirable. How she'd missed that.

If only he didn't affect every other woman he looked at exactly the same way.

Chapter Eight

Ginger set the table, using place mats, while Mac fixed their plates. When they sat down to eat, she was hit with the sensation that this really wasn't happening. But it *was* happening. She was having supper with her ex-husband, barely a week after he'd shown up unexpectedly at the faculty meeting. And they were eating food prepared by his mother, her worst critic.

What frightened Ginger was her own glow of happiness.

"Well. How is it?" Mac prompted, looking as eager and slightly anxious as one of her high-school students might have looked, turning in a project. She shrugged aside apprehension, reminding herself that she was twenty-nine now, not nineteen, and not likely to lose sight of reality.

"Delicious." Ginger chewed her bite of su

roast beef, savoring the taste. "Mary's a wonderful cook."

"She's had lots of practice," Mac replied, forking a bite into his mouth. He'd made the sandwiches open faced, spooning on gravy, so they were using forks. Knives weren't necessary because the meat was so tender.

"So has my mother, and it didn't do her a lot of good. Your mother's just talented in the kitchen."

"I'll tell her you said so."

"I'm sure she'll be flattered no end with a compliment from me. She may not give you any more leftovers when she finds out you shared these with her ex-daughter-in-law."

"That's a punishment I can live with. Food's not nearly so important to me as it once was."

"He said as he took a big mouthful." Ginger couldn't resist teasing him. "You should have seen the relief on your face when I excused you from eating a tuna-fish sandwich. You were like a man given a pardon."

He grinned, reaching over to wipe the corner of her mouth with his paper napkin. "You were pretty quick yourself to put that tiny can of tuna back on the shelf."

"I make a lousy tuna salad. I haven't improved my culinary skills in general," she added.

"That's okay. Out of necessity I've turned into a pretty fair cook," he stated. "I make a mean pot of red beans and a tasty jambalaya."

How did his learning to cook make it "okay" that she hadn't? Ginger decided not to ask that question. "I'm impressed. Barry's a gourmet cook. But I believe I already told you that." It seemed necessary to bring up Barry's name and wreck the harmony.

"Yes, you did."

"He serves me delicious meals, and I serve him restaurant food when he occasionally comes here for lunch or dinner. So in his case he won't have any false expectations if we should eventually marry."

"The same would be true of you and me," Mac countered.

"Except there's no chance we'll remarry."

"I disagree, but let's not argue while we eat. Or talk about Whitfield. Do you mind?"

The request was so mild and reasonable Ginger could only comply. "What *is* there for us to talk about that isn't a sensitive subject?"

"Lots of things. I wondered if you have a kid named James Carlson in one of your classes."

"In my first-period class. So far he hasn't turned in a single assignment, but he isn't a discipline problem."

"He's repeating the ninth grade and just biding his time to turn sixteen and drop out of school. The kid's a natural athlete. I'm trying to get him to try out for the football team."

"I haven't had time yet to talk with the guidance counselors about him and check out his scores. I'm planning to do that tomorrow."

"I already have. James has an above-average IQ."

"What's the family situation?"

They finished their meal, engrossed in conversation, two professional educators rather than estranged husband and wife.

"Hey, this is great, both of us having this kid in class," Mac said, pushing back his chair. "Between us, we have a double shot of getting through to him. Before when we talked about problem students, we were teaching at different schools." He got up, saving Ginger from having to answer. She started to rise, too, a clamped a big hand on her shoulder, holding her in her chair. "Just stay put. Dessert's coming up."

"I shouldn't have dessert."

But she ended up allowing him to dish up a small portion of his mother's bread pudding for her. Afterward he insisted on rinsing the dishes and stacking them in the dishwasher. He even wiped the counter with a wet sponge.

"Your mother would be horrified if she could see us," Ginger commented from the doorway, where she watched, finding the sight of him all too attractive. "Your brothers, too, for that matter."

"Those brothers of mine would definitely give me a hard time," he agreed ruefully. Still holding the sponge, he looked around at the kitchen and then at her as though to ask whether the cleanup passed inspection.

"I couldn't have done better myself," she said. "You don't really need a wife to keep house for you anymore, do you? Your condo wasn't even messy yesterday."

"I've learned to pick up after myself." He tossed the sponge into the sink. "Let's see what's on the news."

Ginger turned and led the way back into the main room. The fact that he hadn't taken advantage of the opening to say he needed a wife to fill other needs besides housekeeping somehow made it all right for her to let him stay a short while longer. Plus she *wanted* him to stay.

The TV remote was on the coffee table. Ginger picked it up and clicked on the TV, biding her time while Mac chose between the love seat and the sofa. When he took a step toward the love seat, she sat down on the sofa. He pivoted and came to sit down beside her.

"That was a neat maneuver," she said dryly.

He just grinned and sprawled back comfortably, stretching his arm along the back of the sofa. With his free hand he patted his stomach. "That's the first meal I've truly enjoyed in six years." His tone was serious.

"Mac, don't feed me a line, pun intended. I'll be thirty years old my next birthday."

"We'll both be thirty on our birthdays, and mine comes before yours."

"I remember the date of your birthday. You wanted to watch the news," she reminded him, turning up the volume.

He shifted his body slightly toward her, keeping his gaze on her face and ignoring the TV. "I think I already mentioned I was over at Don and Brenda's house the Saturday night you were on the news with your teacher's award. When I think how easily I might have missed that newscast, it scares me."

Ginger gave up on the pretense of paying attention to the words of the woman anchor. She lowered the volume again. "Someone who knew us when we were married would have seen it and told you."

"True. But the effect on me might not have been the same. Like lightning striking. I might have stuck with my coaching job in New Orleans another year and looked you up instead of moving over here. You'd have slammed the door in my face, and I wouldn't have gotten to first base."

"Mac, you *haven't* gotten to first base."

"At least I'm in the batting lineup."

He'd been touching her hair. Now his hand dropped lower to massage her neck. Ginger closed her eyes, shivers of pleasure easing the tension in her body, tension she needed to resist him. "I think it's time for the ballpark to close up for the night."

"Before you lock up, can I have a good-night kiss?"
He leaned close so that she could feel his warm breath
on her face. Before she could say no, his mouth lightly
nuzzled her cheek, nuzzled the corner of her mouth.

I shouldn't. I really shouldn't....

Ginger turned her head slowly, letting her lips brush
deliciously against his. His hand curved on her neck,
and he took an audible intake of breath, but he didn't
pull her to him. Not until she'd kissed him, her mouth
pressing and clinging. He groaned and his arms gathered her into a strong, glorious embrace as he kissed
her with passion. They seemed to be resuming where
they'd left off in the kitchen earlier.

Ginger didn't put forth any struggle when he transferred her to his lap. Her arms were wound around his
neck, her lips returning his pressure, her tongue welcoming the invasion of his ardent tongue into her
mouth. Any faint message from her brain bidding her
to resist was drowned out by the chant of delight from
every cell in her body.

There was simply no denying herself this wild, sweet
pleasure of kissing him, of touching him, of being in
his arms, desired by him. Just this one heavenly relapse.
After tonight she would be wiser and more cautious.
That was Ginger's bargain with her judgment.

She moaned encouragement as Mac's hand stroked
her thighs and buttocks with a possessive familiarity.
His palm sliding over her jeans created trails of sim-
mering heat that led directly to her feminine center.

Please, she begged silently, and he immediately responded to her unspoken need, easing his hand between
her legs.

"Oh, yes," Ginger whispered in helpless ecstasy as

he laid claim to her mound. She writhed brazenly against his hand.

"Feel good, sweetheart?" His voice was husky and tender.

"Incredible."

"We're reaching a point of no return here. I'm on the verge of taking off your clothes."

Ginger's answer was to start unbuttoning her blouse while she brought her mouth to his and cut off more discussion. *Take me this once,* she told him with her lips and tongue. Mac's restraint was suddenly gone, and Ginger thrilled to the knowledge that he *couldn't* stop now any more than she could. He tugged her blouse free of her jeans and slid his hands up over her bare skin to capture her breasts.

"Oh, yes," she murmured again, throwing her head back and giving herself up to the swelling, tingling pleasure of fitting *perfectly* into his strong, wonderful hands. All too soon he released her, but only to pull apart her blouse and shove it off her shoulders with her frantic help. Her fingers collided with his as she reached to undo the front closure of her bra. Together they succeeded and Ginger, naked to the waist now, tossed aside her lacy undergarment.

Next came pure heaven. She clasped his head and guided him from one breast to the other while he kissed her greedy flesh and suckled her hard peaks. His breath was hot on her skin, his tongue rough and wet. Ginger was certain she never wanted him to cease and equally certain she couldn't withstand the stimulation a second longer.

Mac's hands had been caressing her back, his palms sliding over her skin. Now he brought her astride of him and unsnapped the waistband of her jeans. Ginger sucked in her stomach as he slid the zipper down and edged his fingers beneath the elastic of her hip-hugger panties. She rose up slightly on her knees, giving him intimate access. He probed her with a skillful fingertip, forcing a sharp gasp of pleasure from her throat. But then instead of dipping deep into her aching wetness, he rubbed her slick cleft. Ginger gyrated her hips in the effort to trap his fingers into penetrating her.

He let her succeed, asking with tender passion, "Is this what you want, sweetheart?"

"You know it isn't." She unsnapped his jeans and located his hard, swollen manhood. He sucked in his breath when she closed her hand around him. After she'd stroked the pulsing length of him once, he withdrew her hand.

"Enough. I want to satisfy you," he said, hugging her tightly.

"When did you ever not satisfy me?" she replied, tugging his shirt free at the same time she was hugging him back.

"You left me."

"My leaving you had nothing to do with our sex life. Mac, let's please don't talk now! Let's make love!"

He laid her on the sofa and stripped off her jeans and panties together. In her urgency to help him, Ginger was almost more of a hindrance. She watched, anticipation sharpening her desire, while he made short work of shedding his clothes. But then other emotions crowded in, including a wifely pride and possessiveness that she knew were no longer appropriate. She shoved the emotions aside. This was just sex, fantastic sex that might clear the air and give them both closure.

"I always loved watching you undress," she commented as he retrieved his wallet from his jeans and took out a condom. "I guess men in general are probably more unselfconscious than women about disrobing."

"The first year we were married, you were shy about undressing in front of me. You would go into the bathroom and put on your nightgown. Remember?"

"I never really got over feeling a little shy," she admitted, adding, "except when I was turned on, like now. Then I would forget about modesty."

"Which was a major turn-on for me."

He knelt down on the floor beside the sofa and leaned over to kiss her breasts. Ginger threaded her fingers into his hair and moaned with the delicious sensations. "That feels so incredibly good. You're such a wonderful lover."

"I'll make a better husband this time. Or die trying."

"Mac, please don't misunderstand...."

His strong, magical hands were caressing her hips and thighs, and he was kissing his way down her stomach on an erotic journey that dissolved Ginger's bones. Clarifying the situation, which hadn't changed since their conversation earlier in the kitchen, would have to wait until later. She couldn't possibly talk lucidly now.

"Don't! I'm too aroused," she warned when he reached his destination. But he made intimate love to her with his mouth and tongue anyway. Ginger soared to ecstasy and cried out with the release that convulsed her body, bringing her whole upper torso up off the sofa. "I saw colored rockets shooting in all directions," she murmured, going limp and nerveless after the spasms of aftershock had quieted.

"Colored rockets. Sounds like quite a sight," he said, planting tender kisses on her inner thighs. His deep voice was husky with male satisfaction.

"You should have listened to me. Now I have about as much life as a Raggedy Ann doll." Ginger opened her eyes. "And look at the state you're in." The sight of him, naked and aroused, immediately flushed away her lassitude.

"Could you help me with this?" He held out the foil packet. When his fingers touched her, she could feel the slight tremor of his passion.

The intimate task reawakened her hot desire. She drew him down to her, as desperate as before for him to couple his body with hers. He entered her, going deeper and deeper, filling the aching emptiness with a completeness Ginger knew in her heart only he would ever be able to do. She hugged his shoulders and murmured his name in a tone that expressed her sublime joy.

"Welcome home, baby," he said, his voice resonant with a similar joy shot with pain.

The trip to ecstasy was slightly longer, although Ginger was completely out of tune with ordinary passage of time. Her climax when it came was even more cataclysmic, if that was possible, and definitely sweeter because Mac climaxed seconds later. There was the added element of companionship. Ginger delighted in the lax weight of his big body, sinking her into the soft cushions of the sofa. For a few more seconds she could delay putting into perspective what had happened.

"I always loved being smushed like this," she recalled, stroking his back. Regret had crept into her voice.

At her words she could feel strength returning to his muscles. He levered his upper torso and looked down at her. Ginger's heart sank at his serious expression.

"My feelings for you haven't changed one bit, Ginger.'' What about *her* feelings for him? he asked silently.

"Mac, we're divorced. Of course, I feel differently toward you now than when you were my husband."

"In my mind you're still my wife. Those divorce papers didn't turn me back into a single man."

She sighed, turning her head aside. Lying on the carpet was the foil packaging, twisted open. "Do married men carry condoms in their wallet?"

"That condom has been in my wallet at least a year. I haven't needed it."

"The women you date probably read the same advice I read—single women should be ready to supply their own protection."

"I've dated damned few women."

"You were free to date as many as you wanted. Could we please get dressed and then carry on this conversation?" She'd grown self-conscious of her nudity as guilt set in.

"Just to give you an idea of what a fool I am, I wasn't intending to get dressed,'' he said, casing free of her. His hurt, bitter tone made her flinch. "I had visions of sleeping with you."

Ginger didn't dare let herself imagine lying in her bed with him, sleeping cuddled up against his body. "I'm sorry," she said. "I was wrong to give in to lust like this."

"So that's what it was for you? Nothing more than lust?" He was picking up his clothing, his abrupt movements conveying the same anger in his voice.

"I'll always care about you, Mac. Even at my most hostile stage, I couldn't manage to hate you." The answer earned her a hurt, accusing look that was almost her undoing.

"Do you follow that so-called advice to single women?" he demanded, scooping up the foil packaging and crushing it in his hand.

Ginger thought about the condom tucked away and forgotten in a zip compartment of her purse. The remainder of her unused supply of condoms from a single purchase was stored in her bathroom. "I made an attempt to be a woman of the nineties, but I'm not exactly a big customer of safe-sex products."

"That makes two of us." He stalked from the room.

"Feel free to use the half bath, across from the kitchen," she said to his back, sounding as guilty and defensive as she felt.

The door of the half bath closed with a loud bang that made Ginger cringe. It also brought the realization that she'd watched him until he'd disappeared, enjoying the sight of his male nakedness for this one last time. Misery welled up, making Ginger want to sink her face into her hands and weep over the mess she'd made of things by her actions tonight. Weeping would have to wait until later, after Mac had gone. Right now Ginger had to get a grip on her emotions and be ready to state her position when Mac returned. A reconciliation *wouldn't* work. Not over the long term. They would both only be headed for disappointment.

After hurriedly pulling on her clothes, she perched on the corner of the love seat, anxiously rehearsing a speech. A speech she didn't get to deliver. The forceful thud of the front door closing sent reverberations through the whole downstairs of her condo.

Mac had gotten dressed and left, without saying good-night.

Ginger sat there, trying to reason away her despair. It was probably good in the long run that tonight had happened. Good that he'd gotten angry with her. Now he would leave her completely alone.

She just wished his anger hadn't been mixed with hurt. Ginger hadn't ever seen that wounded expression in Mac's face before, as though she'd stuck a knife into him and twisted. He'd never seemed vulnerable. He was so rugged and strong physically and so even tempered and not given to moodiness.

I have to make sure he's okay.

Acting on the worried thought, Ginger decided to call him and apologize again. After seven rings she cut the connection and dialed again, on the chance she'd punched a wrong number. His answering machine hadn't clicked on. On the second attempt there was still no answer and no recorded message. Either he'd turned off the machine or it wasn't working properly.

He'd had ample time to get to his condo. Was he too down in the dumps to talk to anyone? Did he guess she was calling him and he wasn't answering to punish her? Of the two possibilities, she would rather the second one be true.

Suddenly Ginger remembered Mary McDaniel's leftover food in her refrigerator. He'd gone off and left it. She could deliver the containers to his condo and reassure herself that he wasn't suffering from rejection.

Minutes later Ginger stood outside the door of D-1. The doorbell worked. She could hear the faint ding-dong when she pressed the lighted button. Not a sound from inside. She pressed again. Waited. Pressed a third time. The sound of an automobile engine made Ginger turn her head in the direction of the parking lot at Mac's end of the complex. From that vantage point she couldn't see whether his car was in its place.

Maybe he wasn't home. While she was working up

a full case of anxiety, he might have sought solace elsewhere. Ginger set the stack of plastic containers and went to investigate. Sure enough, the red Camaro was gone.

"You idiot," she murmured, some of her worry turning to anger at herself. What had happened tonight probably hadn't been as traumatic to Mac as she'd built up in her mind. More than likely he'd just shrugged off the whole experience with his typical resilience. Right this moment he might be somewhere having a beer or a cup of coffee.

Ginger plodded back to her own condo, forgetting all about the abandoned food containers until she'd gone upstairs and gotten ready for bed. Wearily she debated getting dressed again and retrieving them, but there was really no danger of the food spoiling in the tightly sealed containers if Mac got back from wherever he'd gone at a reasonable hour. The contents were thoroughly chilled.

Without doubt he would be just as happy she'd delivered the leftovers in his absence, saving him from having to talk to her. Ginger expected him to avoid her like the plague from now on, going his way while she went hers.

Mac had headed blindly toward the parking lot when he slammed out of Ginger's condo. With no destination in mind, he'd driven to Interstate 12 and headed east, passing exits for north-shore towns that were only familiar names. Abita Springs. Lacombe. St. Tammany. Eventually he came to Slidell, got off and got back on again, heading back, all the windows rolled down and the wind ripping through the Camaro.

He needed the noise of the tires on the pavement, the

battering force of the wind, the roar of the diesel engines propelling 18-wheelers. The last thing he wanted was to be soothed. Mac knew from experience that anger was his only defense against the pain and disappointment that were going to tear into him like a whole squad taking turns with a tackling dummy.

Ginger had played him for a sucker tonight. She'd let him make love to her under the wrong assumption that they *were* making love, not just screwing each other. Sure, she'd said earlier in the kitchen, "Making love one time wouldn't change anything between us. It would only be sex."

But Mac had spoken up and contradicted her. He'd stated in no uncertain terms, "When we make love, I want it to mean we're on the road to getting back together."

So he'd made love to her, and she'd gotten the sex she wanted. Then she'd hit him with the truth when he was as exposed as he would have been playing bare-ass naked in the Super Bowl. "I don't want you back," was her message. He was good for a couple of climaxes, but he couldn't make the grade as a husband in her book.

Fine with him. Let her marry her CPA. It would serve her right if she ended up sexually frustrated. Whatever Mac's faults, she *hadn't* needed to go looking for sex with some other guy.

Mac took the Mandeville exit and headed back home. Rather, he headed to the place he was renting. His spirits were at a low ebb as he got out of his car and walked to his condo. Then he spotted the food containers stacked neatly, one on top of the other.

A string of curses later he muttered, ''She couldn't even keep them in her damned refrigerator overnight!''

The renewed anger made it easier to go inside and confront the infernal loneliness.

Chapter Nine

Ginger welcomed the buzz of her alarm clock. It meant she'd survived the night of torture. Every hour she'd waked up from turbulent dreams and lain there, worrying about the repercussions of making love with Mac.

She'd also worried about whether those darned leftovers had spoiled by the time he returned home? *Had* he come back to his condo, or were the containers still sitting there?

As she dragged herself out of bed, the same anxiety nagged at her. Before she left for school, she would have to walk down to D-1 and put her mind to rest, at least about the leftovers. There wouldn't be any danger of running into Mac—unless he was just getting home from somewhere.

Early-morning sun slanted into his recessed entryway, highlighting its bareness when Ginger carried out her investigative mission. No welcome mat. No planter.

No food containers.

Good. Now she wouldn't have to dispose of spoiled food and deal with that added guilt. Ginger knew darned well that simple relief over knowing the leftovers had found their way into Mac's refrigerator didn't account for the spring in her step as she retraced her route. Okay, so she was also relieved that he'd returned home safely. And had slept in his own bed.

The vision of a sleeping Mac brought a tender emotion to Ginger's breast. With a sigh she banished the attractive picture. She wished she could do something nice for him that wasn't too personal. That bare entryway of his badly needed a homey touch. Just recently she'd seen a welcome mat with a sports motif at a discount store where she shopped. Maybe she would buy it for him when she stopped by the store after school this afternoon to buy Jonathan a get-well present.

Just as Ginger came abreast of her condo, Barbara emerged through her front door, bearing a plate draped with a paper napkin. Barbara wasn't dressed for work, Ginger noticed, but looked as though she might have climbed out of bed, given her brunette hair a quick brushing and pulled on the purple knit leggings she wore with a matching loose-knit pullover blouse.

"Oh, hi, Ginger," Barbara greeted her. "Do you suppose Mac's up? Jonathan insisted I take him a couple of these blueberry muffins I baked for our breakfast."

"I would expect him to be awake," Ginger replied. "He'll have to leave for school in another fifteen or twenty minutes."

"He was so wonderful with Jonathan yesterday. I can never thank him."

"How is Jonathan?"

"Disappointed that he has to miss kindergarten and

can't show all his little friends his bandage. I'm taking the day off from work and keeping him home today," Barbara explained. "Well, I'd better deliver these muffins to Mac while they're still warm. Have a good day at school."

"Thanks. I'll come by and visit Jonathan this afternoon."

"Great! He'll enjoy that and so will I," Barbara called over her shoulder as she hurried on her way with her home-baked treat.

Ginger could imagine all too easily Mac opening the door of his condo, fresh from his shower, clean shaved and virile. He would recover quickly from his initial surprise and accept the muffins with a sincere, hearty appreciation that would cause Barbara to walk away feeling like she'd saved him from starvation. In the future Ginger doubted Jonathan's mom would ever bake blueberry muffins again without Mac coming to mind.

Which was perfectly all right with Ginger as long as Barbara didn't get hurt. Or it should have been perfectly all right with Ginger, given the circumstances. But it *wasn't*. There was no reason for jealousy anymore, but that's what the unpleasant twinges were. Jealousy.

And Ginger had been suffering attacks of the same twinges since the day of the faculty meeting when she'd seen Mac for the first time in six long years and Sharon had gone after him like a barracuda. Why, as much as she liked Sharon, Ginger had almost *hated* her. And disliked Angie the day she'd done nothing more criminal than accompany Mac to the teachers' lounge. Angie hadn't even been fawning over him.

The bout of honest soul-searching left Ginger deeply troubled about herself. Was she a horrible, warped person? Obviously she was, where Mac was concerned. As a wife she'd been overly possessive, distrustful, insecure. Now she wasn't his wife and yet she'd slipped back into the same mold the moment he came back into her life.

Even if Mac had changed as much as he claimed he had and was capable of being a better husband now, a second attempt at marriage would work only if Ginger could change. Those were big *ifs*.

The only given was that it wouldn't be difficult for her to fall in love with him all over again.

"Wow! A Saints football helmet! Thanks, Miss Ginger!" Jonathan's face shone with the same childish excitement in his voice. He wasted no time in ripping his present from the cardboard-and-cellophane packaging, using his uninjured hand.

"He's been dragging me to the toy department and begging for one of those," Barbara remarked, smiling indulgently at her small son, who promptly tried on the helmet. "You couldn't have gotten him anything he would like better."

"I'm glad I made a lucky guess. I hadn't noticed him wearing a football helmet."

"Mom, is it time for my favorite program yet?" Jonathan inquired.

"Yes, it just came on." Barbara turned on the TV set and flipped to a children's cable channel.

He settled himself on the carpet and was instantly engrossed in a popular cartoon featuring ragamuffin children. "How about a cup of coffee?" she asked Ginger. "I just brewed a pot."

"Since it's made, I'd love a cup."

"Let's sit over at the breakfast bar where it'll be easier to talk over the TV."

Ginger moved over to the high counter between the kitchen and the dining area and took a stool. Barbara joined her after she'd served their coffee and brought Jonathan a glass of milk and a saucer with several cookies that looked homemade. She'd set a plate of the same cookies within tempting reach of Ginger and urged, "Help yourself. Jonathan loves for me to bake cookies and muffins," Barbara was saying. "I figure it's the least I can do."

To make up for his not having a father. Ginger finished out the thought for herself. "He's a delightful little boy. You seem to be doing a great job as a single mom."

"Thanks. I try hard. The only thing that really gets to me is seeing how he thrives on male attention." Barbara sipped her coffee. "In theory it would be great to give him a step-dad, but what are the chances of finding a guy like Mac who's not taken?"

Ginger choked on her swallow of coffee. "Is he 'taken'?"

"Yes, he's hoping to get back together with his wife."

"When did he tell you that?"

"Saturday night. Jonathan and I ran into him, and the three of us ate together. In the course of conversation, he filled me in on his reasons for moving here. He said he'd relocated because his wife lived here and he wanted to be near her." The other woman made a wry face. "I guess I gave off hopeful signals, and Mac didn't want me to misconstrue his friendliness."

Ginger remembered the phone conversation with Fay Novak yesterday, remembered how she'd reacted with jealousy and suspicion. It had been a chance meeting, just as he'd described it. Probably he had told the truth on many occasions in the past that had aroused Ginger's suspicion, and she just hadn't known whether to believe him.

Barbara was eyeing her with concern. "Is something wrong?"

Yes, very wrong. Ginger glanced into the living area and saw that Jonathan's attention was still glued to the TV screen. "Can I share something with you in confidence?"

"I think I can guess what you're going to say, Ginger." Barbara had lowered her voice, too. "You're Mac's wife?"

"Ex-wife. We're divorced."

The correction came as a surprise. "He gave me the impression he and his wife were separated, not divorced." Ginger's neighbor went on, "I sort of added one and one and came up with two from seeing you and Mac together. You're both such nice people. I hope everything works out for the best."

"Me, too."

"If it's not being too inquisitive, why the secrecy?"

"I suspect it's a result of poor communication. He's respecting my privacy, and I'm respecting his."

The doorbell chimed.

"Mom, somebody's at the door!" Jonathan shouted.

His mother's reply was patient. "Thank you, I heard the doorbell. Excuse me," she said to Ginger, who wasn't sorry to be given a few seconds to absorb Barbara's account of her conversation with Mac on Saturday night. According to him, he *had* moved to the north shore because of Ginger.

The confirmation of what he'd told Ginger himself was every bit as scary as it was thrilling. I'm so afraid of being hurt again, she admitted to herself.

"Hi, Mac." Barbara had opened the door.

Ginger's heart dropped to her stomach, and she slid off her stool in panic. Mac was *here!* She wasn't ready to face him!

"Come on in. Ginger's here. She brought Jonathan a present."

There was a split-second pause before his reply.

"Then I'll pay Jonathan a visit later."

He didn't want to see her. He was still hurt and angry about last night.

"Mom! Is that Coach Mac?" Jonathan wasn't waiting for an answer. He'd scrambled to his feet and was racing toward the foyer to investigate for himself.

Ginger was torn between an urge to join the rest of them and an urge to huddle out of sight. The latter urge won at least temporarily while she eavesdropped.

"Coach Mac! You brought me something, too? See what Miss Ginger gave me?"

The little boy had been wearing his football helmet when he made his headlong rush for the door. Gestures would be accompanying his eager words.

"Jonathan. Mind your manners," Barbara scolded.

"Looks like Miss Ginger beat me to the punch." Mac's voice was rueful. "I'll have to take mine back and exchange it."

"You're kidding," Barbara said laughingly. "You bought him a Saints helmet, too?"

"Can I have it?" Jonathan asked. "Then when my new friend from kindergarten, Ryan, comes to play with me, he can wear it!"

"Are you sure you won't come in? Ginger and I were having coffee and cookies."

"Homemade cookies," Ginger called bravely.

His pause seemed to last an hour.

"As long as I'm not interrupting," he said finally, reluctance in his voice.

The three of them trooped in, with Mac towering over mother and son. Ginger had climbed back onto her stool. She smiled a self-conscious greeting at him. "I couldn't help overhearing. What a coincidence."

He hadn't smiled back at her.

Jonathan created a welcome diversion as he ripped into cellophane and cardboard and freed his duplicate helmet with exclamations of "Oh, boy! This is neat! Two Saints helmets!"

"Now finish watching your program while Coach Mac has a cup of coffee," his mother instructed. The little boy obediently returned to the living room area, hugging his new helmet. "Sit down," Barbara said to Mac, turning to go into the kitchen.

He had his choice of the two vacant stools, one of them next to Ginger. He took the other one, which would put their hostess in the middle.

"Thanks for the doormat, Barb," he said. "I've been meaning to get one and kept forgetting."

"Doormat?" she repeated, setting a steaming cup of coffee in front of him.

"Someone bought me a doormat. Maybe it was my landlady."

"No, it was me," Ginger spoke up. She'd placed it in front of his door before she paid her visit to Jonathan and Barbara.

You? You're kidding me. His skeptical gaze was so eloquent he might have spoken the words aloud and added, *Why, for Pete's sakes?*

"Your entryway looked bare. If you don't like that particular doormat, there were others you might like better."

"I liked it fine," he muttered.

Past tense. *Liked.* Before he connected it with her.

"Excuse me, please," Barbara said, and disappeared from the kitchen. Shortly afterward there was the sound of a door. Ginger surmised that the other woman had gone into the powder room. Barbara was either heeding nature's call or making herself scarce for a few minutes.

"You're angry?" Ginger said to Mac.

"Damned right I'm angry."

"I'm sorry about last night."

"That makes two of us. Don't worry. It won't happen again." He drew his cup and saucer toward him too abruptly. When coffee sloshed over into the saucer, he cursed under his breath. Ginger silently handed him a paper napkin. He took it grudgingly and mopped up the spillage.

"Your mother's leftovers hadn't spoiled by the time you got home, I hope," she ventured.

He shrugged. "I was only gone an hour, at the most. You sure as hell didn't waste any time dumping them at my door."

"I was worried about you. Returning the food was a good excuse to make sure you were okay. Then you weren't there. You had already gone somewhere in your car." When he said nothing, she asked, "Where did you go?"

"I drove to Slidell and back on the damned interstate."

"To cool off?"

He shrugged his broad shoulders, and Ginger interpreted his body language as an indifferent yes.

The door to the half bath across the kitchen opened and closed noisily. Seconds later Barbara reentered the kitchen. "More coffee?" she asked.

"Not for me—"

"No, thanks—"

Mac and Ginger had spoken in unison as she slid off her stool, and he got up from his. Barbara blinked in surprise.

"I have to go," Ginger said, looking at her watch.

"No, I'm on my way out," Mac said. "You stay and visit."

"I really can't stay. I have plans."

His brown gaze bored into her accusingly. "A date, you mean." He bit the words out between clenched jaws.

"Dinner with a friend."

"Whitfield."

"Yes. At his house." With Barbara there, Ginger couldn't go into details and say she wasn't looking forward to having to tell Barry about what had happened last night. The other woman must be wishing she'd stayed longer in the bathroom and had missed this tense scene between her divorced neighbors. Ginger looked over at her apologetically. "Thanks for the coffee."

"You're welcome. Thank you for coming by and bringing Jonathan a present. He'll want to say goodbye." Barbara came out of the kitchen and summoned her son, who still wore one piece of shiny black-and-gold headgear and carried the other.

"Bye, Miss Ginger. Thanks for my helmet." He looked at Mac hopefully. "You don't have to leave, too, do you, Coach Mac?"

"No, I can stick around a while longer, sport." Mac reached out and squeezed the little boy's shoulder. Jonathan moved closer.

"So long, everyone," Ginger said. "I can let myself out, Barbara."

The other woman's farewell blended with her son's repeated "Bye, Miss Ginger." Mac didn't say anything.

"We're having pizza for supper. Do you like pizza, Coach Mac?" Jonathan was asking as Ginger reached the foyer.

"I sure do," came the reply.

"Mom, can Coach Mac eat supper with us?"

"He certainly can if he wants to."

Ginger made her exit. Of course Mac would end up sharing supper with them. There wasn't one reason in the world he shouldn't.

If Ginger were a better person, she wouldn't begrudge Barbara and little Jonathan his company. But she did.

"Hey, why the long face?" Barry asked after he'd welcomed her with a hug and chaste kiss.

On the way over, Ginger had debated about whether to wait until after dinner to make her shameful confession, but she found herself blurting out, "I did something really wrong last night."

"Are you going to be arrested for it?" he asked, gently making light of it. "Come and have a glass of wine while you confess all."

"You may not want me to stay that long. I slept with Mac—or not actually *slept* with him."

"Made love with him."

"Yes."

"Wasn't it only a matter of time?"

"I guess it was."

Barry hadn't acted shocked at her revelation. Nor did he seem visibly upset. He hadn't recoiled or even taken his arm from around her waist. Ginger realized in a moment of insight that his reaction—or lack of a reaction—didn't come as a surprise to her. She hadn't actually expected him to feel betrayed. Despite those few times they'd made love, they were friends, not lovers.

"I gather a reconciliation isn't a sure thing."

"No."

He sighed. "The timing of your indiscretion is amazingly convenient. I was shoring up my courage before you arrived to unburden my soul."

Ginger looked at him searchingly and saw the guilt in his expression. Also, the anxiety.

"Unburden your soul about what?"

"It's a long, sad story. But let's hear yours first. That is, if you're free to stay."

"I'm free to stay as long as I want. Mac and I are on worse terms than before now. He's not waiting for me." Right this moment he was probably eating pizza with Barbara and Jonathan.

"Poor Ginger. Poor Barry," he said with bleak irony, paraphrasing a line from a depressing play they'd seen the previous winter, *Who's Afraid of Virginia Woolf?*

Ginger accompanied him into his living room, where he poured them each a glass of merlot from a bottle he'd opened in preparation for her arrival. They sat side by side on the sofa. Barry gave her his full attention.

Ginger sipped her wine. It was comforting to be able to confide in Barry since she wasn't causing him pain or arousing his jealousy.

"That's not characteristic of McDaniel for him to stay angry, is it?" Barry remarked. "The way you've described him, his temper would flare up during an argument, but he would soon cool down."

"No, it isn't characteristic. Mac has changed in some ways. And he acted really hurt last night that I wasn't open to reconciling with him. Although I explained ahead of time that making love one more time *didn't* mean anything.''

"He probably didn't believe you based on what he knew of your personality." Barry's gently knowing tone said he wouldn't have put much stock in her claim, either, in Mac's place.

"I'm very ashamed of myself for being weak."

"Don't be hard on yourself." He patted her hand.

"Your turn," Ginger said.

Barry avoided her eyes. "I hate to lose your respect. Your friendship."

Suddenly she could guess the nature of his shameful confession. Barry *was* gay. "I doubt you'll lose either," she managed to say, her mind reeling with the revelation.

"Here goes," he said miserably. "Since my teenage years I've been trying to be heterosexual, but I'm just *not,* Ginger. When I met you, I liked you and enjoyed your company a lot. You were so undemanding and didn't seem to mind dating a guy with a low sex drive. I had about talked myself into thinking marriage would even work. Then—" He broke off.

"Then Dan came along?"

He nodded, making the admission as though he were owning up to a heinous crime.

Ginger's heart went out to him. "Being around Dan made you come to terms with your sexuality," she said, helping him with his painful explanation. "You're not a guy with a low sex drive. As much as you like women and appreciate them, they just don't turn you on."

"I'm sorry. There's no insult to you personally. Any normal man would want to take you to bed." His words were full of self-disparagement as well as abject apology.

"I don't feel insulted," she assured him, patting his hand as he'd patted hers minutes earlier.

"Nothing has actually happened between me and Dan. Or between me and any male. Before now, I haven't faced up to being gay."

"The attraction between you and Dan is mutual?"

"I think it is. So far neither of us has crossed the line and said or done anything overt. He's probably not sure about me because I'm dating you."

"Do you know for certain that he's gay?" Ginger's question was concerned. She didn't want him to get hurt.

"He hasn't come right out and said so. But I can tell he isn't interested in getting women into bed. There's none of the usual sexist guy talk with Dan." Barry went on to explain how the welcome absence of "sexist guy talk" relieved him of being obligated to comment on the anatomy of every female who came along. "You can't imagine how nice it is not to have to pretend that getting into a woman's panties is your main object in life. I'm so sick, Ginger, of being a hypocrite."

"Then stop pretending to be what you aren't, Barry. Be yourself."

"It's not that simple. Society is so intolerant of homosexuality. And we're not living in San Francisco or Key West. I can just imagine the reaction if I came out openly. My neighbors wouldn't speak to me. Probably more than half my clients would fire me. My own family back in Alabama would disown me."

Ginger thought about what her own parents' reaction would be and couldn't honestly soothe his worries other than to say, "You may be surprised how many people prove to be broad-minded. I know for a fact that Sharon Hawkins is."

Barry paled at the mention of Sharon. "For God's sake don't breathe a word to your librarian friend," he implored. "Or to McDaniel, either. Promise me, Ginger."

"Of course, I won't tell a soul!" she protested. "But you could trust Sharon *and* Mac not to gossip."

"I'm even paranoid about you knowing," he admitted. "We're talking my whole livelihood. Promise me."

"I promise."

He seemed satisfied.

They had dinner, and the meal was as excellent as always. There was more conversation about his dilemma and hers and conversation about other things, too. When Ginger said good-night, they embraced one another with warm affection and Barry walked her to her car. A neighbor seeing them wouldn't detect anything out of the ordinary about the familiar scene.

In so many ways, nothing had changed about their relationship, which had been largely platonic before. Yet everything was subtly different now. Ginger hadn't exactly had the rug jerked out from under her feet, but rather firmly tugged from under her. The floor underneath was bare and slippery. With Barry no longer her suitor, no longer a prospective husband, she felt more vulnerable than ever in dealing with Mac's presence in her life.

Of course, that presence might be short-lived, after last night. He might already have changed his mind about a reconciliation and be making plans to move back to New Orleans next year.

I hope—

Ginger couldn't even finish the sentence in her mind. What *did* she hope?

Chapter Ten

"I wonder if Mac is dating someone else," Sharon remarked as she squeezed a packet of thick ranch dressing on her salad.

Ginger tried to make herself say, *I don't know anything about Mac's social life.* The words that tumbled out were, "You mean, besides yourself?"

"I haven't managed to get a date with him yet, and it's not from any shyness on my part." The librarian busied herself with a second packet of dressing.

Ginger squeezed diet Italian dressing on her salad. "He didn't take you on a picnic on Saturday?"

"No. Did he tell you he had plans for a picnic?"

"He tried to make plans for one with me, and I refused. I assumed he had asked you or Angie instead."

"Angie was out of town this weekend. I thought the coast was clear for me. He must have met somebody else, darn it! He wasn't at home last night. I called his number several times and he didn't answer."

"He might have been visiting a little boy who lives in our complex." Ginger explained briefly between bites of salad that tasted amazingly good even though she wasn't crazy about diet Italian dressing. The news that Mac hadn't spent Saturday with Sharon or Angie made her ridiculously lighthearted.

Sharon quizzed her about Barbara Philips and then sighed glumly after she'd elicited a description. "Great. Just what I wanted to hear. More competition. A single nice-looking mom who needs a daddy for her cute kid."

"With Mac there's always going to be plenty of competition, Sharon. It was one of my problems with being married to him."

"And he's not even a big flirt. I guess that's part of his attraction."

Ginger had almost dropped her fork at the first statement. "You don't consider Mac a big flirt? What about his sexy grin that you were raving about at the first faculty meeting?"

"Oh, he has a sexy grin and a way of making a woman feel all woman. But he's not on the make." Sharon made a face. "I wish he were more of a womanizer type." She stretched her arms wide in a melodramatic gesture. "Here I am, available for a mad night of passion, and I can't lure him into my bed. He *is* a terrific lover, I'll bet."

"Could we talk about something else?"

"Your blush gives me my answer. God, you're so prim and proper, Ginger."

"I wouldn't want Mac discussing me as a sex partner," Ginger defended herself. Actually her blush was a sign of guilt rather than embarrassment. Guilt and secretive pleasure that she had enjoyed Mac's skills as a lover just two nights ago.

"Maybe he likes the virginal, hard-to-get types like you."

Ginger could feel her cheeks growing hotter as she saw a vision of herself sitting on Mac's lap on the sofa, frantically unbuttoning her blouse. "Believe me, I was never hard-to-get where Mac was concerned. We had only been dating a month when I came up pregnant."

Sharon didn't seem interested in that thread of conversation. They both devoted themselves to their lunch, thinking their own thoughts. Ginger mulled over her colleague's surprising observations about Mac that contradicted Ginger's own conception of his behavior toward women. *Not* a flirt? *Not* a womanizer? The other woman was far more experienced about men than Ginger was. Was she right and Ginger wrong?

"I'll give a party at my place next weekend! *That's* how I'll get him into my clutches!" Sharon rubbed her hands together gleefully. "I'll invite all the single faculty members. You can come with Barry. Do you think he would make some of those divine canapés he served at your birthday party he gave for you at his house?"

"Barry and I may not be able to come," Ginger protested. "Don't automatically include us."

"Do the two of you have plans? I can work around them." Sharon spoke with the reasonable assumption that Barry's social plans would include Ginger. That was no longer necessarily the case, but Ginger couldn't enlighten Sharon without being bombarded with questions. Ginger would have to lie to protect Barry's privacy, and she wasn't a good liar.

"None that come to mind," she said.

The talk changed to subjects of interest to both of

them as professional educators. Ginger was reminded of why she'd become friends with her colleague in the first place. For all her self-proclaimed man-hungry tendencies, Sharon was first and foremost an excellent school librarian committed to her students. She was also a nice person, generous and helpful. She was upbeat and often funny.

Mac was almost sure to enjoy dating Sharon and vice versa. Since he was certain to start dating someone in the near future, it was horrid of Ginger to cross her fingers mentally and hope that he didn't ask her tall, thin, blond librarian friend out on a first date and discover those good qualities for himself.

Horrid, but not puzzling. Ginger begrudged every woman alive the pleasure of Mac's attention, the special joy of sharing his bed and his life.

She selfishly wanted that pleasure, that joy for herself.

But she didn't want the conflict and arguments, the tears and unhappiness, the jealousy that had led her to divorce him and set him free for the Sharons and Angies of the world to vie for him.

Were those arguments just a smokescreen?

The question rocked Ginger, and she really couldn't answer it other than to admit to herself that she'd never felt woman enough to hold Mac.

Ginger saw Mac out on the practice field directing drills when she was leaving school that afternoon, but he didn't turn his head toward the street. It was the first glimpse of him she'd had all day. Much to her frustration, she couldn't even slow down because the car behind her was right on her bumper and leading a procession of other departing faculty and staff.

Had Mac just been busy today during his plan period and lunchtime, or had he avoided running into her because he was still angry and hurt? Ginger simply had to find out and do something to soothe his anger and hurt if the second explanation turned out to be the case. She'd dealt with more than her share of both destructive emotions, but Mac's personality was such that he hadn't had experience with dealing with them.

This is silly, stewing over his state of mind, Ginger thought, suddenly impatient with herself. Finding out would be as easy as paying him a visit after he'd gotten home from football practice, for heaven's sake. Maybe she could take him a peace offering, like a big slice of carrot cake, his favorite dessert. No, not carrot cake. It would bring up that disastrous attempt of hers to make a carrot cake for him from scratch his first birthday after they were married.

Ginger winced at the memory and then suddenly heard Barry's words from a recent conversation when she'd related her spaghetti dinner disaster, ''Afterward you weren't able to laugh about the whole episode with Mac and put it in perspective?''

Laughter was long overdue, even if it was too late.

''Carrot cake it is,'' Ginger said aloud.

Coffeehouses had become popular on the north shore. She drove to the nearest one that featured a selection of high-calorie desserts, including a sumptuous-looking carrot cake. Ginger's mouth watered as she stood by the glass case waiting to make her purchase and wrestling with the temptation to buy two slices.

If she showed up with dessert for two, he might be more likely to invite her in.

''Can I help you, ma'am?'' asked the college-aged male employee.

"Give me two slices of carrot cake, please," Ginger replied.

Her lack of willpower seemed to unleash other errant impulses. There had been one dish she'd prepared with more or less regular success that Mac had always eaten with gusto. A casserole with Spanish rice and pork chops. Why not cook it and invite him to supper? He would probably be hungry when he got home.

Ginger headed next to the supermarket and bought the ingredients. Pork chops, long-grained rice, canned tomatoes, chili powder, salad makings, salad dressing that wasn't nonfat. Her pantry already included a few staples like onion powder and garlic powder, salt and pepper. On her way to the checkout counter, she picked up a carton of the domestic beer she'd seen in Mac's refrigerator. He might enjoy a cold beer before supper.

At her condo she transported everything inside. Only then did the realization dawn that she was missing one very important item—the recipe. Six years ago when she'd packed up her possessions, she'd left her several recipe books behind along with a folder of recipes clipped from magazines. Her attitude at the time had been, "I'll never cook another awful meal again in my life."

"*Now* what am I going to do?" she asked herself, throwing up her hands in dismay.

The choice was clear. Either she had to abandon her whole plan and be left with all this food on her hands or else she had to put the casserole together from memory.

"I *think* I remember most of it," Ginger coaxed herself, getting out a casserole dish whose sole function before now had been to warm up restaurant take-out food in the microwave.

With the casserole in the oven, she wrote a note extending a casual invitation, walked down to Mac's condo and wedged it under his door where he couldn't fail to see it. Then she hurried back, cleaned up her kitchen mess and assembled a green salad.

The flutter of anticipation was incredibly familiar, bringing back all those occasions when she'd awaited Mac's homecoming. The pangs of dread that her meal would be a flop were just as familiar.

Mac's stomach growled as he got into the Camaro, which sat alone in the deserted faculty parking lot. He'd brown-bagged his lunch, but lunch was six hours ago. Being down in the dumps might kill his interest in food, but it didn't keep him from getting hungry.

That first year after Ginger had left him, he'd survived on fast food and junk food, which he'd washed down with a lot of beer. He'd gone through a six-pack more nights than he cared to remember. Then he'd cleaned up his act and started preparing simple, healthy meals for himself, falling back on frozen dinners and occasional fast food.

No way was he going to relapse and abuse his body. But tonight would be one of those infrequent fast-food nights, he decided. And probably he would drink a couple of beers, but no more than a couple.

Ten minutes later he paid for a large hamburger and large fries at the drive-through window of a burger franchise that happened to be the most conveniently located. His intention was to eat after he got home, but the aroma made him ravenous. *What the hell difference does it make where I eat? There's nobody to give a damn,* Mac thought, and dug the hamburger out of the bag. He wolfed down big bites and fished fries out of

the bag and crammed them into his mouth as he drove
to his condo. Only a few fries remained when he pulled
into his parking slot. Walking to his condo, he finished
them and crumpled the bag, trying to produce a belch
to relieve the case of instant indigestion he'd already
developed.

The sight of the new doormat made him curse vio-
lently under his breath. Last night he'd come close to
throwing the damned thing in the garbage. Instead he'd
left it there as a galling reminder not to be taken in
again by Ginger's mixed signals. She'd actually gone
to a store and bought him a present when she had a date
with Whitfield just hours later. Less than twenty-four
hours after she'd made love with Mac. Correction. *Had
sex.*

He would take the damned doormat back to her right
now and tell her what she could do with it.

Mac was half bent over when he spotted the piece of
paper protruding from under his door. He snatched it
and immediately recognized Ginger's handwriting. After a quick reading, he stood up straight, reading more
slowly. "How about supper? That is, if you're feeling
adventurous enough to take potluck. Dessert is carrot
cake. Don't worry—I didn't make it." She'd drawn a
smiley face. Along the bottom of the page, beneath her
signature, she'd sketched a twig with leaves and labeled
it "Olive branch."

"Olive branch my—" Mac wheeled around and had
gone half a dozen steps on his way to Ginger's condo
when he realized he was clutching her note in one hand
and the balled-up bag from the burger joint in his other
hand. He stopped long enough to hurl the latter back
into his entryway.

His long strides took him quickly to her entryway,

where he jabbed the doorbell button twice. Within seconds the door opened wide, framing Ginger. Her smile was welcoming, and she looked slightly flustered and glad to see him.

Mac could feel his rage dissolving. He waved the paper in his hand. "What in damnation is going on here? Was last night Whitfield's night and tonight's mine? Thanks, but *no thanks!*"

Her smile had died on her lips, and the glad expression had died, too. But unfortunately for Mac, she didn't stiffen and turn proud and righteous. "You're still mad at me," she said with a sigh.

"Hell, yes, I'm mad at you. And I'm going to *stay* mad." He rattled the paper again. "You haven't answered my question. What's going on in that pretty head of yours? Did you tell Whitfield—?"

"*Yes,* I told him," she broke in, her voice low. "Mac, *please* don't talk so loud. Come inside and yell at me where the neighbors won't hear every word."

Mac muttered a crude comment about the neighbors as he stepped inside. He had been talking loud. A food aroma floated out from the kitchen, making him uncomfortably aware of what he'd just eaten.

"Okay, I'm inside," he said, planting his feet in the foyer. "Now fill me in. You told Whitfield you got it on with me Sunday night. How did he take that news?"

She seemed to be forming her answer. "He wasn't surprised it had happened. Barry's more perceptive than a lot of men."

Mac frowned and waited several seconds for her to say more. "That's it?"

Ginger avoided his eyes. "He didn't react with a lot of jealousy, if that's what you're wondering."

Damned right it was what he was wondering. What

the hell was wrong with the guy? "You didn't— He didn't—" Mac couldn't get the question out.

"No, I didn't smooth things over with him in bed," she assured him. "Our relationship has always been mainly platonic."

"So the bottom line is you haven't broken off with Whitfield."

"No. I mean yes. For the time being, I'll still see Barry and stay in touch."

Mac crumpled up her supper invitation, managing somehow not to vent his sick disappointment with more violent action, like slamming his fists into the wall. "Then you'd better feed him my piece of carrot cake and whatever else you're warming up," he said harshly.

"Barry's not your rival, Mac."

"The hell he isn't."

"But I'm telling you he's a man *friend*. There's nothing sexual between us any longer. Stay for supper," she pleaded. "You can leave after you've eaten, if you want."

"I've already eaten."

"Oh. So you're not hungry."

No, but he would have force-fed himself whatever she was serving if she wasn't still dating Whitfield.

"It's probably just as well," she said with forced cheerfulness. "I tried cooking that pork-chop-and-Spanish-rice dish that was one of my minor successes in the kitchen. Remember it? Except I no longer have the recipe. When I took a peek a few minutes ago, the rice looked dry like I hadn't guessed right on the liquid measurement."

"It smells good," Mac couldn't keep himself from saying gruffly.

"Do me a favor and take the carrot cake with you, or I'll end up eating both pieces."

Mac stood there and waited while she ducked into the kitchen. Immediately she returned with a white bakery box. He took it from her, jerked open the door and left while he could still make himself leave.

The reason she didn't have the damned recipe was that she hadn't bothered to pack it with her things when she walked out on him. Mac latched on to the reminder to keep himself from turning around and going back.

He'd thumbed through her several well-used recipe books one of those nights when he'd drunk a six-pack. The food-spattered pages had fallen open to recipes including the dish she'd cooked tonight. Mac's vision had blurred as his emotions nearly got the best of him.

At any point during the past six years, Ginger could have come back to him and he would have jumped at the chance to be a better husband the second time around. That was true now. But it was all or nothing for Mac.

Under different circumstances, Mac wouldn't mind her having a male friend. Or male friends. Not if he and Ginger were reconciled or even on the road to getting back together.

Disappointedly, they weren't. She hadn't said any of the things he had wanted her to say, including the badly needed assurance that she still loved him. And that she was beginning to view him in a much better light as good husband material.

With his status so shaky, Mac was supposed to be broad-minded about her continuing to see a guy she'd been dating for close to a year? The thought was unendurable for Mac. Ginger with another man besides him. She was still *his* wife, damn it, divorce or no divorce.

Whitfield had to go. Ginger had to make her choice between him and Mac.

That's probably Barry or someone else, Ginger thought dully, wiping her hands on a dishcloth to answer the phone. She knew Mac wouldn't be calling her tonight.

"Hi, Ginger." Sharon's voice greeted her. "You were supposed to let me know about your and Barry's plans for this weekend. Is Saturday night okay for you two?"

Ginger pressed fingers against her closed eyes. "I haven't talked to Barry yet. Actually I'm not sure you should invite him and Mac both. It might make for an uncomfortable situation."

I should be honest with Sharon, she thought. And yet where to start? And how much to tell? Once she opened the door of confidence, Sharon would want to know all, and Ginger shrank from confiding things like making passionate love with Mac on her sofa. The experience was too personal, too intimate to share as though it were a salacious scene in an R-rated movie.

Then there was the problem of Sharon's asking, *What about Barry?* Ginger was on pins and needles not to reveal any slight hint that might lead her friend to conclude she'd been right in sizing Barry up as gay. He was so concerned about secrecy, and understandably.

Besides, didn't Mac have an obligation to level with Sharon? With his experience with women, he knew darned well she was chasing him. If he'd moved to the north shore to get back with Ginger, why hadn't he set the librarian straight from the start like he'd apparently done with Barbara?

The party would give Ginger a chance to observe

Mac in a social situation with Sharon and the other single females who attended. Maybe Ginger could come to some conclusion on whether she dared consider reconciliation.

One way or the other, she would bring Sharon up-to-date afterward.

As soon as she'd hung up, she called Barry and filled him in on the party situation. His reaction was exactly what she expected it to be. He didn't object to her going without him, but he expressed concern about her.

"Be careful, Ginger," he stressed, his tone worried. "I would hate to see you get hurt again."

"I don't intend to rush into anything," she assured him. "If I get back together with Mac, it won't happen fast. I want to be very sure this time."

She didn't tell him about her impulsive supper invitation to Mac and the trouble she'd gone to for nothing, although relating the whole story to Barry would have had enormous comfort value. He would naturally want to know why Mac had passed on supper. She couldn't lie and make up something. Barry would end up feeling bad when he learned he was the cause of contention.

This was a fragile time for Barry as he was coming to terms with his sexuality. Ginger wanted to be there for him to lend her support. Mac would simply have to believe her when she gave her word that her relationship with Barry was platonic and there were no grounds for jealousy.

As though there weren't already enough people to consider in the whole complicated situation, Ginger's mother called just about the time Ginger had settled down to get some schoolwork done.

"Your father insisted I check on you," Ellie said

after an exchange of affectionate greetings. "*He's* not bothering you, is he, dear?"

"He" referred to Mac, not her father, Ginger knew from the intonation. She smothered a sigh. "Mac's not harassing me, Mother, if that's what you mean. Quite the opposite. He keeps to himself."

"That's good news. I told John that he would probably get side-tracked pretty soon, running around with a bunch of women."

"Mother, his name is Mac. And I haven't heard any rumors about his running around with women. His coaching job keeps him pretty busy. He puts a lot into it."

"John took Sid Frasier to lunch yesterday and asked his legal advice."

Sid Frasier was a big divorce attorney in New Orleans who'd handled Ginger's divorce mainly as a favor to her father. The two men had grown up in the same New Orleans neighborhood and attended the same schools through high school.

Ginger groaned. "Why did Dad *do* that! You would think Mac was some thug who'd gotten out of jail. He's a decent guy, Mother."

"Don't push all his faults out of your mind, dear. A decent young man doesn't get a nice girl pregnant in the first place."

"I was just as much to blame for getting pregnant. I made As in biology."

"It's a miracle if he didn't get other girls in trouble." Her mother paused delicately. "Not using any birth control. The very least an oversexed boy like him could do was provide protection."

"Mac *wasn't* oversexed. He tried to keep things under control because he figured I was a virgin. I didn't help him much.'' The understatement of the world, Ginger reflected, blushing at the memory. "I was, well, pretty brazen, Mother.''

"You weren't any such thing. Don't be silly.''

Ginger could hear the faint embarrassment in her mother's voice beneath the note of ladylike reproof. No wonder I turned out prim and proper, she thought. While sex hadn't been a taboo subject, discussions between mother and daughter had always been tinged with a Victorian propriety.

"How is Barry?'' Ellie asked brightly.

"Barry's fine." Except for the fact that he recently realized he's gay. Even with Barry's permission, Ginger would never have couched the truth that simply and straightforwardly. She would have launched into a roundabout explanation to soften the impact.

"I hope you'll bring him the next time you come for a visit,'' Ellie was saying. "Your father and I both like him so much. Nothing would make us happier than to learn he's our future son-in-law.''

"I hate to disappoint you and Dad, but Barry isn't going to be your future son-in-law, Mother." Ginger broke the news kindly, but firmly.

"You haven't broken up with him!''

"I'll still see him and stay in touch because we're the best of friends, but we've talked and come to an understanding. We won't be getting married.''

"This is all *his* fault, isn't it?''

Mac's fault. Ginger didn't need her degree in English to supply the antecedent to "his.''

"Honestly, Mother, Mac's not the villain. Barry and I would have reached the same decision if Mac had never moved to the north shore. Lately I've wondered if I gave up on Mac too soon," Ginger continued. "I'm starting to regret that I didn't stick with him and become a better wife.''

"Gave up on him too soon! You stuck with him four years!'' Ellie exclaimed. "He ran around on you.''

"He denied that he did, and he may have been telling the truth.''

"That bleached-blond girlfriend of his called you and told you she was having an affair with him. A week after you'd left him, he was out at a restaurant with her.''

"She could have been lying just to break us up. Please tell me the truth, Mother. Did Mac look happy when you saw him at the restaurant? Did he look like he was having a good time?'' Ginger braced herself during the pause when she sensed Ellie was recalling the scene.

Finally her mother replied, "No, he didn't look happy.'' A troubled sigh came over the line. "Ginger, he told you himself that he wouldn't have married you if he hadn't gotten you in trouble.'' The reminder was gentle. "You cried your eyes out. It broke my heart, and I've hated him to this day for hurting you like that.''

"What he actually said was something like, 'I didn't dream I'd be getting married to anybody until I was out of college and had a good job. But it's okay. I'd be a lot sorrier if I was marrying somebody else besides you.''' Ginger swallowed a big lump in her throat, visualizing Mac as he'd looked, so young and sincere. "I didn't really believe that last part. I was sure he was just being sweet because he felt bad about the fix we'd gotten ourselves into. Maybe he really meant it.''

"Don't look back with rose-colored glasses and build him up into something he wasn't.''

"I'm trying to take off my dark glasses and give him

credit where credit was due. Didn't you admire and respect Mac just a little back then, Mother, for the way he conducted himself? Didn't you think he behaved in a mature, responsible way, insisting we get married and raise our child ourselves?''

''A lot of nineteen-year-old boys wouldn't have handled the situation that cheerfully,'' Ellie admitted. ''He was quite a charmer, all right.''

''For a while he did everything but stand on his head to make you and Dad like him and accept him as a son-in-law. You probably would have if I'd been more mature and hadn't run home in tears every time I got upset with something he'd done or said. Or hadn't done or hadn't said.''

In the eyes of Ellie and John Honeycutt, Ginger hadn't ever had any faults. She was their sheltered and adored only child. The best thing they could have done for her was tell her to grow up when she went running to them for sympathy after she was married.

But they hadn't. They'd taken her side and resented Mac for making her unhappy.

Ginger wasn't blaming them. She blamed herself for not painting the whole picture, for not being a loyal wife.

''Your dad just stuck his head into the kitchen,'' Ellie said. From her cheery tone, Ginger could surmise that her father was standing in the door and Ellie was smiling for his benefit. ''He's ready for his dish of ice cream. He sends you his love. Glad everything's going well, and that ex-husband of yours isn't being a problem. Goodbye, dear.''

''Goodbye, Mother. Give Dad my love. I hope you'll share our conversation with him.''

''Will do,'' was her mother's cheery reply.

Whether or not Ginger ever got back together with Mac, she didn't want her parents to continue to regard him with loathing. Whatever his shortcomings as a husband, he wasn't the degenerate person they made him out to be.

Chapter Eleven

The next morning the rumble of thunder and the sound of rain slashing against the windows almost drowned out the buzz of Ginger's alarm clock. Yesterday's weather forecast had predicted the movement of a system of squalls through the area.

The gusty wind had abated and the thunder had subsided by the time she was ready to leave, but the rain was still coming down steadily. It drummed on her umbrella as she walked quickly to her car, which, sure enough, sat in a shallow lake. Hanging on to umbrella, tote bag, purse and grocery bag containing her shoes while getting the door unlocked wasn't easy, but Ginger managed and was finally seated behind the wheel, slightly damp.

So far so good, she thought, slipping the key into the ignition and twisting it. Nothing. The motor didn't leap to life. Dumbfounded, Ginger clicked the key into the off position and then twisted it all the way to the right again.

Nothing. Not so much as a feeble whirr under the hood.

Several more times Ginger went through the familiar starting routine, failing to coax any response from her dead engine.

"Now what?" she asked in exasperation, watching the rivulets run down her windshield. Off in the distance she heard a faint rumble. Great. Another squall was probably headed this way.

She could call a taxi, but goodness knows when it would get here. Taxis weren't a common sight on the north shore. She could call another teacher and ask for a ride to school. That would be more than a little silly since she could walk down to Mac's condo and catch a ride with him.

Ginger made one last futile attempt to start the car before she swung open the door and braved the elements again. The exercise involved didn't account for her rush of adrenaline as she walked to D-1, her footsteps making splats on the pavement of the walkway.

Reaching the shelter of Mac's entryway, she pressed the doorbell and composed herself, not wanting to look too eager. The keynote she wanted to strike was cheerful acceptance of an inconvenient circumstance, not glee over an unforeseen gift from fate. A glance downward at her damp shoes helped to kill Ginger's flush of anticipation. The shoes weren't planted on the doormat she'd placed there Monday afternoon. Mac must have gotten rid of it because she'd given it to him.

No, he hadn't gotten rid of it yet, just removed it from his sight. Ginger spotted the forest green rectangle over in a corner, upside down, where he'd evidently flung it, probably in anger.

The door swung open. Ginger's greeting died in her throat as she watched the quick play of expressions on Mac's face, half of which was clean shaved and half covered with shaving cream. It definitely wasn't surprised pleasure that left him temporarily at a loss for words, too.

He was bare to the waist, wearing jeans he'd hastily pulled on and zipped up but not fastened at the waistband. Even with the shaving cream, he could have posed for one of those hunk calendars.

"Don't worry," she said, finding her voice. "I didn't come bearing muffins hot from the oven. My car won't start."

"What's wrong with it?"

"I don't have a clue. It started right up yesterday."

He looked out at the rain and then down at his watch. "You'll just have to ride to school with me." An unpleasant solution for both of them, his tone suggested.

"That's what I had in mind. I certainly don't expect you to be my mechanic." He'd done all the routine maintenance on their cars himself when they were married, including messy jobs like changing the oil filter.

"I'll be another five minutes." With those words he turned away, leaving the door wide open.

"I realize we're on your schedule," Ginger said to his gorgeous back as she accepted the less-than-gracious unspoken invitation to enter and wait for him inside, if she chose. He was taking the stairs two at a time. "Can I pour you some juice or something?"

"No, don't bother." The refusal was grim.

Ginger's offer had probably struck a chord of memory with him, too. During their marriage she'd typically gotten up earlier on weekdays. Occasionally he'd eaten breakfast with her, but usually Ginger poured his juice and fixed him a bowl of cereal and fruit so that he only had to add milk. Or she stuck bread in the toaster, ready to be toasted and got out the margarine and jam, to save him those extra steps.

After six years apart, it would have seemed incredibly natural to step into his kitchen and perform those same voluntary acts of love. But she wasn't his wife anymore. And hadn't been blissfully happy much of the time when she was, Ginger reminded herself as she perched on a stool at the counter dividing the kitchen and dining area.

In five minutes he returned, clean shaved and fully dressed, a red knit shirt tucked into khaki slacks securely fastened at the waist and belted. He went straight to the refrigerator and got out the gallon jug of orange juice.

"You nicked yourself," Ginger observed sympathetically. A tiny scrap of toilet paper stuck to his cheek had absorbed a drop of blood.

"I'll live." He filled one of his giant-sized glasses and drank it in gulps as he stood there.

"Don't skip breakfast on my account," she said, enjoying watching him. "When my car didn't start, I resigned myself to arriving at school later than usual."

He put the jug back in the refrigerator, strode over to the sink and rinsed his glass, set it down with a loud clunk. "Ready?"

Ginger expelled a sigh as she slid off the stool. "It's awfully early for hostility, Mac."

"I'm not being hostile."

"Yes, you are. But I'll just have to put up with your bad humor since I need a ride."

The rain was still coming down steadily. "Don't you have an umbrella? You'll probably need it today, don't you think?" she said when he pulled the door closed behind him with nothing but his keys.

"There's probably one in the car."

Ginger opened her umbrella and held it high so that he could walk beside her, but he muttered a curse about the weather and made a dash to the parking lot. It wasn't like him to be ill-natured about weather or anything else. He was venting his anger at her, evidently determined not to call a truce.

The Camaro sat in a good three inches of water. Ginger sloshed to the passenger's side and got in, her feet thoroughly soaked. Having already started up the engine, he shifted into gear while she was getting settled.

"Fasten your seat belt," he ordered her tersely.

"Give me a chance," she snapped back, her temper flaring. "I'm truly sorry for the inconvenience, Mac. If my car isn't back in operation by tomorrow morning, I'll make other arrangements, I promise."

He shoved the stick shift back into Neutral. "Look, I don't mind giving you a ride, dammit."

"You certainly seem to mind. I'll bet you didn't give Barbara the cold shoulder when she rang your doorbell Monday morning. You probably smiled at her."

"What does Barbara have to do with anything?"

"Nothing, I hope."

He shifted into Drive and backed out.

The snippy exchange seemed to have put him in a slightly better mood, for some reason. Ginger's irritableness disappeared, too. Even the discomfort of squishy socks inside her wet shoes didn't detract from a cozy contentment at being his passenger.

"You'll be happy to know the pork-chop casserole

wasn't very good," she told him. "The rice didn't swell up. I probably didn't add enough liquid."

"Why would that make me happy?" He turned up the volume on the radio, which was tuned to a popular New Orleans station that reported news and city-traffic information during the morning hours. Information that was no longer relevant to him.

Ginger decided not to take his hint that he would prefer no conversation with her. She raised her voice over that of the male host. "How was the carrot cake? As delicious as it looked?"

"I don't know. I didn't eat it."

"You threw it in the garbage? Mac, that's criminal. You could have brought it to school and put it in the teachers' lounge. Someone would have enjoyed it."

"I didn't throw it away. I stuck the box in the refrigerator. I meant to bring it to school today."

"But it was raining cats and dogs, and I showed up, ruining your whole day."

"You showed up," he stated.

The scrap of toilet paper was on his right cheek, facing her. "I'm sorry I caused you to nick yourself shaving," she said, reaching her hand toward his face with the intention of gently removing the tissue. He batted her hand away and jerked the tissue from his cheek roughly. Fresh blood oozed from the cut.

"You're bleeding again!" Ginger dug a clean tissue from her purse and held it out to him, but instead of taking it, he stuck the toilet paper back on his cheek. "Go ahead and be muleheaded and petty!" she exclaimed, exasperated and stung by his rejection of all her attempts to smooth things over with him. "After all, why be pleasant when we can be nasty toward each other!"

Ginger jammed the tissue back into her purse and crossed her arms over her chest. Not another word would she utter on the remainder of the drive to school. He wanted stony silence from her. Well, he would get it.

Mac turned down the volume on the radio. "What seems to be the problem with your car?" he asked. "Did the engine try to turn over?"

"No."

"How old is the battery?"

"The same age of the car."

His glance over at her bespoke impatience. "I'm trying to narrow down the problem. You might be a little more cooperative."

"It's not your problem. I'll call a garage."

"You'll play hell getting a mechanic out on a day like this if you're not a regular customer. Plus there'll be enough stalled cars on the highway and fender benders to keep every tow truck on the north shore busy. Take your car key off your key ring," he instructed her.

"Why? I'm *not* letting you take care of this for me, Mac, not after the way you've acted!"

"Now who's being muleheaded and petty? You've probably just got a dead battery. I'll pick up a new one during my plan period, take it over and switch it with the old one. Then you'll have transportation by this afternoon."

"And be out of your hair."

He shrugged his broad shoulders.

"You'll be saving me no telling how much money, and I'll be in your debt," Ginger elaborated.

"Even if your insurance covers towing, you'll probably shell out a hundred bucks at least in labor. You'll also pay a higher price for the battery."

"I don't know if my insurance covers towing." Ginger was getting out her keys. "This is awfully nice of you," she said, handing the car key to him.

"Don't make a big deal out of nothing. I'd do the same for Barbara."

"Or Sharon. Or Angie. I get the picture." When he shot her a look, she made a face at him.

"Angie would be more likely to borrow my car and go buy her own battery and install it herself," he said.

Acting on a perverse instinct to prove something—Ginger wasn't sure what exactly—she reached over a second time to remove the scrap of tissue paper from his cheek. This time he let her.

Ginger purposely spent her plan period in the teachers' lounge, thinking that Mac might return from his Good Samaritan errand before the hour was over and give her a report on the status of her car. It was still raining steadily.

Five minutes before time for the bell to ring, James Carlson, the boy whose name Mac had brought up on Sunday night, appeared at the lounge door and asked to see her. As surprised as she was curious, Ginger got up and went out into the corridor to speak to him.

"What can I do for you, James?"

"Coach Mac said to come tell you your car's in the teachers' parking lot." He held out the key to her car.

Ginger took it. "Thank you."

"He drove it, and I drove his car," James explained.

"I see. In other words, Coach Mac took you along with him to buy the battery."

"Right. He got me out of shop," James explained, referring to his industrial-arts class. "We weren't doing anything anyway since the electricity keeps going on and off today, and that's bad for the power tools.''

"Well, I certainly appreciate your helping him.''

James shifted in embarrassment. "I didn't mind. He's cool, Coach Mac.''

"So my battery was dead.''

"Dead as a doornail. We took the old one back for a rebate. Oh, here's your receipts.'' He dug in his jeans pocket and pulled out a wad of paper. "See you around, Miss Honeycutt. Coach said I could go ahead and get in the lunch line early.''

"Thanks again, James.''

He strode off with a loose-limbed, athletic grace, his posture much straighter and his whole demeanor subtly different, the "I don't care'' body language gone at least temporarily. It had obviously done wonders for his self-esteem to be singled out and given the perk of accompanying Mac on an errand outside of school.

While Ginger would have liked Mac to come to the lounge in person, she couldn't begrudge James his role of responsible messenger.

During the several minutes before the lunch bell rang, she wrote out a check to Mac. According to the receipt, he'd paid with a credit card.

Giving him the check and thanking him provided her with the perfect excuse to seek him out during the lunch hour. On the other hand, she *could* save paying and thanking him until after school hours.

Ginger opted for the latter. As it turned out, she wouldn't have had much opportunity to get him aside anyway. She met with one of her students for fifteen minutes in her classroom, giving some one-on-one tutoring. Then she went to the cafeteria and bought lunch. Carrying her tray into the teachers' lounge, she spotted

Mac, seated at the long table and involved in an animated conversation as he ate his cafeteria meal. A male coach sat on one side of him and on the other side sat—who else?—Angie.

There wasn't an empty seat at the table, much less one near him. Disgruntled because Mac didn't look at her or give any sign that he was aware of her presence, Ginger joined a couple of her English-department colleagues on the opposite side of the room who balanced their trays on their laps. After he'd finished, he got up and left.

That afternoon Ginger was straightening her room after it had emptied out for the final time when Sharon popped in, all smiles. "So far everybody I've talked to who's invited is coming Saturday night." Holding up a slim-fingered hand, she ticked off fingers as she listed names, starting, of course, with Mac.

"The others will probably come, too," Ginger said, trying not to be a wet blanket. It was hard to muster any enthusiasm about the party with relations so strained between her and Mac. But then if relations were better between them, she would have to level with Sharon. *I should level with her anyway.*

"Several people offered to bring their favorite Mexican dips. I said, sure," the librarian was saying.

"Do you have time to sit down for a few minutes?" Ginger asked. "There's something we need to talk about. A matter concerning Mac."

"Something serious from your expression." Sharon slipped into a student desk.

Ginger followed suit. "I haven't been totally honest with you," she began. "I've given the impression I'm totally indifferent about what Mac does and who he dates. That's not true. I'm *not* indifferent and I don't dislike him.''

Sharon raised her eyebrows, looking slightly perplexed. ''Okay. Are you posting a Keep Your Hands Off My Ex sign?''

''No, of course not. I have no right to post any Keep Off signs.'' Not as things stood now. ''Those signs didn't work when I had the right,'' she added.

''But the old wifely instinct to scratch out the eyes of another female who makes goo-goo eyes at him is still there. Is that what you're saying?''

Ginger sighed, nodding.

''Does Barry know about these leftover feelings you have for your ex?''

''Yes, he knows.''

''Anything else?'' Sharon braced her hands on the desktop, poised to maneuver her tall body to a standing position.

Ginger shook her head.

She hadn't accomplished a thing by the partially candid heart-to-heart with her colleague. Yet how could Ginger be more candid when, in addition to being protective of Barry's privacy, she was uncertain about what she wanted to happen between her and Mac? Sure, she could admit she couldn't stand the thought of another woman as his date or lover or wife, but was she willing to try married life with him a second time and risk heartbreak again? The answer to that question right now was, *I don't know. I'm afraid.…*

Sharon paused on her way out. ''I'm glad we had this chat. Now I won't pay you any attention if I see you looking daggers at me when I'm making goo-goo eyes at Mac at the party Saturday night. Bye now.''

Outside, the rain was continuing to fall from a gray

sky. Ginger changed back into her athletic shoes, which had dried out by now, and splashed her way to her car, her eyes seeking out Mac's red Camaro parked several spots away.

Despite the weather, football practice probably hadn't been canceled, but rather moved indoors where the coaches would utilize the time to go over plays and strategies for the offense and the defense. Mac wouldn't be leaving early, Ginger reflected with an insider's knowledge she'd gleaned from being a coach's wife.

At her condo she kicked off her water-soaked shoes and stripped off sodden socks just inside the door. She'd made it as far as the kitchen and was reaching for the handle of the refrigerator when the phone rang.

"Hi. Are you climbing the walls, too?" Barry asked. "I've got a bad case of cabin fever."

"You sound depressed." She'd detected a note of real desperation beneath his ironic tone.

"That could be because I am depressed. I would drive off a cliff if cliffs weren't so hard to come by in south Louisiana."

"Don't say things like that even jokingly!" Ginger admonished. "Would you like to come over for some hot spiced tea? I was planning to make a pot."

"Let's go to a movie. Something light and entertaining. I'll buy you a giant bucket of popcorn," he cajoled.

Seldom had Barry ever pressed Ginger like this. He obviously badly needed company. And it would probably do her good, too, to go somewhere and get her mind off Mac. "As long as you promise not to buy it with butter, not even when I beg or threaten you," she said.

"A deal."

He insisted on picking her up rather than meeting her

at the theater, and Ginger agreed to the arrangement. Later when she got home, she would take the check to Mac at his condo.

Going to a movie had been a good idea. Ginger felt better about life in general. Barry seemed much more cheerful, too, as he walked her to her door, ever the gentleman. And wonder of wonders, the rain had finally stopped.

"Want to come over to my place tomorrow night?" Barry asked. There was no urgency behind the casual invitation.

"No, I think I'll stay home and catch up on some schoolwork."

He kissed her on the cheek, and they gave each other an affectionate good-night hug.

It was a quarter to ten. Ginger stood in her foyer, debating with herself about the wisdom of taking the check to Mac tonight. The hour was late for dropping in on someone, but Mac wasn't exactly a new acquaintance. She knew his habits well enough to be certain he wouldn't be in bed yet.

He'd delivered a check to her just as late. The reminder tipped the scales. Ginger was out the door of her condo.

The route to D-1 had become familiar, she realized, following the paved walkway. The accumulation of rainwater had drained off into the saturated lawn.

Mac's entryway was dark, the doorbell button a tiny beacon of brightness. Ginger pressed the button and waited, straining her ears for the sound of movement inside.

All of a sudden the two wall light fixtures flanking the door lit up. While Ginger was blinking at the sudden relative brightness, she heard the key turning in the lock, and the door jerked open. Mac towered in the space. A scowl came over his face, and he glared at her with a kind of angry bafflement. It wasn't necessary for him to say aloud, "What the hell do you want?"

"I brought you a check to pay for the battery," Ginger said lamely. She groped inside her purse, searching for her checkbook.

"Put it in my faculty mailbox." His tone was harsh.

She kept searching. "And I wanted to thank you."

"Well, now you've thanked me."

Ginger finally located the checkbook and pulled out the loose check stuck inside it. She handed it to him, and he snatched it and jammed it into his jeans pocket.

"What have I done now?" she demanded with a touch of impatience, as well as bewilderment.

"Don't pull that innocent act on me. I know you were with Whitfield tonight."

"How—?" Ginger broke off, hearing her guilty inflection. She hadn't done anything to be guilty about. "I don't have to 'pull an innocent act.' My date with Barry *was* innocent. We went to a movie and had something to eat afterward. He brought me home and said good-night at the door."

"Then you hotfooted it here. What am I supposed to do, supply a little sex to round off your evening?"

Ginger's mouth fell open with her indignation. "All you were supposed to do was behave with some minimal courtesy! *Not* insult me like you have!"

"I'm the one who has a right to feel insulted. Make up your mind, Ginger. Whitfield or me."

"It's not that simple."

"It's every bit that simple."

"Mac, regardless of whether I'm friends with Barry,

you and I would need to take things slowly, not rush into a reconciliation."

"Until he's completely out of the picture, we're not taking things fast or slow. There is no 'we,' period. Am I making myself clear enough?"

Ginger sighed. "Can't we be friendly in the meanwhile?"

"Hell, no, we can't be *friendly*. It's all or nothing."

"It can't be 'all' just yet."

"Then stay the hell away from me." He closed the door, effectively ending the discussion.

Equal amounts of frustration and dismay made Ginger reach out her finger and press the doorbell button. The door jerked open again. She spoke hurriedly before he could get a word in. "I thought I should tell you that I'm *not* abiding by your rules. What's at stake is *too* doggone important. Furthermore I certainly hope you won't start dating a lot of women just to spite me. Thank you again for fixing my car. It was very good of you to go to all that trouble even if you did want to make sure I wouldn't be bugging you for rides to school. Good night."

She made a hasty departure, bracing herself for him to slam the door closed this second time. But he didn't even close it for long seconds. Evidently he glared at her back while he zapped her with the hot current of his anger. She heard a forceful thud only after she'd branched off his narrower walkway to the main walkway.

For all her brave words, Ginger's heart was heavy as she walked more slowly to her condo. She just *couldn't* abandon Barry at this difficult time in his personal life. Even if he'd given her permission to reveal his newly discovered sexuality to Mac in confidence, erasing any jealousy factor, there would still be problems. Mac apparently viewed reconciling with her as a very cut-and-dried matter. Either she wanted to get back together with him or she didn't. No *if*s, *and*s, or *but*s.

For Ginger there were a lot of *if*s, *and*s, and *but*s. She wasn't about to act as impulsively as some of the women protagonists in the romance novels she enjoyed as recreational reading. Marriage *wasn't* something to rush into, not even marriage number two to the same person. Long-term happiness had to be based on more than great sex, based on more even than a man and woman loving one another. She and Mac needed to iron out all their differences on important issues like money management and financial security. Issues like trust and fidelity. Issues like family loyalties and in-laws. And, yes, her own insecurity where he was concerned.

Darn it, couldn't Mac understand that Ginger would marry him again in an instant, but she didn't think she could survive divorcing him again? If he had acted reasonably tonight, they could have sat down in his living room and discussed all these thoughts churning in Ginger's head as she let herself into her condo and went upstairs to get ready for bed.

A blush heated her cheeks as she visualized Mac's big man-size sofa. If he had invited her in, she would have wanted to do more than just sit primly and carry on a discussion. Of course, with his instincts about women, he'd probably guessed that, which was why he'd blocked the doorway, keeping her out.

Had he cooled down enough to talk to her? It would be so easy to find out. Ginger hurriedly finished brushing her teeth and settled on her bed with the telephone.

He answered on the second ring.

"Mac, it's me. Don't hang up," she said quickly. "I

remembered something I wanted to tell you. Actually a couple of things. First that was a really good idea you had today, getting James Carlson out of class and enlisting him as your helper. It did wonders for his self-esteem. I won't be surprised if you manage to recruit him for the football team.''

"I have recruited him. Dammit, Ginger, I *don't* want you calling me," he continued with fierce emphasis before she could respond.

"Then you shouldn't have moved to the north shore and taken a job in my school. You brought all this on yourself, Mac. Of course, you can get an unlisted number. Speaking of which, I wanted to give you mine." She rattled off the digits.

"What the hell do I have to do to get through to you?" he demanded. "Don't you understand plain English?"

"This is the grown-up me, Mac. I'm not the shy, reserved college girl who fell head over heels in love with you."

"You can say that again." His voice was harsh with bitterness. But it was his note of weary disappointment that struck fear in Ginger's heart.

"You don't like this new me?"

"I don't like much of anything at the moment." He hung up.

The new grown-up Ginger managed not to behave like the old Ginger and break down into unhappy tears.

Chapter Twelve

"I'm just not getting prepositions and conjunctions, Miss Honeycutt. Could I come after school and have you go over them?" asked Sally Shawnfelt, a student in Ginger's second-hour English class.

Ginger smiled at the tiny girl who wore oversize glasses. "Could you come the first fifteen minutes of lunch instead, Sally? Immediately after sixth period I'm scheduled to meet with the homecoming-float committee for the sophomore class." She was a faculty sponsor for the sophomore class. And, coincidentally, so was Mac, as Ginger had discovered just that morning when she'd gotten a calendar of scheduled activities.

He would be at the meeting this afternoon, too, along with several other teachers. Which accounted for Ginger's enthusiastic tone. She tended to carry out extra-curricular duties more cheerfully than some of her colleagues who resented extra demands on their time and energy. Still, she'd never felt *eager* before about extending her school day.

"Sure, I can come at lunch. Thanks, Miss Honeycutt," Sally called back over her shoulder.

"What? Oh. Good, Sally." Ginger made a face at her own expense, grateful that her student hadn't seemed to notice anything odd about the way her normally composed English teacher was behaving.

Pull yourself together and get on with your day as usual, dearie. Ginger acted on that sheepish advice and put the meeting out of her mind.

During fourth-hour plan period she bought a diet soft drink from the vending machine in the teachers' lounge and drank it at her desk in her room, reading essays. When the lunch bell rang, she returned to the lounge and used the microwave oven to heat a frozen diet dinner she'd brought from home. Mac didn't put in an appearance.

Perhaps he was avoiding her. Perhaps he wasn't. Either way Ginger knew she would see him after sixth period. She meant to get him aside and share encouraging progress about James Carlson, progress for which Mac could largely take credit. The boy had actually brought a pen and notebook to class today. He'd paid attention for the first time and even jotted down the homework assignment.

The float-committee meeting was being held in a classroom in the same wing as Ginger's. After her sixth-period students had all bolted out the door, she used up a few minutes restoring her room to order and giving the corridor a chance to empty out. Anticipation built as she gathered up her purse and tote bag and walked to the classroom.

Two of the other teachers arrived at the same time

and entered with Ginger. They were greeted by four or five students who had already gathered and were huddled together and talking excitedly. Ginger smiled in amusement at their lowered tones and furtive manner. Traditionally each class was very hush-hush about its float design, going so far as to post guards at the site where the float was constructed.

Several more students filed in, and several additional teachers showed up, including a coach, Dave Cooper, whose name Ginger didn't remember reading on the list of sophomore faculty sponsors. She was about to get out the list and double-check it when he clapped his hands, quieting down the chatter and taking charge.

"Why don't we get started with your meeting?" he said to the group of students.

"But where's Coach Mac?" asked one of the girls, voicing Ginger's own question.

"There's been a change. Coach Mac is a junior-class sponsor." Cooper opened his arms, grinning. "What can I say? You get me instead."

The girl who'd spoken up mustered a smile, as did several of the other girls, smiles that didn't mask their disappointment, which couldn't possibly have been as great as what Ginger was experiencing.

Mac had asked the other coach to switch with him to eliminate being a cosponsor with her.

Tonight I'm going to call him up and tell him—

No. She wouldn't call him up and tell him anything, darn it. He wanted her to stay away from him and not bother him. Well, that's exactly what Ginger would do.

But she was still going to Sharon's party Saturday night and intended to have a good time. Let him give her the cold shoulder if he wanted to.

* * *

"Hey, you look pretty!" Sharon complimented when she opened the door to Ginger on Saturday night.

"So do you." Her taller blond colleague wore a short, tight black skirt with a ruffled crimson blouse. Ginger's own turquoise blue shift seemed conservative by comparison.

"Your timing is perfect. I was just starting to put the food out. You have that knack for arranging a bowl of dip and a basket of chips and making the whole effect like a picture in a magazine. With me it looks like I plopped down a bowl and a basket." Sharon was talking gaily as she led the way to the kitchen of her town house.

"I guess I learned that knack from my mother. She and I both depend on distracting guests with our food presentation so they don't notice the taste so much," Ginger said with light irony. Mac must still be coming, she was thinking with relief. Otherwise Sharon wouldn't be quite this bubbly.

Still Ginger waited for her opportunity to make certain. "I take it you haven't gotten any last-minute regrets," she remarked when there was a break in conversation, the two of them working compatibly.

"No, every single person I invited is coming. I saw most of them yesterday at school. Come to think of it, everybody but you."

"I always try to get as much schoolwork done as possible on Friday so I don't have to do it over the weekend." Plus a stubborn sense of "I can play this game, too" had kept her out of the teachers' lounge so that she wouldn't run into Mac if he ventured into the lounge.

"God, you're so disciplined."

"It's just the way I am."

Sharon raised her eyebrows at Ginger's defensive-ness. "That *wasn't* a criticism. It was a compliment."

"People who are less organized and conscientious and more scatterbrained are generally more fun and interesting, I guess."

"Do I detect an inferiority complex underneath all that poise and competence?"

"I have moments when I feel a little dull and ordinary," Ginger admitted. "I guess all of us 'prim and proper' women secretly wish we could dance on tables once in a while."

Sharon laughed her gusty laugh, obviously entertained by the image. "If the mood hits tonight, just let me know and I'll put on some show music for you."

"Show music wouldn't go along with your Tex-Mex theme. I love the colorful piñatas. Where did you find them?" Ginger changed the subject, knowing she wouldn't dance on tables tonight or any other night. It simply wasn't in her nature to be an exhibitionist.

After they'd finished with their preparations, Sharon made a batch of frozen margaritas. She'd just handed Ginger a salt-rimmed glass when the doorbell chimed, heralding the arrival of the first guest. Forty minutes later the party was well under way, the whir of the blender mixing with a hubbub of voices and laughter. Only two people were unaccounted for—Mac and Angie.

I wonder if he's bringing her. If he does, that's the end of any thoughts of reconciliation, Ginger told herself. A sense of dread grew as she mingled and sipped her original margarita, making it last. When her ears caught the doorbell chime, she turned her back, unable to bear the sight of Mac arriving with his attractive coaching colleague. She heard his deep voice responding to greetings, but she didn't hear Angie's.

Then the chimes pealed again.

"That must be Angie," Sharon said.

Mac had come alone. The realization brought a mixture of shaky relief and euphoria.

Other guests crowded around the main refreshment table, but Mac wasn't among them. Ginger kept track of him as he headed over to the margarita bar and took over bartender's duties. He could avoid her if he wished, but she wasn't going to avoid him, she decided, picking up an empty guacamole bowl and a nearly empty salsa bowl to take them to the kitchen for a refill. Her route took her past the margarita station.

"Hi, Mac," she greeted him, noticing that he'd uncapped a bottle of beer for himself and already drunk most of it.

"Hi, Ginger," he returned without any show of friendliness.

"Could you make me one of those without the tequila, please?"

Her request brought teasing inquiries from several people standing around who asked if she were volunteering to be the party's official designated driver. Ginger good-naturedly admitted that she wasn't a heavy drinker. For one thing, she added, her few hangovers in the past had been bad enough to convince her that getting inebriated wasn't worth the morning after. Mac, who'd been there for those hangovers, didn't participate in the conversation, instead applying himself to dumping ice and margarita mix in the blender.

After tending to her assistant-hostess duties, Ginger circled back to get her nonalcoholic frozen margarita. Mac was twisting off the cap of a fresh bottle of beer for himself. His response to her thank-you was a brief nod.

Ginger didn't hang around, since she obviously wasn't welcome. This was a party, and she intended to enjoy herself. But while she was socializing, she kept close enough tabs on him to know that he was drinking beer after beer and refusing the offers from those who were willing to relieve him as bartender.

Naturally he didn't lack for female company. Angie and Sharon in particular seemed to vie with each other in keeping him from being lonely, though without any encouragement from him. Likewise they both brought him plates of snack food, which he accepted and put aside.

As the hour grew later, finally Ginger couldn't stand it any longer. She walked over near him and waited her chance to say to him in a low voice, "Mac, don't you think you should eat something? You're getting drunk."

"That's the general objective," he said, and lifted his bottle of beer to his mouth and drained it.

"When you get ready to leave, I'm driving you home," she informed him. "You're not getting behind the wheel of your car with that much alcohol in your system."

"Hey, listen to this, everybody!" crowed Pete Carisco, an industrial-arts teacher who'd downed his share of margaritas by now. He'd evidently overheard her last two statements. "Ginger's acting just like a wife, telling Mac here what he can and can't do."

"You got that wrong, Pete. I was acting like an ex-wife who doesn't want to see her former husband kill himself or anybody else on the highway." The words came out on their own, and there was no taking them back. Nor did Ginger want to.

"*Ex*-wife? You're kidding! You and Mac were married?" Silence had fallen in the immediate area, and Pete's half-skeptical voice rang out.

Everybody at the party gathered around, all the faces except Sharon's mirroring astonishment. And even she—and Mac—looked surprised.

"Is that true, Mac?" demanded Angie. "Ginger's your ex?"

He shrugged. "Yes, it's true."

"So what was the big secret?" Angie's question was almost drowned out by a half-dozen variations of the same curious inquiry.

"It was nobody's business but ours," Mac said. And still wasn't anybody else's business, he clearly implied. He shifted his weight, reaching out a hand to the wall beside him to steady himself.

He *was* inebriated, Ginger realized.

"I think I'll have another margarita if the bar's still open," Pete said, either taking Mac's hint or losing interest.

The party resumed with nobody pursuing the subject. Mac opened himself another beer.

At midnight Ginger made coffee and put out trays of delectable-looking cookies and brownies. There were plenty of takers, but Mac wasn't among them, even though Sharon and Angie both urged coffee on him. Ginger held her tongue as she gave in to temptation and savored every bite of a cookie and a brownie.

A general exodus began when the first guest departed. "Anybody who isn't sober enough to drive home is welcome to sleep on the sofa," Sharon announced.

There were glances in Mac's direction.

"I think she's talking about you, Mac, old buddy," someone said.

Angie went over and slipped her arm through Mac's. "I'll see that my fellow coach gets home safely."

Not in this life, Ginger thought. "That would be pretty silly," she spoke up. "It's not out of the way for me since Mac and I live in the same condo complex."

"What the heck? I don't mind—"

"I'll drive him," Ginger stated, enunciating each word firmly. She could sense the curious reaction among those standing by.

Angie looked inquiringly at Mac, giving him a chance to decide for himself. Seeing that his slightly bleary-eyed attention was focused on Ginger, the trim brunette shrugged and withdrew her arm.

"Damn, why didn't I go into coaching instead of industrial arts?" grumbled Pete. "Maybe I would have two good-looking women fighting over who would drive me home."

Someone made a joking, insulting remark at Pete's expense that provoked laughter, and Sharon accompanied her guests toward the door, with Ginger and Mac bringing up the rear. He seemed to be concentrating on putting one foot in front of the other.

"Just leave everything and I'll come over in the morning and help clean up the mess," Ginger offered as the last person in front of them departed.

"You've already done enough," declared Sharon. "And Mac nearly wore out my blender making margaritas." She reached and patted his cheek. "I would give you a big hug and kiss, Mac, but I doubt Ginger would allow it."

Ginger smiled sheepishly in response to the other woman's knowing grin.

"Good night. Sorry about getting…" Mac didn't finish his sentence. Evidently he wasn't so drunk he didn't realize that the male slang terms for *drunk* were too crude for female company.

"No apologies necessary." Sharon called after them, "Have fun, you two, or as much fun as you can."

With Mac's alcohol level, she meant. Ginger easily interpreted the suggestive advice and wondered whether Mac did. How much of tonight would he remember tomorrow?

Everyone else had left by now. Ginger glanced at her car, parked in a visitor's bay, and then located Mac's Camaro some distance down the street. She doubted he would be in favor of leaving it there overnight. But she wasn't sure how he would react to letting her drive it. "Do you have a problem with me driving your car home?" she asked a little uncertainly.

He fished into his pocket and drew out his keys and handed them to her. They walked side by side along the street. Ginger was prepared to grab his arm and steady him if he lurched or stumbled, but he did neither.

"I hope I didn't embarrass you at the party," she said. "Blurting out in front of the whole world that we were married after you'd kept it a secret. And then confronting Angie the way I did. It just didn't make sense for her to go out of her way. Of course, you may have preferred to have her take you home." When he didn't make any reply, she sighed. "Don't you have anything to say?"

"Where the hell was Whitfield tonight?" he asked.

Ginger had to switch mental channels. "Barry made other plans for himself. Sharon and I agreed that it wasn't a good idea to invite him and you. Naturally she chose to invite you."

"Other plans? The guy's dating you, and he makes 'other plans'?"

"He had dinner with his associate, who happens to be a man. If his associate were a woman, though, it wouldn't matter. Barry and I are good friends and nothing more, as I keep stressing."

"Why wasn't I told that the SOB wouldn't be there tonight?"

"He's not an SOB. And I haven't had a chance to tell you anything the past two days since you weren't talking to me," Ginger protested. "Tonight you might have said two words to me at the party."

They reached his car. Ginger unlocked the passenger's door for him before she went around to the driver's side. He was lying back in his seat, his eyes closed, when she got in.

"Feeling dizzy?" she inquired sympathetically.

Without turning his head or opening his eyes, he reached out his hand and stroked her cheek with his knuckles. "You looked pretty tonight in that blue dress. And damned sexy."

Sweet emotion made Ginger's voice husky. "Thank you. I appreciate the compliment."

His arm dropped and his breathing became deep and regular. Ginger lifted his inert hand and kissed it lovingly before she laid it on his hard thigh.

He slept soundly during the fifteen-minute ride. Glancing over at him, Ginger was fiercely glad she'd done battle with Angie and claimed this role for herself. He didn't rouse up when she pulled into his parking spot and killed the engine.

"Mac. Wake up. We're here." Grasping his shoulder, she gently shook it. His only response was to mumble something unintelligible. After additional attempts to wake him proved just as futile, Ginger got out of the car and went around and opened his door. She brought his seat upright and resorted to shaking him harder, finally getting his eyes to open. "No, don't close them," she half pleaded and half threatened. "We've got to get you to your condo and up to bed."

After more coaxing, he unfolded his big body from the car with her help and they set out for his condo, Ginger's arm around his waist. She talked him along, not sure that he wasn't sleepwalking and wouldn't just topple over suddenly. "It's not much farther. You can do it. You can do it." She giggled. "I sound like one of my exercise videos."

They reached his entryway. Fortunately he'd left the light on earlier. With her free hand Ginger unlocked the door and pushed it open, then stepped over the threshold with him. "Now let's get you upstairs."

"I'll just crash on the sofa," he said drowsily, bracing his hand against the wall.

"Won't you be more comfortable in your bed? Come on. I'll help you undress."

Side by side they mounted the stairs. Again Ginger's help didn't seem altogether necessary. Mac grasped the railing, propelling himself upward without any noticeable effort and without leaning on her. "You have wonderful balance, even with a high alcohol level," she commented. "I guess it comes from being an athlete. But that doesn't account for the fact your speech isn't slurred, does it?"

"I'm not that drunk," he replied. "I was only drinking beer, not whiskey."

"You must have gone through two six-packs, though."

"More like three. I guzzled one for Dutch courage before I got to the damned party."

"Because you were expecting to run into Barry and me together, I suppose."

"Why did you come without him?"

They'd reached the top of the stairs. The floor plan of all the condos was the same. Assuming that he'd taken the larger bedroom with adjoining bath for his use, Ginger guided them in that direction as she answered his question. "You know why. Because you were going to be there. Along with Sharon and Angie and several more single females." None of whom he'd shown much attention to tonight.

"How many times do I have to tell you I'm not interested in any other woman besides you?"

"Oh, I don't think you could tell me that too many times. It's music to my ears." He'd left the light on in the bathroom so that the bedroom was also dimly lighted. "Here we are," she said as she maneuvered them through the open bedroom door and toward his queen-size bed. "I'm impressed. You made your bed."

"It never looks quite as neat as it would if you had done it."

He stripped the shirt over his head and threw it aside, baring his powerful chest and shoulders. Ginger looked on, enjoying her view, while his hands moved to his belt.

"You still have your shoes on," she reminded him when he dropped his slacks without ado, revealing white briefs that cupped the bulge of his sex. "Sit down and I'll take them off for you."

He obeyed, and Ginger knelt to remove his loafers and dark socks before she tugged his slacks off. "Don't bother with that," he said when she began to shake them out to fold them. He took the slacks from her and tossed them aside, then grasped her by the waist.

"Mac!" she protested as he lifted her and brought her onto his lap. His arms came around her and he hugged her tight. Reveling in his strength and in being this close to him, Ginger hugged him back. "Drinking too much hasn't made you a weakling," she murmured.

"Lie down with me."

"Mac, I'm fully dressed!" He was laying her on the bed and stretching out beside her, paying no attention to her weak objection. Ginger managed to kick off her shoes and cuddled against him willingly as he embraced her tightly. Her cheek pressed against his hard shoulder. She turned her face and nuzzled his skin and planted a kiss. "This is so nice," she said softly.

"There's something I have to know."

"What?"

A feeling of suspense built as long seconds passed.

"What?" Ginger said again.

He sucked in a breath. "Do you still love me?"

"Isn't it obvious?"

"Not to me."

"I still love you, Mac." She could feel his whole body go lax as though with enormous relief. "Isn't that your cue?" she asked wistfully. "Remember our ritual? I would say, 'I love you,' and you would say…"

"Same here. Those words definitely apply." His relaxed muscles all turned to iron as he hugged her, squeezing the air from her lungs.

Ginger wriggled for breathing room and made a startling discovery. His embrace loosened, and she wriggled her lower body against his again to make sure she hadn't been imagining things. "Mac, you're— I mean, haven't you had too much to drink?…" Ginger blushed at the feminine delight in her tone.

"Too much to get you out of those clothes without

doing some damage to them. Especially those damned panty hose.''

''We can get around that problem. I'll take off my clothes myself.''

He released her, and Ginger made quick work of undressing without getting out of the bed. By the time she'd stripped off her panties and was nude, he'd managed to shuck his briefs, moving with more deliberation, and lay back naked and splendidly aroused.

Ginger couldn't resist stroking him. He groaned and expressed his pleasure frankly with words, reaching for her and drawing her to him so that they could kiss. Joy blossomed inside Ginger as she moved her head, letting her lips cling to his at different angles. ''I always loved kissing you,'' she confided softly.

''Same here.''

Their tongues mated.

The kissing became more passionate, because his hands were stroking her now, caressing her shoulders and back, sliding down to her hips and buttocks. When Ginger took a break to suck in air, she whispered breathlessly, ''I love the way you touch me.''

''It's mutual, sweetheart, believe me.'' His low, husky assurance was breathless, too.

''Oh, my—I love that, too....'' He'd grasped her at the waist and brought her higher so that her breasts were accessible to his mouth and tongue.

The lovers' conversation grew more graphic and earthy as the level of desire escalated to a fever pitch and Ginger was freed of inhibition. When she'd reached the point that foreplay was torture and she *had* to feel Mac inside her, she was getting astride him when suddenly she remembered birth control.

''There's probably no danger, with the drinking,''

Mac said. "And what does it matter? I want us to have a kid pretty soon. Don't you?"

"Let's not put the cart before the horse. Marriage comes before baby."

"Marriage will happen quick if I have my way."

The discussion of such a delicate issue could wait until tomorrow. Right now Ginger wanted to make love. "Just tell me where you keep your supply of condoms."

The precaution turned out to be necessary, after all. For just a second or two Ginger was deeply sorry that common sense had prevailed and Mac wasn't spilling himself into her. She sensed that he was hit by the same fleeting regret.

Chapter Thirteen

"I should get dressed." Ginger sighed.

Mac's arms tightened around her. "Stay with me." He kissed her hair. "You can use one of my T-shirts for a nightgown. I know you never liked sleeping in the raw." The last words were drowsy. His breathing slowed and his body relaxed. He'd fallen asleep.

She hadn't actually agreed, but she wanted to stay and sleep with him more than she dreaded exiting from his condo tomorrow, wearing tonight's party outfit.

"Good night. I love you," she whispered, kissing his chest and snuggling closer. It was true she'd never been completely comfortable sleeping nude, but rather than disturb him, she would forego his offer of a T-shirt.

In the morning they would probably shower together, make love again. Anticipation curled through Ginger. Later they would have to talk seriously about the past and the future. Surely Mac would agree with her that even though sex between them was as wonderful as before, they couldn't rush into marriage a second time.

When Ginger opened her eyes the next morning, she saw that daylight had filled the room. Mac's bedroom. He'd gotten up already. Disappointed, she lay in the bed alone. According to his digital clock, it was a quarter past eight.

Where had he gone? Ginger turned her head so that she could see into the bathroom. She listened hard. No sound of shower spray. With a sigh she sat up and looked around for her dress and underwear and shoes. They had disappeared! So had Mac's clothes. Only her purse remained.

"Mac!" she called out. "Are you downstairs?"

No answer.

Maybe he'd gone out to buy breakfast and had taken her clothing to make sure she wouldn't leave. It was the only explanation that made any sense. Ginger plumped her pillow and lay back down, curling on her side and pulling the sheet up under her armpits. She'd dozed off when a quiet thud woke her again.

The thud had been the door closing. Ginger rolled over on her back, hearing muted rapid footsteps on the stairs. Soon Mac appeared in the doorway, wearing the slacks and shirt he'd picked up from the carpet and carrying a cardboard box.

"Hi, sleepyhead," he greeted her.

"Hi." Ginger yawned and stretched her arms. "Where did you hide my clothes?"

"I didn't hide them. I took them to your condo and got you a different outfit."

"Another outfit? You're kidding!"

"No, I'm not kidding." He dangled her keys before he tossed them toward her purse. "It wouldn't have taken me so long if I hadn't gotten involved picking out some underwear.''

"What a sweet thing to do!''

"I figured you'd be embarrassed for the neighbors to see you wearing the same clothes you'd left in last night.'' He set down the box and walked over to the bed, where he kicked off his loafers and began unbuckling his belt. Quite evidently he was getting undressed again.

"You're coming back to bed?'' Ginger rose up with a languid movement and stretched her arms.

"That was my plan.'' Mac paused in the act of unzipping his trousers to follow the progress of the sheet slowly sliding down to her waist, revealing her breasts. Under his intent gaze, her nipples pebbled. Ginger blushed at her own brazenness.

"Why is it that you're the only man in the world who makes me feel this sexy?''

"I don't know, but I'm all for keeping it that way.''

She watched him strip, enjoying her ringside seat and the fact that he was obviously in a big hurry to shed his clothes and join her in bed ''Wow,'' she said when he shoved his briefs down, freeing his engorged manhood.

''You can take full credit. This is what you do to me. But I expect fancier language than 'wow' from my national-award-winning English-teacher wife.''

"Believe me, it's a superlative.'' Ginger hadn't corrected him with the reminder she was his *ex-wife* because now still wasn't the time for candid discussion and baring of doubts and fears. "You're incredibly gorgeous, all of you, not just—'' She tipped her head back to make it easier for him to kiss her as he leaned over her. "Yum. You taste like orange juice.''

"Don't change the subject. Finish what you were

saying," Mac chided her, flipping back the sheet. "Not just…"

Ginger finished her sentence and added, "One reason I was always so jealous was that it never seemed entirely real that I'd landed you." Amazingly it did seem real now, although the delicious intimacy could account for the feminine smugness that had always eluded her before.

"You landed me, all right, and kept me hooked." Mac's words were muffled against her sensitized skin. Crouched over her, he was kissing a hot trail down her stomach while his hands caressed her body and found every erogenous zone. Ginger lost count of the times she moaned or gasped or cried out, "Oh, *yes,* I love that.…" The message in her heart was just as joyous— I love him, I love him, I love him. Surely he could hear it, too, feel it in her touch.

When his masterful lovemaking brought them to the point that birth control was a factor, Mac paused to sheath himself without any reminder from Ginger.

Last night he'd argued against the need for taking precautions, saying "What does it matter? I want us to have a kid pretty soon. Don't you?"

Had that been the alcohol talking? This morning in the light of day, was his outlook different?

Ginger pushed aside those questions and rode together with Mac to ecstatic release.

"Just in case you might be a little uneasy, I'm sure I'm healthy, sex-wise," Mac said later as he stood before the bathroom vanity, shaving. He was clothed in a towel. "I always used protection, regardless."

Regardless of whether the women he'd slept with were on oral contraceptives. Ginger filled in the rest for herself and experienced the inevitable and unpleasant curl of jealousy. How many had there been? She would never ask because she really couldn't bear to know the number or their identity.

"In case you're uneasy, I'm positive I'm healthy, too," she replied from the bedroom, where she was donning her underwear. They'd showered together and were planning to go out for brunch. "The few times Barry and I made love, he used a condom."

Mac uttered a low, violent curse.

Ginger glanced and was dismayed to see a bright red blotch amid the white froth of shaving cream on his cheek. "Mac, you cut yourself!"

"It's nothing," he growled, dabbing with a wet washcloth.

"Don't be so rough!" Ginger went swiftly, took the cloth from him and held it, stanching the flow. She kissed his shoulder. "I hope I didn't cause this merely by mentioning Barry."

"Do me a favor and don't bring him up again. Okay? Even better, don't think about him."

"Mac, you shouldn't be jealous. There's no reason."

"The hell there isn't. He slept with you. I'd like to—" He broke off, his jaw clenched.

Ginger sighed as he resumed shaving and she went back into the bedroom, where she got dressed in the jeans and blouse he'd selected.

With his easygoing personality, surely he'd come around and realize Barry presented no threat.

"Here. I'll help you."

Mac had finished shaving and entered the bedroom, not wearing a stitch, as she was making up his bed. He stationed himself on the opposite side, and together they drew up the sheet and the bedspread. Ginger was touched by his painstaking efforts to duplicate her movements.

"That went fast with two of us," she remarked.

"I'm going to do my share this time around," he said, getting clean briefs from his chest of drawers.

His comment created a perfect opening for the inevitable honest discussion, but Ginger was hungry and knew he was, too. Discussion could wait.

"Shall I go ahead to my condo?" she asked. She wanted to fix her hair and apply a little makeup before they went to a restaurant.

"I won't be long. We'll go together."

Her arm didn't need to be twisted. She gladly perched on the edge of the bed and chatted with him while she enjoyed watching him get dressed in jeans and a knit shirt. When we're married, I'll have this pleasure often again, Ginger thought.

It was surely a matter of *when.* Not *if.*

"Did you want to watch TV? There's probably some kind of sports on," Ginger offered when they entered her condo.

"I'd rather come upstairs with you, if you don't mind."

"Of course I don't mind. I'll give you a guided tour," Ginger declared, slightly flustered but not at all displeased that Mac preferred keeping her company to tuning in a sports channel.

At the top of the stairs she led the way toward the smaller of the two bedrooms, explaining, "I use this room as a combination study and guest room."

"You have a computer," he observed from the doorway.

"Yes, I use it mainly as a word processor for schoolwork, but I browse the Internet, too, and visit educational sites.'' Ginger continued over to her desk, where her answering machine was blinking. ''Let me catch these messages while I'm here. One is probably from my mother. She usually calls on Sunday morning.'' Ginger pressed the button and, sure enough, Ellie Honeycutt's voice spoke from the tape.

''Ginger, dear, it's Mother and Dad calling. I'll bet you've gone out to breakfast at some lovely restaurant with Barry. Don't close your mind to romantic possibilities, dear. Barry would make you such a fine husband. Now, don't scold. I know it's your life and Dad and I shouldn't interfere. But we love you and want the best for you. Have a wonderful day. I hope you-know-who still isn't making a pest of himself.''

''Sorry,'' Ginger apologized, cringing at the last statement.

To her relief Barry's voice played next. There was no danger of his saying anything offensive to Mac.

''Hi. How was your party last night? Call me. If you're not busy, come over later.''

''Not on your life, buster,'' Mac said fiercely.

Ginger clicked off the machine without playing any more messages. ''I guess that wasn't such a good idea, was it?'' she said, sighing.

''Call him right now and tell him you're going to be busy from now on. With me.''

''I'm too hungry right now to call anybody,'' Ginger insisted lightly. ''Feel free to play with my computer while I do my woman thing.''

But he wasn't to be sidetracked. ''You *are* breaking off with Whitfield?'' It was more a grim order than a question.

''I won't be 'dating' him, not in the man-woman definition of dating,'' she replied, slipping past him in the doorway. ''But we'll remain friends.''

He caught up to her with a couple of long strides. ''Meaning exactly what.''

''Meaning that I'll call Barry when I have the chance and talk to him. Tell him about the party. About us. Listen with interest to what's going on in his life.''

''In other words he can pick up the phone whenever he damned well pleases and call you.''

''Barry's not the type to be pushy and intrusive, Mac. He's a sensitive person. This is my bedroom.'' She stated the obvious. ''Make yourself comfortable. I won't be long.''

''Take as long as you want. I've lost my appetite anyway.''

''Well, I haven't, naturally. Mac, do we have to fight today?'' Ginger stepped up close to him and hugged him around the waist. ''I'm fond of Barry, but I love you.''

His arms came around her, but there was no capitulation in his embrace. ''I don't want to fight with you any day, and I'll give in on a lot of things, but not this. I'm not sharing you with Whitfield. Period.''

''The situation will take care of itself. I promise. Right now Barry is going through a very difficult time personally. He needs my friendship and support. Plus he's someone important to me, though in an entirely different way than you.''

''What kind of 'difficult time'?''

Ginger hesitated, remembering her promise to Barry. ''I can't explain without violating his confidence.''

Mac dropped his arms, uttering a curse of pure frustration. With a sigh Ginger turned to go into the bathroom, bracing herself for him to storm out. But he paced around her bedroom in angry silence, inspecting her furniture and framed photographs and memorabilia while she was using her curling iron and making up her face as well as she could while paying more attention to him than her reflection in the mirror.

"I'm ready," she announced lightly.

He stood in front of her dresser, glaring at the open top tray of her jewelry box. "Did Whitfield give you this pin?" He stabbed a finger at the pretty diamond-and-sapphire pin fashioned in her initials, *GH*.

"No, that was a Christmas gift from my parents a couple of years ago. Barry hasn't given me any jewelry or any expensive present, for that matter, other than the leather tote bag I use as a briefcase."

"The one you're carrying every time I see you. With *GH* monogrammed on it."

Ginger smiled and lifted her arms as though to say she wasn't carrying it now. "Shall we go?"

He didn't budge. "I don't guess you kept any of the cheap junk I bought you."

"Yes, I did." She went over and pulled out the bottom tray of the jewelry box. "See, here are those Mardi Gras earrings you got me in the French Quarter." She picked up a dangling rhinestone-encrusted mask. "And the charm bracelet from the jazz and heritage festival with all the little musical instruments."

Ginger glanced at his face and saw he wasn't paying attention. His gaze was trained on her wedding rings. "That diamond chip is even smaller than I remembered," he said, reaching and picking up the engagement ring.

"Don't sound so derogatory. I loved my diamond. I cried the entire day when I took those rings off. Quite obviously I couldn't bear to get rid of them."

"Does it still fit?"

Her heart sank as Mac reached for her left hand and slid the ring on. But he took it off again immediately and returned it to the jewelry box. For all her relief that he hadn't insisted she keep it on and start wearing it, Ginger was also sad to see it replaced again next to her narrow gold band. The small diamond caught the light and twinkled so cheerfully. She wished she could put both rings back on with blind, brave optimism.

And maybe she *should* just put aside her doubts and fears....

"You want to wait for me downstairs?" Mac asked, pushing the tray in. "I need to use your bathroom."

"Certainly."

Evidently he'd tired of the sentimental journey that hadn't seemed to rouse much sentiment for him.

When Mac joined her several minutes later, he seemed more his usual self. Outside they encountered Jonathan, wearing one of his Saints helmets. They stopped to talk to the little boy and get a report on his fast-healing injury.

"Great kid," Mac said when he and Ginger were walking hand in hand, headed to his parking lot. "You know, I want at least two."

"Before, you were holding out for three or four," she recalled.

"Well, we messed around and lost six years. So two's okay with you?"

"Two's a nice even number. You haven't forgotten that I miscarried?"

He squeezed her hand. "I grieved over that little unborn character too much to forget. Hey, I don't mean to be putting pressure on you. So don't get all anxious. Like you said, marriage first and then babies."

"I would be more anxious if the doctor hadn't assured me I was perfectly capable of bearing children in the future."

"That was good news to me, even at the time. Boy, am I starving."

He'd passed right over the opportunity to ask, *When are we getting married?* Apparently he wasn't in nearly the big hurry to set a date as she'd thought he might be.

"Will I ever see you again?" Barry inquired, a note of seriousness beneath his drollness.

It was Thursday afternoon. Ginger had called him after she'd gotten home from school. The period when Mac was tied up with football practice during the afternoons was about the only free time she had to sandwich in a phone conversation with Barry.

"I think Mac may be making sure I don't have that opportunity," Ginger admitted in answer to his question. "He's very jealous of you despite my efforts to convince him you're not a rival."

"You haven't told him—" There was a note of alarm in his voice.

"No, of course not," she quickly assured him.

His sigh came over the line. "Today I had a business lunch with one of my richest clients. Just making polite conversation, I expressed interest in his children. It turns out his oldest son is gay and lives in San Francisco. My client has cut off all contact with him and disinherited him. He harped for fifteen minutes on the evils of the gay-rights movement. You can't imagine how debased and hypocritical I felt, sitting there and not saying a word."

"How horrible for you!"

"Not only would he take his business elsewhere if I came out openly as a homosexual, but he would exert all his influence in the Covington community to pressure my other clients to fire me. The financial repercussions are scary, Ginger."

"I wish I had some words of wisdom to help you with your dilemma, Barry, but I don't." Ginger's only role was to listen and sympathize and hope everything worked out happily for him.

"So are you and McDaniel ironing out all your former conflicts? His womanizing and free-spending tendencies, in-law problems and so on." He listed the divisive issues Ginger and Mac still hadn't gotten around to discussing.

"No. It's almost like we skipped over that part and skipped the wedding, too, and got started on a honeymoon."

"Has the subject of a wedding come up?"

"Not really. Of course, it's less than a week that we've been..."

"Back together?" he supplied.

"Yes. Except that we haven't fallen into old patterns. Mac puts himself out to be helpful and considerate. He insists we alternate being responsible for evening meals. He loads the dishwasher. He hasn't watched sports on TV. He's very attentive and hasn't caused me the first twinge of jealousy."

"Why that faint undertone of anxiety? Are you wondering if this state of harmony can last?"

"The problem is I want so much for it to last that I'm on pins and needles. Enough about Mac and me. Did you go to see the new Harrison Ford movie?"

They chatted about other subjects before they said goodbye.

Hanging up, Ginger thought about how good it had felt to voice her worries to Barry, who truly was a dear friend she wanted to keep as a friend.

She had bought Chinese food from a good local restaurant for dinner that night. Ginger had the table set when Mac got there. He filled water glasses while she microwaved the several containers.

"Let's go to the movies this weekend," he said. "I'd like to see the Harrison Ford movie. Dave Cooper said it kept him on the edge of his seat."

Barry had said the same thing, but Ginger didn't dare pass along his recommendation. "We can go Saturday afternoon."

"How about Saturday night? I was planning to drive over to New Orleans during the day and run some errands."

"Oh. Okay." What errands? Ginger was naturally wondering. It was the first she'd heard of any such plans. She wanted to ask if he wanted some company, but didn't quite have the nerve. "Maybe I'll go across the lake and do some shopping myself. I could use a new all-weather coat. Plus you have a birthday coming up in a couple of weeks."

He looked startled. Or was that alarm flashing across his face? "Where will you be shopping? If you do go," he added.

"The Lakeside mall. And possibly the Esplanade shopping center. Why do you ask?"

"Just curious." The reply was too casual.

No suggestion was forthcoming that they might ride together across the lake and coordinate their trips. Don't be suspicious, Ginger reprimanded herself.

But something told her she wouldn't be accidentally running into Mac in the vicinity of either of those shop-

ping malls she'd named. He would be running his errands elsewhere.

"It's such a pretty day. I hate to waste it shopping,"
Ginger said.

"Then do something else," Mac suggested, stacking
her cereal bowl in his and picking up as many of their
breakfast dishes as he could hold. They'd eaten out on
her patio after he returned from his Saturday-morning
run and showered and changed.

"You can't put off your errands?"

"No, I'd rather not. I'm off." He kissed her on the
mouth and departed quickly, leaving Ginger to ask herself the questions bothering her. Where was he going?
Was he seeing anybody in particular? What *were* his
mysterious errands?

He was obviously looking forward to his day without
her. Ginger had caught him several times with a slight
smile and an abstracted expression as though whatever
he was thinking gave him pleasure. The explanation was
probably entirely innocent.

"I guess I'll go shopping," she said aloud in a glum
tone. "And try to avoid the cookie counter." In her
present down mood, she could easily find herself
munching on comfort food like a walnut brownie with
calories too high to be tabulated.

Guilt added to Ginger's mix of gloomy emotions as
she drove across the causeway. Normally she arranged
to have lunch with her mother when she planned a shopping trip on the south shore. But one glance at Ginger's
face and Ellie would be demanding to know what was
wrong. There was too much risk that she would pull the
story out of Ginger, suspicions and all.

This time around Ginger was determined not to cry

on her mother's shoulder. Even if "this time around" didn't last more than a few weeks.

The huge parking lot surrounding the Lakeside mall was jam-packed on a Saturday. Ginger drove from one section to another for a full twenty minutes before she finally lucked up on getting a spot when another car was pulling out.

Inside, the mall was crowded with shoppers of all ages. Ginger joined the throngs and felt herself perking up. She would adopt a "shop until you drop" attitude, she decided, and give her mind a rest from its worry about Mac's whereabouts today.

Several hours later Ginger was lugging a couple of shopping bags and heading generally for the mall entrance closest to the section of parking lot where she'd parked her car. She hadn't bought an all-weather coat, but she'd found some bargains on sales racks and splurged on several full-price items for Mac for his birthday present.

"Ginger." A woman coming out of a store that sold party supplies and decorations spoke her name.

Ginger halted, taking a second or two for the woman's identity to register. She was Meg McDaniel, one of Ginger's former sisters-in-law. "Why, hello, Meg. How are you?"

"I keep busy. Keith and I have four kids now."

"Yes, Mac told me."

Meg's raised eyebrows and expression said, *Oh, so you and Mac are talking to each other. That's interesting*. Ginger didn't read any disapproval.

"He certainly got the whole McDaniel clan in an uproar when he moved to the north shore," Meg said, giving her head a shake.

"I can imagine."

"Mary had a hissy fit when he admitted he was hoping to patch things up with you. Then he added insult to injury by saying that if you two got back together, he didn't ever want to hear another word of criticism of you from his family."

"He said that?"

"In a tone that didn't leave any doubt he meant it." Meg went on when Ginger didn't respond by either confirming or denying the chances for a reconciliation. "You know, Mac hasn't been serious about another woman since you two split up. Sally and Libby and I don't think he's dated that much." Sally and Libby were married to two of Mac's other brothers. Obviously his social life had been a topic of discussion among them.

"Well, it was nice seeing you again, Meg," Ginger said. "Say hello to Keith."

"Will do. He took the kids to the zoo today…" Her ex-sister-in-law seemed to be debating with herself. Resolve flashed across her face, and she hefted the oversize bag she held. "I was just buying decorations and paper plates and stuff for a surprise birthday party Keith and I are throwing for Mac weekend after next at our house. It'll be his thirtieth. If you'd like to come, consider yourself invited. It's on Sunday at 2:00 p.m. Same address."

"A family birthday party?" Ginger couldn't help but cringe at a mental picture of herself walking in and facing a gathering of her former in-laws.

"Family and relatives and all his old friends. It'll be quite a crowd. No need to RSVP."

Meg said goodbye and hurried off. Ginger was just as glad her former sister-in-law hadn't pressed her for a definite answer or suggested that she be in on any sort of plot to get Mac to the party because Ginger couldn't have given a definite answer.

There was no guarantee she and Mac would still be a twosome a couple of weeks from now.

Mac was whistling a tune when he showed up at her condo at five o'clock.

"How did your day go?" Ginger asked.

"Great. What about yours?"

"It went fine."

"Good. Where would you like to go for dinner?"

End of conversation about their day apart in the city.

Ginger made another oblique attempt to open the subject later in the evening when she said, "By the way, I ran into Keith's wife at Lakeside."

"Did she have the kids with her?"

"No, they were with Keith. He'd taken them to the zoo."

"Good for him. Meg needs some free time once in a while. Your mentioning the zoo reminds me. I heard on the radio coming home across the causeway that some monkeys had escaped from the primate center over here on the north shore where some kind of research is conducted with monkeys."

End of conversation about the day's encounters with other people.

Surely he'd run into someone she knew. Surely he'd done or seen something she would find amusing or interesting. *Why* was he being so secretive?

Chapter Fourteen

"I'm taking you out to a fancy restaurant tonight," Mac announced when he returned from his run on Saturday morning. He named the restaurant, which had a four-star rating.

"You have to get reservations weeks in advance, Mac."

"I have reservations."

"You do?" Ginger blurted in surprise. He was a spontaneous, last-minute kind of person. Or had been that kind of person before. "Are we celebrating something?"

"Sharon's party was two weeks ago, so tonight's kind of an anniversary." He kissed her on the mouth. "I'm going to my condo to shower and change. Then I have some things to do. So I'll be out of your hair for a few hours."

"Oh. Okay," she said.

It was perfectly reasonable that he had "things to do" on a Saturday and didn't feel the necessity to explain what they were, Ginger told herself. After all, he was used to being single and looking after himself. She would *not* let twinges of vague distrust spoil this weekend.

Instead she would count her blessings and look forward to a wonderful evening dining out at an exclusive restaurant noted for its romantic atmosphere. Maybe—just *maybe*—he was setting the stage for a proposal?

The several hours to herself would allow her time to clean her condo. After she finished, she would manicure her nails and give herself a facial. Tonight she wanted to look her prettiest.

The phone rang when Ginger was about to vacuum the downstairs carpet, having already finished dusting the furniture. She paused to take the call. Sharon gaily identified herself and explained, "I figured it was okay to call. I knew I wouldn't be interrupting Saturday-morning sex because I saw Mac heading for the causeway toll booths earlier. Does Barry have a cappuccino machine? I need to buy a wedding present for my sister Diane, who's getting married again."

"Yes, he has one." Ginger's voice sounded hollow, which wasn't surprising. She *felt* completely hollow, like a brittle shell enclosing dead air.

Not only had Mac gone to New Orleans again today, but he'd carefully refrained from mentioning his intention. Why would he do that if he didn't have something to hide?

After Sharon had thanked her for the information and said goodbye, not having noticed anything amiss, Ginger numbly returned to the vacuum cleaner and stood there grasping the handle with fingers that had no strength.

All her incentive was gone. What did it matter if her condo got cleaned? What did *anything* matter if she couldn't trust Mac out of her sight?

The doorbell roused Ginger out of her dull stupor.

Outside her door stood a delivery woman from a local florist. Mac had sent her a dozen long-stemmed red roses. The card read "Love, Mac." Or it read that until the writing was blurred by Ginger's tears of anguish and confusion.

It didn't make sense that he would deceive her and send her roses the same day.

At six o'clock he called. "Hi, I'm at my place. I'll be over in about an hour. Our reservations are for seven-thirty."

"Have you been there long?" Ginger asked. She knew for a fact his car hadn't been parked in its spot thirty minutes ago because she'd walked down there and looked.

"A while," he said. "I watched some sports on TV this afternoon. Did you get my roses?"

"They're beautiful. Thank you."

"See you in an hour."

Since he would presumably show up dressed for dinner, Ginger got dressed, too, and did the best she could applying makeup with tears of unhappiness welling up in her eyes.

Please let there be an innocent explanation, she prayed.

Ginger was coming down the stairs when Mac let himself in with the key she'd given him. "Hi," he greeted her. "You look pretty. I like the dress."

"You look very handsome yourself." Heartbreakingly handsome in a dark suit and dress shirt and tie.

"Is something wrong? You haven't been crying, have you?"

She'd reached the bottom of the stairs, and he was getting a closer view of her face. "Actually I have shed a few tears today."

"Nothing bad has happened to your parents, I hope."

"No, this has nothing to do with them." Ginger led the way into the living room. "It has to do with us. Sharon called about thirty minutes after you'd left today and innocently mentioned she'd seen you headed for the causeway."

"I saw her, too, and blew my horn. I was kind of hoping you wouldn't talk to her."

"The north shore is a small world. You can't get by with much." Ginger seated herself on the love seat.

He remained standing, eyeing her with concern. "So are you saying you got upset because I didn't tell you I was going across the lake?"

"Yes, I got upset. Two Saturdays in a row you make a mystery trip to New Orleans. What am I supposed to think?"

He stared at her a long moment. "I'm not believing this," he said finally, shaking his head. "You don't actually suspect me of screwing around on you?"

Ginger threw up her hands. "Where did you go? What did you do? What's the big secret?"

"The big secret is this." He reached into his slacks pocket and drew out a small white jeweler's box and flipped it open to reveal a ring. Ginger got a quick glimpse of a large diamond flanked by two smaller diamonds before he snapped the box closed again. "I sneaked your old engagement ring out of your jewelry box. At first I was just going to take it along to make sure I bought the right size. Then I decided you might like the idea of using the diamond in the setting of a new ring. That meant going to a jeweler rather than just buying a ring." He tossed the box into her lap as though he were getting rid of something he no longer wanted or cared about.

"I'm so sorry," Ginger whispered, cradling the box in her hands. "And so relieved."

"This is never going to work. You don't trust me any more now than you did six years ago!"

"It *will* work! I've truly learned my lesson. And at least this time I kept my doubts to myself. I didn't cry on my mother's shoulder, and I didn't even breathe a word to Barry when he asked how things were going with us."

"Just when did this conversation between you and Whitfield take place?" he demanded, jamming his hands into his pockets.

"One afternoon last week. I went to his house for a cup of cappuccino."

"You went to Whitfield's house?"

"It was perfectly innocent," Ginger protested. She went on. "Barry gave me some good advice, which I should have taken. Then maybe I could have saved us this painful scene. He said I should propose to you myself and open up a discussion of our expectations of one another instead of waiting on you to propose."

"Expectations," he repeated, biting out the syllables.

"Could you please sit down?" Her request was beseeching.

"I'm fine standing. So what are your expectations of me, which I'm sure you've already outlined for Whitfield."

She sighed at his belligerent tone. "We need to communicate, Mac."

"So communicate. I'm listening."

Ginger tried hard to order her thoughts. "Number one on my list is fidelity. I would also ask you to get along with my parents. In return I would do my best to get along with yours."

"What else?" he prompted grimly.

She picked her words carefully, trying not to offend. "Before, we had a conflict about managing our income. I tended to be thrifty. You were more a free spender. I insisted on saving up until we could afford to pay cash for big items we wanted, like new furniture or a nice stereo. You were all for using credit cards."

"I have only one credit card, and I pay off the full balance when I'm billed."

The information wasn't delivered in a friendly tone, but at least he'd volunteered it.

"I do the same," she said. "Not that I'm never tempted to splurge and go into debt for something extravagant and impractical that I really can't afford on my schoolteacher's salary. Last Saturday, for example, when I was shopping for an all-weather coat, I stopped off in the fur department at Dillards and fondled a black mink coat." The little velvet box was still cradled in her hands. She opened it and gazed at the gorgeous ring he couldn't afford on his schoolteacher's salary.

"I can read your mind," he stated flatly. "I bought you an expensive ring on credit and we'll be paying for it the next ten years."

It was exactly what Ginger had assumed. "You didn't buy it on credit?"

"As a matter of fact, I wrote out a check."

"I'm sorry for jumping to the wrong conclusion." She rose with the intention of going to him.

He backed up a step, holding out his hand to ward her off.

"Mac, please. Put the ring on my finger. I'll be thrilled to wear it!" She held the little box out to him, imploringly.

He pushed her hand away. "Do whatever you want with it. Put it in your jewelry box with the other stuff I gave you, for all I care. I'm out of here." The last bitter words were spoken over his shoulder as he headed for the door.

"Mac, *don't* go like this!" Ginger begged, following behind him.

"Here's your key." Passing the kitchen doorway, he tossed the key onto the counter. It slid into the toaster and made a metallic ping.

"Please stay and talk things over!" She clutched at his arm.

"Talk won't change anything." He pulled free of her grasp. "I was a fool to think we could make it together."

"You're hurt and disappointed."

"Yeah. You got that right."

"Mac, I love you. And you love me, don't you?"

He gave her a hard, disbelieving look and walked out.

Ginger would have followed him to his condo or to his car and continued to plead with him, but she knew pleading wouldn't accomplish anything. His bitter note said clearer than words that they were finished, that he didn't want anything more to do with her.

"Going to a birthday party, Miss Ginger?" asked Jonathan, eyeing the large wrapped package she was carrying.

"Yes, a surprise birthday party for Coach Mac."

How welcome I will be is another matter, Ginger thought, feeling another case of jitters coming on.

"I hope he blows out all his candles and gets his wish."

Ginger was hoping Mac's wish wasn't for her to get lost and never bother him again.

During the long week that had passed, Mac hadn't called or made any attempt to see her. At school he'd steered clear of her. Apparently he wasn't any happier than she was. Both Angie and Sharon had gotten Ginger aside and questioned her, "Did you and Mac break up?"

"So that's what's eating him," Angie had said, and Sharon had expressed the same sentiment in different words.

Up until last night, Ginger hadn't mustered the necessary courage it was going to take to attend the party at his brother's house. Her former in-laws would all be there along with a host of aunts and uncles and cousins she'd seen only a few times. Dozens of old friends of Mac's like Don and Brenda Sweeney would certainly be gathered around him. However Mac greeted her, with forgiveness, with gladness, with coolness, with hostility, a whole audience would be looking on.

Ginger's hands were clammy on the steering wheel of her car as she drove across the causeway. She took deep breaths to calm her rapid heartbeat, her mood fluctuating from hopefulness to pessimism. "At least I'll *know*, one way or the other," she said aloud to herself.

Her supply of courage seemed to dwindle as she caught sight of the south shore. It temporarily deserted her altogether when she reached the neighborhood where Keith and Meg's home was located. Cars of every description lined the street. Out front was a neon sign flashing the news, Mac's An Old Man Of Thirty! Black balloons with insulting slogans floated over the sign.

"I *can't* go in there with all those people!" Ginger murmured. She could imagine the confusion and the noise inside the house, the loud voices and laughter. Her background was so different from Mac's, with smaller, more sedate gatherings. She didn't *belong*....

Mac was in there. Those people were his family, his friends. If by some miracle he wanted her there with him, she would fit in, by golly, or die trying to fit in.

Ginger held on to her resolve as she drove a couple of blocks and found a parking spot, immediately in front of Mac's cherry red Camaro, got out and walked back to the house, past the garish sign, up the front walk to the door. Quickly, with resolve, she pressed the doorbell button and stood with heart pounding, a smile fixed on her face, waiting for someone, hopefully Meg, to open the door.

Long seconds passed. Ginger pressed the button again. More long seconds passed. Either the doorbell didn't work or nobody had heard it.

Now what? Tentatively Ginger tried the door. It was unlocked. As soon as she'd pushed it open a few inches, she could hear the hubbub inside. Here goes nothing—or everything, she thought and stepped over the threshold.

Heading toward the noise, Ginger soon came to the doorway leading into the large family room. The whole room was festooned with black crepe paper and hung with huge banners that had been printed on a computer.

People milled about, a blur of bodies and faces. Wrapped gifts were piled on a table. Through another doorway at the far side of the room she could glimpse more movement in the adjoining dining room. Suddenly she felt light-headed with a surge of panic.

What on earth was she *doing* here? She should leave before someone noticed her.

"Ginger. Hi. Long time, no see." A woman dressed in bright red leggings and a matching red overblouse came up to her with bouncy steps, her hands outstretched. "Want me to take that present and put it with the rest?"

Ginger blinked and focused on her face, recognizing her finally as Brenda Sweeney. "Hi, Brenda. I guess I'm kind of late."

"No, not really. Mac just got here himself a couple of minutes ago. I'll take you to him."

"He's not exactly expecting me to come. I might just leave the present."

"I'll bet the best present you could give him is to wish him happy birthday personally. He might actually enjoy his party. Plus Don would like to see you. Come on. This way." Brenda grabbed Ginger's nearest hand, which happened to be her left hand. "Wow!" she exclaimed, glancing down and then lifting the hand for a closer view. "What a gorgeous ring! Mac wasn't kidding when he told Don he wanted to give you a diamond big enough to see this time. The ring wasn't quite ready when he went to the jeweler's last Saturday so Mac killed some time at our house watching a football game with Don on TV," Brenda rambled on in her talkative way.

The fact that he *hadn't* been lying when he told Ginger he'd watched sports on TV during the afternoon last

Saturday made her that much more unsure of her reception, but Brenda was forcibly pulling her along.

"Ginger, you came, after all!" Meg hurried up, all smiles. "I told Mac I'd invited you, and he said you wouldn't be here. I could tell he wasn't very happy about it. You were just fooling him!"

"Look at the engagement ring Mac gave Ginger," Brenda instructed, hauling up Ginger's hand again.

"Oh, isn't it beautiful! Sally! Libby!" Meg turned her head toward the dining room and bellowed the names of her sisters-in-law. "Come and see this ring our husbands' baby brother bought for his soon-to-be-wife-again!"

Sally and Libby both appeared and had to elbow their way through the cluster of other women who'd crowded around, oohing and aahing. Trapped in the middle, Ginger could feel herself blushing with embarrassment. She looked up helplessly and gazed straight into Mac's eyes. He stood just inside the doorway, flanked by his brothers and taking in the whole scene she'd created.

"What's going on? What's all the fuss about?" demanded a voice she recognized as that of her former mother-in-law.

"Make room for Mary," someone said.

A path opened up, but Mac made use of it before his mother could. In a few long strides he'd reached her. Ginger turned toward him uncertainly. "I didn't mean to attract all this attention and put you on the spot. I hoped to get you aside and ask you to forgive me for my lack of trust. Then if you still wanted a reconciliation, your birthday party seemed the perfect opportunity to make an announcement...."

He put both arms around her, picked her up and kissed her on the lips in front of everybody. And prim, reserved Ginger wound her arms around his neck and kissed him back, happiness coursing through her that he was over being angry. There were whistles from the men and applause and a chorus of delighted outcries from the women looking on.

Ginger knew her cheeks must be beet red when Mac set her on her feet again, keeping one arm around her waist.

In the meanwhile both the elder McDaniels had made their way into the center of the crowd and were standing nearby. Mike McDaniel gave his wife a nudge with his elbow. "Let's see that ring everybody's talking about," said Mary.

Ginger held out her left hand, and the older woman surprised her by clasping it with her own hand. "My son has good taste, all right."

"Thanks, Ma," Mac said gently. He leaned forward and kissed her on the cheek. She patted his face lovingly.

"I want to thank you, too, for raising such a wonderful man as Mac," Ginger said. Acting on impulse, she kissed Mary on the cheek and got her own pats in reciprocation.

Mike Sr. slapped his son on the back and expressed gruff, sincere congratulations. Suddenly all three of Mac's brothers were there, shaking his hand, slapping him on the back, hugging Ginger and kissing her and welcoming her back into the family.

Finally Meg asserted herself as party hostess, clapping her hands and raising her voice loud enough to be heard, "Everybody, into the dining room. It's time to light the candles on the birthday cake. We have the fire department standing by."

Mac kept Ginger close by his side as the assembled

guests swept them along into the adjacent room. Amid the mayhem, the two of them managed a brief, important conversation.

"We'll deal with any issues that crop up this time," Ginger said. "Money management, in-laws, whatever."

"You bet we will," Mac replied, his confidence enforcing hers.

"Later I have something confidential to tell you about Barry that will erase any jealousy concerning our friendship."

"Whitfield's not a problem for me. Not after today."

"And Sharon and Angie aren't a problem for me. I'm *not* going to be an insecure wife."

Cries of "Make a wish, Mac!" ended the exchange. Everyone was eyeing him expectantly during a sudden hush.

"I don't have anything to wish for now that I'm getting my wife back," he declared, giving her waist a squeeze.

Ginger wondered if a person's heart could actually burst with happiness.

"That turned out to be a good idea, going by my parents' house after we left your birthday party." Ginger had had her doubts, but Mac had insisted.

"I think the visit broke the ice," he said. "I'm determined to make them like me."

"You won half the battle with Mother by buying me this gorgeous engagement ring. I'll bet we weren't out of the house before she was calling her bridge friends and bragging to them. And Dad was very impressed when you brought up the stock market and told him about your mutual-fund portfolio."

"You remember Bernie Winkler from SLU? Tall,

skinny guy with glasses who was a whiz in math? Well, he's a stockbroker with a discount investment company. I went to him for advice during that first year after we split up. He explained dollar-cost-averaging and recommended I set up automatic monthly contributions to an investment account. I did that and also invested extra money I earned at summer jobs. Partly I acted out of an urge to make you sorry you'd written me off as a lost cause.''

"I *am* terribly sorry I took the immature way out. I wish I'd stuck with our marriage and dealt with our problems. I *would* have if I hadn't doubted in my heart of hearts that you really loved me."

"You don't doubt it anymore."

"No. It's still too good to be true, but you're mine, Coach.'' The conversation halted while she staked her possession with a kiss. They were lying in her bed, naked under the sheet and satisfied after making love.

"About the ring. The jeweler would probably give me a refund on the diamond—"

"I'm not giving up my ring," Ginger cut in to announce. She held up her hand. "Look at how it sparkles even in this dim light. I can't wait to wear it to school Monday and announce our engagement.''

"Our *short* engagement," he stressed. "I want to get married right away."

"Our short engagement," Ginger agreed. She sighed happily, continuing to admire her ring. "Oh, while we're tying up loose ends here, Barry gave me permission to tell you he's gay.''

"You're kidding."

"No. He just recently acknowledged his sexuality, coincidentally about the same time you showed up.

Now he's struggling with the decision of whether to come out openly.''

"Tough decision. I don't envy him."

"Barry needs my support and friendship. Plus I would want to keep on being friends with him anyway."

"Sure."

"I'll try to be as tolerant of your platonic friendships with women you like," she promised.

"Are you going to admire that ring all night?" he asked with a note of pleased indulgence.

"I guess you can turn off the lamp now."

He did and plunged the room into darkness. Ginger sighed contentedly, snuggling close to him.

"One other thing, since you're so solvent. And this is for future reference only since we'll be wanting to make a down payment on a house and buy nursery furniture in the near future. Just don't forget that my favorite fur is—"

"Black mink. Don't worry. I have that information filed away," he assured her drowsily.

"Good." She kissed him on the shoulder. "Good night. I love you."

"Same here. I love you," he added, hugging her closer. "Now close your eyes and go to sleep."

"Okay." And she did, with a smile curving her lips at the thought, No dream could be more wonderful than reality.

Epilogue

Ginger stopped off at the supermarket on her way home from her doctor's appointment. She'd clipped a recipe for spinach lasagna from the food section of the *Times-Picayune* in yesterday's Sunday edition, and she wanted to buy the ingredients and cook it for dinner tonight. Yes, *wanted* was the right verb.

Amazingly her whole negative attitude toward cooking had undergone a miraculous change during the ten months she and Mac had been husband and wife again. Slowly but surely Ginger was developing confidence in herself in the kitchen. One day soon she was even going to try her hand at making her mother-in-law's famous roast beef and gravy. At Ginger's request Mary McDaniel had written down directions, step by step.

And her confidence in other areas as a woman had soared, thanks to Mac's love and devotion. Ginger and

Mary were getting along well these days. Both Mac's parents had been delighted over the news that another grandchild was on the way.

Life was good. Incredibly good. Ginger loved the house she and Mac had bought in a nice subdivision. They'd made friends with their neighbors, most of them married couples with children. Mac had gone from being a condo dweller to a proud home owner with his typical enthusiasm. Ginger teased him, claiming he was going to wear out his new lawn mower within a year if he kept mowing the lawn so often.

"Hi, Ginger."

The greeting from Barbara Philips, Ginger's former neighbor, roused Ginger from her happy reverie.

"Hi, Barbara. It's good to see you."

"You're starting to show!"

"I'm five months." Ginger slicked the loose folds of her maternity dress to display her gently burgeoning stomach.

The two women chatted a few minutes, standing by their grocery carts in the aisle with the pasta. Jonathan's name came up and so did that of Jack Cassidy, the single divorced man who'd bought Ginger's condo. Barbara and Jack were dating each other. Ginger wouldn't be at all surprised if they ended up getting married eventually.

It was icing on the cake that the changes in Ginger's life would generate happy changes in the lives of other people her life touched.

For a while she'd been concerned about Barry, but he'd been doing fine ever since he reached a decision the previous Christmas to come out of the closet discreetly. He and Dan had moved to New Orleans and bought a house together in the Garden District. Ginger's phone conversations with Barry had grown less and less frequent because he was involved in his world and she was involved in hers. But she would always consider him a dear friend and have a warm spot for him in her heart.

Yes, life was good.

In that mood of contentment, Ginger purchased her groceries and drove home. She was just setting her plastic sacks on the counter in the kitchen when the phone rang. Her mother's voice came over the line. Ginger could tell at once that something was bothering Ellie Honeycutt.

"How did your checkup go?" Ellie asked brightly. *Too* brightly.

"It went fine. Dr. Palmer says I'm healthy as can be."

"Did she do an ultrasound?"

Ginger answered her mother's rapid-fire questions, the intuition growing that something was wrong. "Mother, is there some bad news you have to tell me?" she finally asked, bracing herself for a dreaded announcement that John or Ellie had developed a serious health problem.

"Not necessarily bad news. I saw Mac today."

"You did? He didn't mention that he was going to New Orleans," Ginger commented with mild surprise. "Did he say what his errand was?"

"I didn't talk to him." A pause. "I don't think he saw me." Ellie went on in the same oddly reluctant voice, explaining the circumstances. She'd been passing by a large sporting goods store on Veterans Highway and happened to spot her son-in-law emerging from the store.

"You should have pulled in and said hi to him."

Another pause accompanied by a sigh. "He wasn't by himself. He was with someone. A blond woman. I would almost swear she was the same one...." Ellie sighed again. "But my eyesight isn't as good as it used to be."

"Would you finish your sentence, please? What same woman?"

"That blond hussy your father and I saw with Mac at the restaurant shortly after you two were separated."

"Oh. Trudy Miner."

"Probably they both just happened to go to the store and ran into each other, dear. Mac certainly seems to dote on you. He wouldn't—"

"No, he *wouldn't* fool around on me, Mother. You're absolutely right about that. Whoever the blond woman was, Mac didn't arrange to meet her." Ginger's words weren't wifely bravado. All she had to do to banish any slight uncertainty was to close her eyes and remember saying goodbye to Mac that morning. He'd hugged her tight and kissed her, patted her stomach and included their baby in their farewell conversation.

Ginger would bet her life that he hadn't been planning a clandestine date with another woman.

After she hung up, she busied herself with dinner preparations. The lasagna was in the oven when she heard Mac's car in the driveway. Eagerly she went to greet him.

"Hmm. Something smells good," he declared, entering through the door from the garage into the utility room. "I'm starved. I skipped lunch today."

"You did? Why?"

Was it her imagination, or did a guilty expression cross his face?

"Too busy," he said, opening his arms and enveloping Ginger in a bear hug. "I made a run over to New Orleans at noon time."

"Mother said she saw you."

"Where?"

Ginger pulled back, hearing his anxious note. "Coming out of Sports Unlimited on Veterans Highway."

"Oh. Right. I stopped by there to pick up a couple of pairs of new running shorts."

Why did he seemed relieved?

"Good. Your old ones are threadbare. Who was the blonde?" Ginger asked.

"Trudy Miner. I don't remember her married name," he admitted absently, his mind obviously not on the conversation. "She's pregnant, too. With her second child."

"Did you do any other shopping?" Surely he hadn't driven across the lake just to buy running shorts, Ginger reasoned.

"Some major shopping." His answer might have been a confession. "I bought that nursery furniture we looked at this past weekend."

"Mac, you didn't!" Ginger's voice held more delight than reproof. "When's it going to be delivered?"

"Tomorrow. Look, I know we agreed it was too expensive and we would keep our eyes open for an ad in the classified section of the newspaper for the same brand and buy second-hand furniture and refinish it, but dammit, this is our first baby and—"

Ginger cut him off with a kiss before she finished his

sentence for him. "And we can economize in other ways."

"You're okay with me going ahead and buying it?"

"I'm very okay," she assured him happily. "In fact, I couldn't be *more* okay."

* * * * *

FOLLOW THAT BABY...

the fabulous cross-line series featuring the infamously wealthy Wentworth family...continues with:

THE MERCENARY AND THE NEW MOM
by **Merline Lovelace**
(Intimate Moments, 2/99)

No sooner does Sabrina Jensen's water break than she's finally found by the presumed-dead father of her baby: Jack Wentworth. But their family reunion is put on hold when Jack's past catches up with them....

Available at your favorite retail outlet, only from

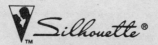

If you enjoyed what you just read,
then we've got an offer you can't resist!

Take 2 bestselling love stories FREE!

Plus get a FREE surprise gift!

Clip this page and mail it to Silhouette Reader Service™

IN U.S.A.	IN CANADA
3010 Walden Ave.	P.O. Box 609
P.O. Box 1867	Fort Erie, Ontario
Buffalo, N.Y. 14240-1867	L2A 5X3

YES! Please send me 2 free Silhouette Special Edition® novels and my free surprise gift. Then send me 6 brand-new novels every month, which I will receive months before they're available in stores. In the U.S.A., bill me at the bargain price of $3.57 plus 25¢ delivery per book and applicable sales tax, if any*. In Canada, bill me at the bargain price of $3.96 plus 25¢ delivery per book and applicable taxes**. That's the complete price and a savings of over 10% off the cover prices—what a great deal! I understand that accepting the 2 free books and gift places me under no obligation ever to buy any books. I can always return a shipment and cancel at any time. Even if I never buy another book from Silhouette, the 2 free books and gift are mine to keep forever. So why not take us up on our invitation. You'll be glad you did!

235 SEN CNFD
335 SEN CNFE

Name	(PLEASE PRINT)	
Address	Apt.#	
City	State/Prov.	Zip/Postal Code

* Terms and prices subject to change without notice. Sales tax applicable in N.Y.
** Canadian residents will be charged applicable provincial taxes and GST.
  All orders subject to approval. Offer limited to one per household.
  ® are registered trademarks of Harlequin Enterprises Limited.

SPED99   ©1998 Harlequin Enterprises Limited

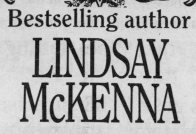

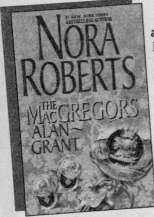
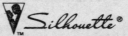

Silhouette®

SPECIAL EDITION®

COMING NEXT MONTH

#1225 BABY, OUR BABY!—Patricia Thayer
That's My Baby!
When Jake Hawkins returned to town, he discovered that one unforgettable night of passion with Ali Pierce had made him a daddy. He'd never forgotten about shy, sweetly insecure Ali—or how she touched his heart. Now that they shared a child, he vowed to be there for his family—forever!

#1226 THE PRESIDENT'S DAUGHTER—Annette Broadrick
Formidable Special Agent Nick Logan was bound to protect the president's daughter, but he was on the verge of losing his steely self-control when Ashley Sullivan drove him to distraction with her feisty spirit and beguiling innocence. Dare he risk getting close to the one woman he couldn't have?

#1227 ANYTHING, ANY TIME, ANY PLACE—Lucy Gordon
Just as Kaye Devenham was about to wed another, Jack Masefield whisked her off to marry him instead, insisting he had a prior claim on her! A love-smitten Kaye dreamt that one day this mesmerizing man would ask her to be more than his strictly *convenient* bride....

#1228 THE MAJOR AND THE LIBRARIAN—Nikki Benjamin
When dashing pilot Sam Griffin came face-to-face with Emma Dalton again, he realized his aching, impossible desire for the lovely librarian was more powerful than ever. He couldn't resist her before—and he certainly couldn't deny her now. Were they destined to be together after all this time?

#1229 HOMETOWN GIRL—Robin Lee Hatcher
Way back when, Monica Fletcher thought it was right to let her baby's father go. But now she knew better. Her daughter deserved to know her daddy—and Monica longed for a second chance with her true love. Finally the time had come for this man, woman and child to build a home together!

#1230 UNEXPECTED FAMILY—Laurie Campbell
Meg McConnell's world changed forever when her husband, Joe, introduced her...to his nine-year-old son! Meg never imagined she'd be asked to mother another woman's child. But she loved Joe, and his little boy was slowly capturing her heart. Could this unexpected family live happily ever after?